ALSO BY JULIE MYERSON

Fiction

Sleepwalking

Me and the Fat Man

Laura Blundy

Something Might Happen

The Story of You

Non-fiction

Home

Not a Games Person

JULIE MYERSON

The Touch

VINTAGE BOOKS
London

In memory of my tutor Roy Littlewood (1928-1984)
Who told me I could write

Published by Vintage 2007

2 4 6 8 10 9 7 5 3 1

First published in Great Britain in 1996 by Picador

Vintage
Random House, 20 Vauxhall Bridge Road,
London SW1V 2SA

www.vintage-books.co.uk

Addresses for companies within The Random House Group Limited can be found at: www.randomhouse.co.uk/offices.htm

The Random House Group Limited Reg. No. 954009

A CIP catalogue record for this book is available from the British Library

ISBN 9780099499329

The Random House Group Limited makes every effort to ensure that the papers used in its books are made from trees that have been legally sourced from well-managed and credibly certified forests. Our paper procurement policy can be found at: www.randomhouse.co.uk/paper.htm

Printed in the UK by CPI Bookmarque, Croydon, CR0 4TD

PART ONE

one

It is freezing cold on the day he lets them find him, cold as if Our Saviour the Lord Jesus Christ had deserted the planet, drained it of light and heat. As if he had pulled the plug – whoosh! – stopped the natural gas supply. Nice one, Jesus!

A Sunday in early February – traffic is moving stealthily along the edge of the Common and Alsatian dogs are worrying away at sticks, coats muddy, eager beards of saliva shaken from their lips. Everyone's out – after the Sunday roast and whatnot – swishing in nylon coats and boots, over the grass, under the leaky winter sun.

And poor old Frank lies here, beat up and bleeding, waiting for them to come and get him. It won't be long. Now and then he makes his eyes focus on the leafless trees, the sky now bright blue with daylight, now blooming violet with the flush of his own blood.

Everything is going according to his plan. He won't be able to admit it when he gets to Heaven, of course: 'What did you do, Frank? Lure poor innocent travellers into trouble?' Ha! that's a good one. A scheming mermaid – a seventy-year-old pensioner, beating his stinky fishtail on the frozen grass.

He knows precisely how he got here, though he must

make them believe he came from nowhere. He can appear and disappear at will, see all, hear all (it is part of Jesus's gift to him) – though one fine day he may crack open his poor useless mouth and have no sound come out, nothing at all.

The truth is, no one has ever listened, let alone understood him, said a decent please or thank you. No one has taken any notice. He could have had an audience, sure, he could have bought one, couldn't he? Could have gone public, taken advertising, used pounds sterling to cause a stir. Many false prophets do.

But he refused, so instead his preaching fell on deaf ears. Ears stopped up with wax, with soil, with flakes and dust and ashes and spit, with every sort of human debris.

But his time is coming, yes it is. The next months will show who is in control.

Speaking of which, here they come, advancing over the icy Common, a proper little army – sleeves and scarves and mitts and billowing breath. A young man, two young women – sisters in fact, though you wouldn't necessarily know – and a child and, yes, the kiddy's seen him all right. Now for the shouting, the sticks pointing, fingers extending, flash of the crippled girl's silver. Coats flapping – what a drama – as the pretty little tableau is gobbled up by dusk.

He'll close his eyes now, the pupils dull and sticky and hurt. He is a poor old man on the ground.

They don't know what they are in for.

'Jesus Christ,' one of them will say – the cocky man with the lazy smile. Fond of himself: black hair and long jaw and dimples. Jesus Christ? On the right track, there, yes sir! So he stands safely holding his pockets, a grey man-mountain, this smarmy young man, looking down. Scared to touch – scared to soil his office hands?

No matter if they don't recognize him, don't listen to him, so long as they stay. He is the Lord's messenger now, his cohort. He has the ability to change shape at will.

He'll have proved it to them by September, several times.

*

'How's work?' Gayle asked Will as they left the path and moved over the Common. 'Busy right now, are you?'

He thought, not for the first time: why does she go out of her way to look like shit? OK, she had nice big eyes, Donna's creamy-bluish skin, but she doggedly neglected herself – bit her lips, let the skin chap and redden, did nothing with her long frizzy hair. Her clothes were past their best, pilled, buttons missing. The look was Oxfam Shop reject and she was way too old for it to seem interesting or romantic. Here I am, she was saying: a thing worn down, thumbed and used and broken and tangled and split, not to be desired. The opposite of Donna, in fact, who bravely made the most of everything she had, despite her pain, despite her twisted spine.

Gayle wasn't much older than him, only four years, but you wouldn't think it to look at her. OK, she had the last proud flash of youth on her side, but not for much longer. She would have to watch it. Motherhood had blurred her edges, allowed the shadows to settle under her eyes for good. A pattern of fine red veins was creeping over the side of her nose and the pale carpet of hair on her cheek threatened to darken to moustache where it traced her lip. Will, who had a strong visual sense, who noticed these things, recognized that Donna would have done something about that – Donna, who put on lipstick even for the osteopath, even when she could barely stand up.

Donna told him that Gayle couldn't get excited about something as superficial as the way she looked when there was so much misery and inequality in the world. She explained this idea to him rather touchingly as if it was something new – as if her sister was right and admirable and special. Will roared, of course. He had no respect whatsoever for such humourless and immature self-flagellation. Donna was simply blinded by loyalty and charity and love of her sister. Donna was infinitely trusting, surprisingly devoid of cynicism.

Once, he remembered, Donna had lured Gayle (God knows how) to the hairdressers and brought her back with a mane of corkscrew curls. 'All natural,' Donna had announced as she showed her sister off in the doorway, 'just finger-dried and scrunched.' He had been briefly impressed, but Gayle had been straight into that bathroom, messing it with her fingers, brushing it, tearing out the curls. 'People pay money to have hair like yours,' Donna shouted miserably as Gayle left the house.

What it boiled down to was selfishness. Gayle had no sense of humour. She was prickly, edgy, chippy, charmless. In her heart, she probably did make an effort to get on with him – for Donna's sake – but all her questioning about his work (which she clearly despised) only made him less likely to tell her anything. Something about Gayle made him want to run a mile, be wordless and abrupt, misbehave.

But anyway, he told her business was good, even briefly

referred to the LexCom pitch, though not by name. She widened her eyes, shivered. 'American,' he explained, not intending to give much away, 'computer games. Big bucks.' The account was in fact massively lucrative – would be if they won it. He wondered idly whether she understood – whether she had any idea how much money might be involved.

'Oh,' she said.

'We won't know if we've got it till the autumn,' he added.

'The autumn?' She pulled a miserable scrap of pink tissue from her pocket and blew her nose on it. 'That's ages. What do you do in the meantime?'

'Well,' he was bored now, sick of this walk, of the cold, didn't know why he'd agreed to come, 'we pitch.'

'Ah,' she said.

In his pockets, his finger ends were numb despite his calfskin gloves. When he got back, he would turn up the heating, roll a joint, lie on the sofa and zap the TV channels, close his eyes. Get pleasantly stoned.

*

Donna – the lovely, delicate young woman with the twisted spine and the walking stick – stops and stands over him.

He senses the unsteady lopsidedness of her walk, the muffled vibration of the stick. Clouds of white escape from her mouth. From down here, he sees the two dark pinpoints of her nostrils, the glittery movement of earrings. She's pulling the kiddy against her. In a moment her voice will crack with concern.

He knew she would get to him first.

The walk was all her idea. Despite her so-called

disability, she is the lively one – well, isn't it always so? 'Fresh air,' she'll have said optimistically, responding to his call without knowing why – and they will have headed up Clapham High Street, past the Burger King Drive-Thru, through a landscape of dustbins and satellite dishes, over a stained and filthy pavement – littered with discarded takeaways and bird carcasses.

The child will maybe have picked up a wishbone still tufted with brown flesh and her ma will have yelled at her to drop it. Naughty, dirty, let go. Tears, and then someone will have had to pick up the tot and carry her. Ought to be the fancy young man, but no, he won't do anything to please the tot's mum. And Donna – lovely, frail Donna – can't carry anything, so Mummy will have gathered her in her arms and they'll have continued towards him in all innocence – tricycle squeaking, sticks snapping underfoot, exhaust from the street circling their legs. Fresh air, what a joke!

Come on, come on, he's had a long wait – he's tired, he's an old man of seventy. Blood tickles his mouth, his eyes. He's live bait.

'Hey!' Donna shouts (there you go). 'You two! Over here!'

The ground hums then with their approaching feet.

When he gets to Heaven's Gates, he will say, 'I preached the Gospel, healed the sick,' and the Lord Jesus Christ will give him a big rib-crunching hug and say, 'Well done, my good and faithful servant.'

*

Something was going on. Donna was shouting at them to come. There was a long black shape spread on the ground at her feet.

Gayle began to run.

'Oh God, oh God,' Donna was saying.

A man's inert body was stretched out before them on the frozen ground. Kitty could not stop moving her legs in her excitement. Her nose was running, a clear shining line from nose to lip.

Gayle caught hold of Kitty's duffel hood to stop her poking wildly with her stick, then bent to the body. Just then a pattern of geese or ducks passed overhead, breath and feathers, loud crying, then sucked up by gloom. Kitty screeched and danced as they passed. 'It's all right,' said Gayle, 'he's breathing,' – and then Will caught up.

'Jesus Christ,' he said, 'what's wrong with him?' and Gayle thought, Yes, that's the thing about Will – he never acts, he always stands there on the fucking sidelines and waits to be told.

*

'We are sure, are we, that he's not just drunk?' said Will after a moment. If it was up to him, he'd have gone on walking. He saw his joint on the sofa slipping away from him. But the girls ignored his comment. They were on their knees around the man. He kept his hands in his pockets.

The man had thick white hair, snaked with grease. He was big, sturdy. It was impossible to tell from the back of his head, his clothes – heavy black coat, grubby nylon trousers, newish trainers – what sort of person he was. How old, how clean, how sober or alive. Big, solid fingers curled on the concrete path, black-rimmed trampish nails.

'I'm going to turn him over,' Gayle said, with an officious eagerness he found unnecessary. Drama and accident attracted her, even off duty. He'd noticed before.

'Go on then,' he said, so relaxed as to rile her.

'Careful.' Donna moved back, pushed her fringe from her face.

'Hold on.' Gayle dropped to her knees and placed her gloved hand on the man's shoulder, rested it there a moment. She pulled off her glove, felt for a pulse.

'Hello,' she said, 'hello there? Can you hear me?'

*

'Hello, have you been born again?' the pastor asks him on 23rd September 1958, the year fat, disruptive Tommy is born.

He wanders into that church by mistake – takes in the muscular arcs of wood, the ordinary plain-glass windows. No angels, no fuss of velvet, no flowers. He has no purpose in coming in – strays in by mistake, sick of Daddying, sick of all the crying and Lola's pink, pleased face. Wanting peace. Well, that's exactly what he gets.

Born again? 'I suppose so.' He rolls pocket fluff and grit between his thumb and first finger. 'Somewhere along the line.'

He is afraid to move away. The pastor's shoes rock on the tiled floor. Sweat polishes him, gives him an angelic shine. He has a whacking great mole the size of a sultana on his chin and his beard has been forced to grow around it.

'Somewhere along the line? You don't get saved somewhere along the line. It's an Act of Conscience, you know.'

He wasn't interested, of course, not then. He supposed himself to be a Christian – what else could he be? – but beyond that he hadn't the faintest idea. Personal Redemption was not something he was looking for – no sir! – not something he was aware he needed.

But the Good News jolted his heart.

He'd always up to now lived in terror – of his life, of his stored-up death. His mum warned him wolves would come for him in the night if he misbehaved – break his neck and strip the flesh from his bones. Why did she want to frighten him like that? He has never known the answer – and she died with him still fearing her, still thinking she was right.

Until the pastor told him the Good News – of how Christ climbed willingly up onto that cross for him – and for his mum. So they need not fear. Such News! He'd have hammered on her pink granite stone and woken her and told her, skeleton in muck that she was, had he been able to.

Instead, he went to Patel the newsagent's and blew up some snaps of her angry sepia face on the photocopier (six for one-fifty, not bad) and pinned them on the living-room wall. She glared down at him and he laughed because she couldn't stop him – and anyway, now his wife's dead, he can have what he likes on his wall. So what if he wants his mum back? (Even if he never had her.)

An Act of Will, ha! Sometimes the world kills him, it is so comic. You don't keep secrets, they keep you. He can tell you that for nothing. Lying there, with the pretty, crippled girl standing over him and her lean, sulky boyfriend, and bossy big sis trying to say hello right into his ear.

*

No reply. 'OK,' said Gayle.

Donna watched her strain against the weight, careful not to let the head fall back and hit the path. You knew she was a nurse, you could tell, because there was no awe, terror or smugness in the way she touched him. Then she rested back on her heels and a face lay at their feet.

'Come here, Kitty,' Donna said because of the blood which was all over his eyes and nose. But she was already getting a good look.

'Is that how babies come out?' Kitty hopped, furious with excitement. 'All blooded up?'

The man moaned. 'I thought he was going to be dead,' said Donna, 'I really did.' It was a strong face, as far as she could tell – elderly but defined, large nose, large mouth, clean-shaven. He moaned again. She felt inexplicably frightened.

'Better not move him,' Gayle said. 'Where's the nearest phone box?'

'Will,' Donna pulled at his sleeve. Why did he stand there so quietly?

'Over there,' he said.

'Go phone an ambulance, quick.'

'I'm going,' he said, turning slowly.

Kitty had lost interest and had sat down on the path and was pulling her boots off, then her tights. Beyond them, beyond the leafless web of plane branches, street lights were coming on. The grass by the path was sparse, mostly mud. On a nearby seat, next to the bin, a baby's bottle had been left behind, mud and grass on the teat, half full of pinkish water.

'What's the matter with Will?' Gayle said almost to herself and rocked back on her heels. She sighed and without looking round, said, 'Put your clothes on please, Kitty.'

*

Soon after he buried his wife – soil chucked on polythene, by the way, no ashes or dust involved – he sat and wrote a letter to Tommy:

Dear Tommy,

I did not know it was Lola's wish she should leave all her money to the Church after Funeral expenses. But I don't see why not, after all she saved it out of her housekeeping money and her pension so it was her own to do with as she liked. I thought she had about £450 and I thought that this together with the grant would be enough for a GOOD FUNERAL. I do not mind in the least for after all you can do what you like with your own.

But as far as her already wealthy Church is concerned, I have preached the Gospel for years and been a Pastor myself and have never charged a penny for my services or my tracts, although I have often paid out for postage etc and made gifts towards expenses of printers.

Oh, one correction! I once preached in a church in Arizona, nothing to do with Brother Wilson's message, and they sent the Collection Plate round and gave it to me. I didn't want it but thanked them – it was their custom for a visiting Preacher and it is 'more blessed to give than to receive' etc etc and it was a rich church and they couldn't return everyone's money. But this is the ONLY TIME.

Still, I don't mind IN THE LEAST. I'm very well off on my £63.61 a week and NO RENT TO PAY. But I'm going on too long. It's twenty past midnight,

God Bless you,
(officially) Your affectionate father
Frank F Chapman
and love 'DAD' or 'DADDY'
(don't know what you prefer)

PS I have no opinions. I say what He says which just shows I agree. I'm trying to stop. You will have to forgive me if I've said Too Much. I'm going to bed.
May the Lord bless you and all my offspring. By the way, Isaiah declared that he saw us True Believers in Heaven and all our offspring with us.

PPS I can't include my (Roman Catholic) in-laws in this, but I hope of course that they will come too.

When he'd finished the letter, he sat there staring, appalled by the silence. The electric fire had heated his left trouser leg and the smell of hot nylon filled his mouth and nose.

The clock said ten to four. He was so alone that the hands barely seemed to move. He tried to think about Colossians 3:17 which declares, 'whatsoever you do in word or deed, do All in the name of Jesus Christ' – but for the first time it didn't work. He laid down his biro and wept.

*

The ambulance arrived in twelve minutes. Two men ran towards them over the grass and, after examining the man and commenting briefly, lifted him onto a stretcher. He moaned loudly and gripped randomly at one of the ambulancemen's wrist. 'Hey, now, matey,' said the first one, who was red-haired and freckled like a child, 'hey.' There was a wet smudge of blood on the tarmac where the old man's face had been, and the red-haired man stepped around it.

'Police will want a word with him,' said the other one, who was black and older. He laid a blanket over the man and tucked it so his arms were held to his sides.

'I'm surprised anyone could mug him here, so close to the road,' Gayle observed, 'and it can't even have been dark at the time.' She mentioned that she worked at the hospital. One of them muttered something and she laughed loudly. When they reached the ambulance, Donna and Will, who'd been following behind with Kitty, watched as she climbed in with the stretcher and the red-haired man. 'You don't mind?' she called, mainly to Donna. 'Someone really ought to go.'

'Oh,' said Donna, 'right.' Great, thought Will, we get to spend the rest of the afternoon babysitting. Kitty minded too – flung herself down on the frozen pavement and cried.

'I'll see you at your place in an hour,' said Gayle as the doors closed.

'Fine mother she turned out to be,' said Will.

'Oh, come on,' said Donna, and she squatted to speak to Kitty, promising her videos and marshmallow fluff on bread and to paint all her finger- and toenails red. Kitty stopped crying. 'Can you pick her up?' Donna said to him, levering herself up with the help of her stick. Pain ghosted for a moment over her face.

'Are you OK?' he asked her, holding out his hand.

'Let's get home,' she said. Then everything was drowned by the vehicle's tearing screams.

*

Gayle had to grip the rail as they dodged through traffic, as the blue light and alarm noise rolled all around them through the streets. The man with the red hair said he was called Jeshel.

'What?' said Gayle.

'Jeshel. My mum made it up.'

In front, the driver laughed. 'Believe that and you'll believe anything.'

Gayle was looking at the old man. 'Don't worry,' Jeshel said, 'he'll be fine. The wounds look pretty superficial.'

'I don't know him or anything,' Gayle explained.

The driver looked at her in the mirror. 'I thought he was your dad, you know?'

Jeshel chortled.

'Christ, no,' Gayle said, 'we just found him. He was just lying there. There were people all over the place, but no one seemed to have noticed him; I suppose he just blended in. Anyway, we couldn't leave him.'

The old man lifted his head and looked at Gayle. Beneath the blood, his eyes were very pale, his gaze hard and discerning. When he spoke, what he said was, 'Where's Donna?' – and let his head drop back again.

'What?' Gayle froze, a gust of blood rushing through her body. 'What?'

'Not much of a weekend break for you – on tomorrow, are you?' Jeshel was saying, but she wasn't listening. She was staring at the man who had just called her sister by name and was now saying, 'Hallelujah, hallelujah, Holy Spirit, Holy Angels,' over and over again, like the nagging whine of a machine just plugged back in.

*

He hoped for Donna, but he's got the other one, the nurse. Too bad, can't be helped, he will have to make do.

Memory is exploding in his head in delirious technicolour: boiling yellow sun on the concrete slabs by the outdoor toilet where the washing blows. Dull green stinging nettles which push through the broken slats in the toilet door, furry-burning your knees when you're sat there doing your business. Every summer he hacks them down, every summer they grow back.

When he brings his wife Lola to Lassingham Lock in 1957, her thick accent and blue-black hair scare the villagers – whisperings about gypsy blood. Not true. Hungarian blue blood. 'Show them what's what,' he urges, 'tell them your father was a general. Tell them about being presented at court in a white dress. Tell them you like Cliff Richard.'

But they won't have her in the WI. Full up, his elbow! She comes home and rants that it's all his fault, that he should never have married her. She never gets over being an orphan and only five foot in her stockinged feet.

When he bends to kiss the tawny skin on her neck, standing there among the catering tubs of ketchup and salad cream, she pushes him away. It's 1957 and he does not yet know the Lord. She'll beg him later, for his physical favours, sure she will (forgive his modesty here).

He remembers the *Princessita*, her deck treacly with

varnish, slipping over the brown water on the Broads. And the Holy Ghost laying a cool cheek against his. Like balm.

He, meanwhile, lays the back of a hot teaspoon on his son's bare thigh at breakfast time, to make him jump. It's a joke. It leaves behind a mark crimson as sin.

Now, there are three things which can ruin a minister:

1 Giving your affections to someone other than your wife.
2 Wanting to be a Big Name.
3 Going after Money.

Many are guilty on all three counts. But not he.

Christianity began on the Day of Pentecost, but he's gone beyond any old ordinary redemption. He knows things he shouldn't – things no one should have to know. The vortex isn't black, as you'd think, but multicoloured, like an oil slick, a sherbet rainbow sweetie.

The frizzy-haired nurse jumps out of her skin when he names her sister – his Chosen One. Donna, Donna, Donna. The word rocks and wobbles in his mouth – speaks of woman's flesh waiting to be healed.

*

'He's been in before,' the duty nurse told Gayle, 'several times. Though from what I can gather never this bad.'

She punched some buttons on the computer and brought up his file. 'Frank Fergus Chapman. Yes, in and out like nobody's business. Three times since November.'

'Really? Three times?' Gayle looked down at him and was going to speak to him, but he grabbed her hand suddenly, thick, horny nails digging at her flesh. She drew back.

'Look, love,' he said – hand frisking the air to find her again.

'Heavens,' said the nurse, stepping sideways to answer the phone. 'I'll get some help, shall I?'

Gayle pushed him off again.

'I baptize you,' he cried, lifting his head heavily, eyes rolling, 'in the name of the Alpha and the Omega, the Beginning and the End,' and his fingers fluttered and snapped at the air, sought her again. She moved right away. People were looking at them now.

A man was wheeled in in a chair, his head doubled over his legs, his foot weeping black blood. He was groaning. A young woman with long blonde hair and a fur coat and no tights or shoes on was standing next to the fire extinguisher, crying.

'Calm down, will you?' Gayle whispered to the man, Frank whatever his name was. 'You've had a shock. How do you know my sister's name?'

He clasped his hands, looked away, closed his eyes.

Another nurse came up and felt his pulse. He did not grab at the nurse. In the background, the blonde woman had now taken off her coat and was shouting something to the people waiting on the seats.

'Mr Chapman?' The nurse bent close. 'Are you in pain anywhere? Can you remember what happened? Are you his daughter?' she asked Gayle.

'No bloody fear,' Gayle said. She saw that he was looking at her again. His eyes were rapt, unseeing. The skin was stretched white and tight around the edges of his mouth. He had a strong face, big, even features. She could not think why such a strong and well-preserved face should be so physically repellent. 'No,' she told the nurse, 'I just brought him in, that's all.'

'A piece of pie the cat dragged in,' he sniggered as the nurse walked away again.

Gayle shivered. 'Pardon?'

'I can heal her.'

She looked at him and he adjusted his grin, toned it down. 'What do you mean? Who?'

'I'll tell you something interesting. Christianity began on the first day of Pentecost. So you can forget your good works, your penances, rosaries and indulgences. You can't substitute the Church and the Virgin Mary for Christ—' His voice had changed. He was murmuring, rapt.

'I'm not religious,' Gayle said quickly. 'What do you know about my sister? How do you know about her? I don't see how you could know anything.'

'Aren't you a Roman Catholic?'

'No.'

'Oh,' he looked abashed, 'I thought you were one of the Pope's girls.' He closed his eyes. 'This is a plain invitation to come to Jesus. So Donna isn't a Catholic?' He stared at her, excited.

'I don't know what you're talking about,' Gayle said, 'you're concussed.'

'If he's being a pain, do go,' the duty nurse called from the counter, 'it was good enough of you to bring him in.' Gayle nodded. She thought she'd been there long enough. She ought to get Kitty to bed.

'Donna needs the help of the Lord Jesus Christ,' he said then and once again the sound of her sister's name in his mouth made her shudder. Donna, Donna, Donna. 'He works through His Messenger, Frank Chapman.'

'I'm sorry.' She picked up her bag. 'I haven't got time for this,' she said, 'I told you, I don't believe. I'm an atheist.'

'Well, it's better than a Catholic,' he said. From somewhere on his dirty, bloody person, he produced a small card, printed with the words *Something Real*. He put it into her hand. She looked at it. 'Grace and Truth came by Jesus Christ. What must I do to be Saved? Remember John 3:16 and obey Acts 2:38. Then see yourself in Luke 12:32.' On the back, it said *Frank F. Chapman* and there was a phone number.

'My calling card,' he told her, 'you can take it or leave it. I only preach the word of God as found in the Bible. I have Donna's good in mind. The Bible could not be more clear on the healing of the sick.'

'What makes you think she's sick?'

The nurse came back. 'OK, we'll take him through now,' she said.

'Jesus came to me with a diagnosis,' he said.

Gayle laughed, despite herself. 'Jesus is a GP, is he?'

He ignored her. 'I pray for Donna,' he said, 'all those devils twisting her spine.'

How did he know about Donna's spine? She felt suddenly angry. 'You can leave Donna out of your prayers,' she said. 'It was us who wanted to help you. We did and that's that.'

'If you're ready, Mr Chapman,' said the nurse, who was feeling the man's pulse and ignoring their conversation, 'we'd like to do a wee X-ray now.'

He turned his head to Gayle. 'Cheer up, young woman.

Come for a chat another day. No extra charge.' As he smiled she saw how large and white his teeth were, with flashes of silver.

'Thanks,' she said, 'but I won't.' She realized he had already stopped listening. His eyes were fixed on a far point of the ceiling and he was licking his lips and saying, 'Praise the Lord!' over and over again and, as the trolley began to move, he raised his bunched fist in the air in a kind of salute.

'Watch him,' she told the nurse as he was wheeled off. 'He's angry – like a great big baby,' she added loudly, and specifically for him to hear.

*

His wife's a nice enough girl when he meets her, but she's a foreigner and a worrier and never gets used to the city filth and the monotonous city cold.

Some days, lying in the dark in his (joyfully) thin bed, he still sometimes forgets and waits for her to drop her hairpins in the dish and set the alarm clock in its chubby pink shell.

He could have been an adventurer – could have seen the world, had it not been for her.

And she's so chicken-boned and weightless that she can't take him on top of her for long, and if he pulls her onto him she just lies with her lips touching the outer flesh of his ear and he knows she's secretly picturing the larder shelves and making shopping lists.

I haven't got a wife, he used to think, I've got a list maker, an egg-timer. He'd congratulated himself on the neatness of marrying an orphan – no baggage, no ties – and he converted her from Catholicism, easy as pie, but still she wouldn't worship at his church, had to choose another where they all held hands and forged fellowship with each other instead of with Christ. Well, it's no skin off Jesus's nose. He's not short of a disciple or two, is he?

At her graveside, in the driving rain, he opens up his carrier bag and tries to give out sandwiches – potted meat, Hartley's seedless jam on Mother's Pride.

'Rejoice,' he tells the mourners (all, of course, from her upstart church), 'she's with Jesus, yes, sir, out of the rain, what's more.' But they don't recognize the Truth when they hear it. He unscrews his thermos and offers coffee, made that morning by his own fair hand (pouring boiling water on granules, reading the jar, unsure of everything now she isn't here), but no one wants refreshment or to look on the bright side. Coats flap open, damp hair snakes across mouths, great gusts of water chuck themselves from the roof guttering.

'Hallelujah!' he shouts. 'May Jesus shine His Holy Light on these sandwiches!'

'Shut up, Dad,' hisses Tommy from under his big black umbrella. 'Go away, get lost, shut up.'

And, yes, Tommy's still insisting upon wearing his girl's T-shirt with the lace-up front, but he looks fine. Back from the dead, but nothing would surprise Frank now. Tommy always loved his mum best. Frank blinks his eyes and finds tears there, digs his nails into his palms and discovers it hurts.

He saw her top-to-toe naked on the day she died, his wife of thirty-six years. The nurse bullied her to stand so she could change the sheets on the sofa bed in the front room, peel off her soiled nightdress. She could barely hold her body straight, but he watched, frozen by the back door, as she raised her arms in the air like a kitten punching at string, saw her sway slightly as the failing heart pumped its last rounds, did its last brief shift.

Four hours later she was dead on those clean sheets, her lips pulled tight, her body still privately hot.

'She married me because she was an orphan,' he dictated into his tape recorder that evening, 'for my nationality and because I had a gas-fired home with twin beds.'

But now when he leans back and shuts his eyes all he sees is Tommy's umbrella over the open grave – a winged shadow, waiting.

*

It was past eight that same evening by the time Gayle finally came to fetch Kitty, who had cried and cut up rough and refused to eat any tea. Overtired and unmanageably hungry, she'd coloured in Donna's drawing of a shark and then burst into tears again. In the end, they let her watch a programme about monkeys on TV, gave her crackers and milk, wrapped her in a blanket. Donna had fallen asleep on the sofa and eventually so had Kitty.

'She's been great,' Will lied in the freezing hallway, 'really good.' He hoped Gayle would go quickly.

'Thanks a lot.' She stood there in the semi-dark in her coat, an unlit cigarette in her hand, her fist held bunched to her as if she were worrying about something. 'I appreciate it.'

'Don't be silly,' he said. He was tempted to wake Donna. He was too shattered to make an effort with Gayle. He offered her a drink which she thankfully declined, but she stood instead and smoked the cigarette in the cold kitchen, bending to light it off the cooker. He shook some matches at her, but she waved them away, already inhaling. She'd left a little charred mark on the ring.

'So was everything OK?' he asked her finally and reluctantly. 'Did they sort him out?'

She stood there with the smoke curling loosely from between her fingers and said yes, the man had been admitted. She'd left him there being X-rayed. Presumably the police would talk to him – assuming it was a mugging. 'Actually,' she said, 'he was incredibly uncooperative. He's some sort of a born-again Christian – can't stop saying hallelujah and going on about Jesus and all that.'

She laughed and then frowned.

'Uh, great,' said Will, with little interest. He didn't want to get into having to discuss the whole thing with Gayle – as Donna no doubt would have, had she been awake. 'I'll wake Donna,' he said, 'she didn't want to miss you.'

'No,' Gayle said quickly, 'don't. There's more. Something else.'

'Oh?' Will folded his arms, leaned against the table and waited. Some of the felt pens Kitty had been using rolled and fell on the floor. Gayle bent to pick them up.

'His name's Chapman. Frank Chapman. He lives in Brixton. The weird thing is, he seems to know something about Donna.' She put a lid back on a pen.

'About Donna?'

'Yes.' She stubbed her cigarette out on the edge of the sink, then held it in the air while she looked for the bin.

He took it from her. The end was still moist from her lips. 'He knows her name and – this is weird – he seems to know about her back. He said various things. Said he wanted to cure her.'

'What?' Will said.

She told him everything the man had said.

'I don't see how he could possibly know anything about any of us,' Will said, 'I mean, we just found him there.'

'Quite.'

'So what did you say? Did you ask him how the hell he knew?'

Suddenly, she blinked and laughed. 'Look, it's not that important, I wouldn't worry.' She hooked her hair behind her ears, picked up her bag, Kitty's coat. 'He's a bit of a lunatic. He's making it up, he must be. It's all nonsense. I just felt I should tell you.'

She was backtracking – why? 'But if he said it, he must have got it from somewhere,' Will said.

She touched his sleeve, nurselike. 'Look, Will, don't you see, he's got a problem. He's not all there. I deal with people like this all the time. It means nothing.'

Will found her sudden dismissiveness infuriating. 'So what are you saying? It obviously means enough to tell me. You can't have it both ways. Either it means something or it doesn't. Christ, it might be a matter for the police.'

'Oh, for Heaven's sake. He must have heard us say her name or something – there are a million ways.'

'Oh, yeah, and we all discussed her back problem as we were standing there on the Common – like you do?'

Gayle laughed, unruffled. 'Well, maybe he knows someone we know?'

'Maybe,' Will said, furious at being drawn in and then dropped like this.

'I don't see why you're so annoyed.'

'I'm not annoyed.' But he was. As usual, she annoyed the hell out of him. He let out a long breath, looked at the clock.

'Let's not mention it to Donna,' she said.

'I don't see any point,' he agreed tersely. Not that he was going to play her game and make some big dramatic secret of it either. Then Kitty wandered in, imperious and sleepy, clutching the blanket to her chin.

'I'd drive you,' Will said without looking at Gayle, 'only my car's at the garage.' It was less than a mile to where they lived in Stockwell.

'Sure,' she said, and dug in her purse for a mini-cab number, swept the yawning Kitty over her shoulder. As they waited for it to come, he heard Donna shift on the sofa next door and sigh. 'How's she been?' Gayle asked him, as she stroked Kitty's hair.

'So so. The same.'

'Is it hard for you?'

He shrugged. 'It's worse for her.'

'I am sorry,' Gayle said. Then added, 'It was good of you to have Kitty, I'm sorry it took so long.'

'Don't mention it,' he said as coldly as he could, relieved to hear the cab outside.

'Don't give that man another thought,' she said as she went out of the door. 'He's not worth it, right?'

He said nothing. He shut the door and as he did so, Donna's stick, which had been propped in the corner, clattered loudly to the floor.

two

Donna's stick had a silver handle, a rounded knob with a loveheart stamped on it, a present from Will two Christmases ago.

He'd given it to her in bed, this long, thin gift wrapped in scarlet tissue paper and tied with a dark green ribbon like foliage. She'd known before she'd unwrapped it what it was. She'd fingered the loveheart engraved over the spherical end, cold and smooth and hard. 'Just in case,' Will had insisted, because he knew what a jump it was for her, 'think of it as ornamental.'

But of course she'd used it. Once she'd grasped what a help it was, once she'd understood that it didn't have to mean she was branded a cripple for life, then she'd cursed herself for not giving in before. All that unnecessary pain – or extra pain, anyway.

They – Will, Gayle, her mother, doctor, friends – had all put it down to vanity. Just as she still tried now and then to wear high heels and to dance at parties (well, it seemed a reasonable enough thing to want to do, at twenty-eight, though next day she would be tearful, hunched over with muscle spasm, which was hardly glamorous). But it wasn't vanity that had made her refuse the stick, it was optimism – the idea that help might be just around the corner. Every day, she seemed to read somewhere about something which might make the difference, which might mean she didn't have to give in. 'Queen of the alternative therapies' Will called her, and certainly she took a million vitamins and did yoga stretches, had tried massage, acupuncture, shoe inserts and relaxation tapes, as well as osteopathy, kinesiology, chiropractic. The list was endless.

But she was still waiting for someone to sort her out. To diagnose her and prescribe relief. Because the truth was, though it had been called a scoliosis, no one really knew why her muscles forced her spine to twist like a sketchy letter 'S'. And because no one knew, there was still hope. There was no point acting disabled if you might be cured at any moment.

Not that she was actually disabled of course, far from it. But certainly there were good days and not so good days. On a good day, she was a little stiff, a little achey, but her body was relatively straight and strong. She could bend down and bring in the milk off the step without thinking twice. But on the whole her sacroiliac joint had a mind of its own and, on a bad day (well, she tried not to call them 'bad' – her hypnotherapist had said it wouldn't help) it moved around so much that her pelvis tipped over to one side and she could not place one leg in front of the other without a lot of pain. Some mornings she woke and hurt so much that even rolling out of bed and getting to the lavatory was a major event.

On a day like this she just had to phone work and be late. Lie low. Lie, in fact, on a pack of frozen peas (which eased the inflammation) and take two Nurofen and wait. She watched a lot of daytime TV.

And that was the trouble: she was always lying down, vegetating. She no longer read books. It was as though her back trouble had frozen her mind, halted her in the middle of a train of thought. Long ago, she'd dreamt of being a teacher; instead, look at her, she worked in a shop.

The condition had crept up in her teens. She couldn't pinpoint an exact time. She had a stiff back now and then – exacerbated by a period or a batch of exams. Then, just before her sixteenth birthday, she'd gone with Gayle to see Genesis play Wembley and by the time she got back home had seized up to the point where she could barely walk.

At first, her mother was convinced she'd taken drugs or something at the concert. Gayle said no way. She'd had to lie on her back for six weeks. They'd injected her with everything they could think of – painkillers and muscle relaxants and tranquillizers – and she'd just lain there and tried to get her head together to revise for exams, waiting for it to pass.

It never did pass. By the time she'd recovered enough to walk – and do badly in her exams – one side of her pelvis was so much higher than the other that she was referred straight to the hospital where she had a series of tests, including a scan where they put you in a long box and look inside your tissue and bones.

'I'm glad to say we can find no reason,' the consultant said, 'I mean that's good news or bad news, depending upon how you look at it.'

'Well, it's good,' her mother had said, after a pause. 'But there's no operation?'

'Nothing to operate on. An operation would not be appropriate. It's what we call a functional scoliosis –

functional, because it's only the muscles doing the mischief.'

Donna looked at the doctor's lean, perky, clean-shaven face. In his open briefcase, she could see an apple and a Mars bar. She stood and held onto the back of a plastic hospital chair. She couldn't sit for very long that day. Gayle had had to help her get her socks and jeans on and even the short car journey had been painful. 'Only the muscles?' she repeated and her voice sounded as though it were coming from another room. That morning she'd lain on the floor and cried, beaten the musty, wiry carpet with her fists.

'Look.' The consultant did not look at her, but grabbed a plastic spine and pelvis off the desk, shoved a biro in between the bones and jiggled it. 'There's nothing wrong with the joints at all. The muscles are just spasming for no reason, and when they do,' he forced the knots of the spine together with his palms, 'compression and pain.'

Without meaning to, Donna began to cry. Short little gasps. She put her fingers to her eyes and felt them growing wet.

'OK, fine, so what next? What do we do?' her mother asked him. She'd moved into her you-can't-fool-me-because-I've-been-around voice. She reached behind her and patted Donna on the leg.

'What indeed? Well, you might want her referred for some other sort of help.' The consultant pushed a box of tissues at Donna. His tie had a pattern of leaping kangaroos on it. His lips were pastel, lilac-pink and new looking, wet in a healthy way.

'This isn't just some sort of hysterical condition,' her mother told him.

He sighed and looked down at his papers, as though he wasn't going to say it, but he couldn't be so sure. 'We'd be happy to prescribe painkillers. Some of the newer ones are more effective than you'd imagine.'

'I thought they wrecked your liver,' Donna told him as she compressed her tissues into a hard, tight ball.

'Not in the short term,' he said with a display of patience, 'not in the short term.'

They'd gone and had coffee in the hospital canteen. A brand-new baby lay in a carry-seat. Donna looked at her flowering of black hair and the pink metallic balloon tied to her seat. She stared back and fisted the air, agitated. The baby's mother leaned across and laughed, 'Someone's keen on you,' she said.

'Don't you worry,' her mother blew on her watery coffee, 'we're not going to take no for an answer.'

But they had, of course. They'd had to – what else was there? No one knew what was wrong with Donna – it did not look like anyone ever would. And meanwhile, what was the point of not managing? People had worse to put up with – look at the people Gayle worked with, for a start.

She wasn't dying and her brain was intact. She had a stick with a silver knob, which had become her fetish, her worry bead – had slowly turned into a part of her. She took care not to leave the house without it. Even on a good day, it was a prop. Friends insisted it was intriguing, glamorous. Kitty said that when she was a big girl, she would have one too.

*

Will watched Donna take her clothes off and chuck them on the chair and wondered why she was so angry. She pulled a plaid nightshirt over her head and lay down on the carpet with a book under her head, to do her exercises. 'What did Gayle say?' she asked him, staring at the ceiling, fingers on her abdomen.

'Not much,' he said, 'he's going to be OK.'

'She doesn't know what happened, then?'

'No. He wasn't very forthcoming.'

'Oh.' Donna pulled each knee to her chest. She dabbed at her tongue to remove a hair from her mouth. Will watched as she performed her slow, deliberate movements – aligning her spine, breathing, allowing her shoulders to drop. Donna was never absent from what she was doing, never. Her concentration on her body and her pain was a fierce, dark thing, which made the rest of her harder to see.

She was still a schoolgirl when he met her – dazzlingly pretty, ears pierced in three places, smelling of Nivea Cream. She had a limp, and was briefly embarrassed by the fact that, in bed, she had to lie flat on her back. His first virgin – but half a bottle of wine and half a dozen Bob Dylan tracks later, she was simply his.

All through his twenties he messed around with her, often unfaithful, holding her at arm's length, refusing to claim her absolutely. He made her promise not to get involved. He never said he loved her.

One summer, he gave up his job and went off travelling, told her not to wait. On a different continent, he slept with someone else and he wrote and told Donna about it – a death wish of a letter.

But when he got back, she was waiting. If he looked for obstacles, she smoothed his path. He made a point of not kissing her for several days – an excruciating private experiment – until he finally saw how much he'd hurt her.

When he gave himself up – submitted all over again to her black hair and fragile, slippery limbs – he just went for it: asked her to live with him.

That was two flats ago. Four Christmases. Now they still lived together in a scared and temporary way, with their books on separate shelves, half their things in boxes in the spare room.

'We had nothing to say to each other,' he remarked now, 'absolutely nothing.'

'Who?'

'Gayle and me.'

Donna lifted her head off the ground and looked at him, then dropped it back, as though nothing she could say would be worth the physical effort – and she was probably right. He thought about moving in on her right there on the bedroom floor, pressing her mouth against his, burning his knees on the carpet, but he hadn't taken off his own clothes yet, and by the time he got into bed, she was already turned away from him, her shoulders stiff, her hand cradled under her cheek like a child.

'What is it?' he asked, without knowing whether it was a specific expression of discontent he was responding to, or just a general certainty that everything was wrong.

'I don't think I can go on like this,' she said at last to the wall.

'Like what?'

'Like this,' she said, her voice dangerously calm and dry, 'without a baby.'

He flinched inwardly and clasped his hands behind his head and looked at the blank TV screen. All his energy for this conversation had gone – drained away. He didn't want to be the one to remind her of what the doctors had said. She could not even lift Kitty onto a swing, let alone carry an entire, growing child of her own. 'I know,' he reached out his hand and felt for hers, but she moved her fingers so he could not take it, 'I know.'

She made a noise in her throat, but she didn't cry, for which he was relieved. Why was most of her fury directed at him? Because he could not be sufficiently devastated? Because he could not view the situation as tragic? Because he loved her whether or not she was supposed to bear children?

'Can't you see, I love you?' he'd said to her at Christmas when she had the miscarriage a year ago. 'We could wait ten years before we have any kids.' She'd turned up the collar of her jacket and looked at him as if he were shit.

'You must be patient with her,' Donna's mother pleaded on the phone, adding as a second thought, 'I know you are, of course.'

Yes, he was. They all knew he was. He guided her as best he could through the world out there and if he saw a pushchair he steered her across the road. 'Why're we crossing the road?' she'd ask.

'Because I want to see if the print shop's open.'

Or: 'What's wrong with the pavement on that side?'

'Nothing. I just fancied a change, that's all.' She followed him. He held her elbow, put an arm around her thin shoulders, kissed her cold cheek in the wind. Sometimes he wondered whether she knew what he was doing – and when he wondered, he realized that she must. But mostly, he gave it no thought at all. Just carried on steering her, oblivious.

'There is nowhere for this conversation to go,' he said.

She remained silent.

'What do you want me to say?' he asked, finally. 'Tell me and I'll say it.'

'I want a baby,' she said, in a voice which was metallic with grief.

'So. Tell me what to say to that.'

She said nothing so he leaned across and kissed her neck. She made a spluttery sound and he couldn't tell if it presaged tears or not. Rain was drumming on the window. Her feet touched the warmed arch of his own in the bed. He worked his hand in gently between her legs and she didn't stop him and he felt how dry and hot she was. He licked his fingers. 'I'll make you feel better,' he said.

'Don't laugh at me,' she began, but he felt her move to let his fingers in.

He only heard her watery breath as he rode there in the dark – could only hope she shared the familiar amnesia which flushed across his belly and brain, zapping all doubts, recreating tolerance and calm. 'I haven't got my diaphragm in,' she said suddenly, just before he overflowed.

He pulled out in time and felt the semen spray up disappointingly between her breasts. But he was grateful she'd given him the chance to pull out. 'Love you,' he whispered, 'love you.' But the words were unconvincing, scripted – seemed to come from a long way off.

*

At six thirty next morning as Gayle got the bus to work, she made a deal with herself: she would check on Mr Chapman but that was it. She wasn't going to get into a conversation or waste any more time thinking about him.

A freezing rain was falling. She was shattered, her body loose and light and fidgety for lack of sleep. She had a whole shift to get through before she could go and get Kitty from Hilary-the-childminder's and lie on the bed and share a banana and watch Tots' TV with her.

Kitty always slept over at Hilary's when Gayle was on earlies – it was a long-term arrangement and it made sense, since she had to be out and on her way by five fifteen at the latest. It meant Kitty could wake at her usual time on Hilary's camp bed and eat a bowl of Coco Pops (a treat reserved for Hilary's) and watch a video whilst Hilary no doubt smoked her first cigarette in the kitchen and listened to the Flying Eye.

Hilary said it was no trouble, and only charged her a babysitting fee for the evening. The idea was of course that it was less disruptive for Kitty, but all the same a run of days like this would leave her cranky and tearful. And Gayle could never get to sleep when Kitty wasn't in the flat. You'd think it would be the other way round, but no, she'd wake on and off all night, staring at the black walls, gulping in the silence, the nagging absence of breath.

One day, she promised herself, she'd do something else,

find another way of supporting Kitty. No more commodes and catheters, no more enemas and shrouds. No more having to peel off all her clothes and shower the moment she got home – shampooing her hair twice over – before she could bring herself to put her arms around her daughter. Because death got everywhere: into your skin, your hair, under your nails, between your teeth.

She had these persistent, vivid daydreams about sunlight: Kitty crouching on a rock, squinting into the yellow air, watching a lizard scatter itself earthwards – razz of sea and raw glitter of sky, flowers hard and tight in the smoky afternoon shadows – paperbacks curling in the midday heat. The faraway roll of waves; the silvery rub of crickets in the *maquis*, the watch left ticking in a canvas shoe.

Once she'd seen a programme about epileptic children who had 'absences', each one lasting a matter of seconds. Sometimes Gayle felt as if most of her life was an absence, and the only conscious moments were those in between – when she imagined herself somewhere else. When she came to life.

*

Annie Corbaci met her outside the locker room. She had bruiselike shadows under her eyes and wisps of hair escaped her heavy plait. 'Swift is dead,' she said, 'just now, after hanging on all night. Perfect bloody timing.' She bit her lip angrily.

'I'll do her,' Gayle said immediately.

'Don't be silly, we'll do her together,' said Annie. 'But I need a cigarette first.

Outside, the dawn rain was clearing and weak lines of

sun patterned the concrete floor of the sluice. 'Well, well,' Annie said and laughed. Annie was pretty, with her wide, pale face and her black hair, eyebrows shaped like a film star's. If it hadn't been for the port-wine birthmark down the side of her face, she could have been a model, she was that good-looking. But it spread from the edge of her left eyebrow down across her left cheek almost to her jaw. The size and shape of a small banana. Some days it was pale, under the skin, waiting to happen; other days it was livid, marking her like a wound.

'You're not shocked, are you,' Gayle said, 'that she's gone?'

'I'm always shocked,' said Annie, 'I'm that type,' and took a Bic lighter from her pocket. They stood together by the rinsed-out bedpans and stiffened J-cloths. Gayle banged a lavatory lid shut and sat down, and Annie pulled up the sash window so the chilly air blew in, rested her elbows on the sill and gulped the smoke. 'They said you brought someone into A&E yesterday?' Gayle nodded. 'Why'd you go and do that? Can't keep away from the place?'

'He was mugged,' Gayle said, 'we could hardly leave him.'

'Not much bloody fun on a Sunday, though.'

Gayle shrugged. 'They said they were going to admit him to Mellor.'

'Going to pop up and have a look at him, then?'

'Maybe. If I get a moment. If no one else decides to die first.'

Annie laughed.

She was the only one on the ward Gayle could talk to. Her father was Italian, her mother Irish. Her hair was long enough to sit on and she wore an ankle bracelet under her tights. She rode to work on a moped and, after late shifts, she went out clubbing, condoms in her bag. 'I wouldn't rely on those,' Gayle had warned, 'that's how Kitty came about.'

'You're kidding?'

'Not that I have any regrets.' Kitty, whose hair smelled of warmed-up honey and without whom life would rattle around pointlessly.

Despite her birthmark – or maybe because of it – Annie didn't have a coy bone in her body. She shook a Femidom out for them in the canteen at coffee to show how they crackled. 'Like one of them Co-op carriers,' she said.

'You'd be good in Family Planning,' one of the nurses laughed, 'you know, blowing up Durexes and that.'

All Annie wanted was to settle down. 'I haven't had a steady boyfriend since I was seventeen,' she said, 'seventeen. Thought my life was beginning. If I'd known then it was grinding to a bloody halt.'

'You don't stand still for long enough,' Gayle said, 'you should forget about men and look after yourself, eat properly for a start.'

'Easier said than done,' said Annie, who existed on crisps and Diet Coke and chagrin. 'What I need is a new face. That would change things.'

'But no one notices. I didn't think you minded it?' Gayle was momentarily shocked. It was very rare for Annie to mention her face.

Annie gave her a look which she'd never forgotten. 'It has ruined my life. I hate it.'

'But no one notices,' Gayle said again. 'You're so pretty.'

'You should try going on the tube with my face,' Annie said. 'Try walking anywhere.'

'Would make-up cover it?'

Annie laughed. 'This is after the make-up.'

Annie lived alone above a betting shop with her pet cockatiel. 'One of these days,' she told Gayle, 'you and that kid of yours will have to come round.'

'Love to,' said Gayle, but Annie never followed it up and Gayle never pressed her.

*

Curtains had been drawn around Emily Swift's bed and the hospital sheet, with its darns and grey laundry marks, seemed so flat to the bed you could imagine there wasn't a body there. Annie pulled it back and touched the beaky nose. White skin so pouchy and wrinkled that the recesses seemed black.

'Anyone coming?' Gayle asked.

'Oh well, they've informed the son, but I wouldn't hold your breath.'

The porters came with a trolley. They were talking about football. One had a black jewel in his nose and he winked at Gayle. 'Give us a bell when you've finished, love.'

'It's not love,' she said.

Emily Swift's limbs were light as a baby's but without the fight. Annie soaked the cotton wool in formalin and Gayle stuffed the orifices of the body using tweezers. 'Wish that woman would shut up,' Annie said. In the Day Room Ruby Jones was screaming her high-pitched, continuous screams.

'Have you got a biro?' said Gayle and she filled out the

name tags and taped them on the shroud and they pulled off their gloves and binned them.

'Bye, bye,' said Annie as she swished the curtain shut and went off to dish out porridge to the living, whilst Gayle moved from bed to bed with a stack of clean drawsheets, whipping off each mound of covers to see who'd had a shit in the night.

*

It was almost eight and Will had been in the office an hour and a half and the vegetable market was already loud beneath his closed window.

He'd done nothing but blow on a cup of coffee and bite his lips and stare out at the crates being stacked and chucked. He hadn't even looked at the papers. He always argued (to himself and others) that he needed thinking time – that a certain amount of staring into space reflected itself later in his creativity, that the thoughts took their best and most productive shape when he was doing nothing. A balls of an argument. This morning his head was empty. He'd just had to leave the flat.

Because there were days when he knew he'd go crazy if he didn't leave the very minute he woke. Sometimes he didn't even bother to shower – he kept a toothbrush and shaver at the office – just opened the curtains and dressed in the glare from the street lamp, pulling the front door behind him as he stepped into the freezing space of the street.

It wasn't Donna's fault, it was him. He was choking. Sometimes she lifted her pretty chin and said, 'What are you thinking?' and he knew she meant it innocently and lovingly enough, but it was as if an abyss had grown up around him and he knew that if he stepped back it would be straight into darkness.

At eight fifteen Betty, his PA, arrived. It was good to see Betty, it always was. Things edged up a notch when she came in. Betty was a brilliant assistant – small and curvy with a red mouth and cap of black hair, engaged unfortunately to some jerk who taught PE. 'No one gets engaged any more,' he'd mocked when she'd announced it. 'What the hell's the point of hanging around?'

'We're waiting till Mat finishes his teacher-training,' she told him, a little haughtily.

'Aren't you even going to live together?'

'We want to do it properly,' she said, 'save for a place. Get a mortgage.'

Will had laughed bitterly and said nothing. He didn't know why Betty's careful arrangements irked him so. Ten years ago, he'd have ignored it and just fucked her, got her out of his system. She had a beautiful, moon-shaped face, big eyes, big, offered-up tits. Maybe he looked beyond the body these days, maybe that was it. Anyway, he made do with a safe, constant flirtation. They sometimes went to wine bars at lunchtime, bought each other drinks. All very innocent. 'How's Donna?' she'd ask, and he'd say, 'Fine. How's Mat?'

'He's fine,' – all this gravely and without irony.

The agency had an eye on her for an account handler, and she knew and deserved it – they made a point of being good promoters, good recognizers of talent. Though not, of course, if she went off and started sprogging with her gym teacher. The choice was hers.

'Well?' She slapped her briefcase on the desk and went

to hang up her coat. The air where she'd stood for a moment smelled powdery, girly. 'So what's new?'

'Not a lot,' he said.

'Oh, come on,' she flicked the switch on her computer – a static flash.

'I rescued this old chap on Clapham Common yesterday.'

'No!' Betty took a tissue and blew her nose.

'I did.'

'Right, I want the whole story.' She prised the lid off her cappuccino and sat down. He told her how they found the old man. He didn't exactly make it clear that it was Gayle who had gone to the hospital, nor did he mention what the man had supposedly said about Donna.

Betty seemed quite impressed. 'It was good of you to stop. Lots of people might've, I don't know, just walked on or something.'

He smiled. 'Yeah? Well, we couldn't just leave him there – poor blighter.' He glanced out at the freezing Soho sky. 'His name's Frank,' he said, 'Frank somebody or other.' And he laughed.

*

Gayle went straight up to see Frank Chapman in her morning break.

He was propped up on pillows, mildly sedated, and he'd been cleaned up. He was better looking than he'd appeared the day before – a strong, even face, large features. His glasses were on the bedside cabinet, though one lens was missing, and the flesh around his eyes was bleached and soft. There was a dressing around his chest. 'He's pretty good. We're keeping him in till Friday,' the nurse said, 'then we'll reassess.'

Gayle thought he was asleep at first, then he opened his eyes and said, 'Well, well.'

'Hello, I've brought you a paper.' She put the *Mirror* on his table. 'How are you?'

'All the better for seeing you. Hallelujah, praise the Lord!' Gayle felt like Red Riding Hood. She drew up an orange plastic chair. 'I've been expecting you,' he said.

'Really? So. Have you told them what happened?'

He blinked. 'I've never been able to resist a bargain, you know. I'm a born businessman. I've made money out of anything and everything – birdbaths, electric and manual typewriters, violins. I once went to Majorca for five days for £25 – a bargain, including flight and hotel. They may not have provided lunch, I can't remember.'

Gayle laughed.

'Of course,' he continued, 'I could never persuade Lola to leave home – she would not and could not fly. But she didn't mind me going off to Bedford now and then to attend the Seven Thunder meetings, where I was much blessed. I had the edge, you see. I knew the Truth as told by the Lord Jesus Christ. I wasn't happy to eat yesterday's food with warmed-over gravy.'

'Look, Mr Chapman,' she said, 'have you told them what happened?'

He stared at her. 'Are you Donna?'

'No, I'm Gayle. Her sister.'

'Look alike, don't you?'

'Not really.'

'Where is she?'

Gayle swallowed. 'Why?'

'Lola will be waiting in Heaven for me,' he said, folding his arms.

'Is Lola your wife?'

He nodded, but more to himself than to her. 'Waiting to thank me profusely, for getting her justified and sanctified. She thought she'd find the Truth at her so-called 'Christian' centre, you see. How daft can you be?'

'Look,' Gayle began.

'In those denominational Churches they serve yesterday's food. Lola swallowed it, oh yes she did. Me, I'm an eagle. Flying high – feasting on freshly killed meat. Amen! The best thing that could happen to the Church would be to make it illegal to speak about Jesus. That would really purify 'em. That would sort 'em out.' He paused, licked his lips. 'Why should I tell them what happened?'

'Well, if you agreed to make a statement they could probably do something.'

'Do something?' He coughed and laughed. 'Why should anyone do anything?'

'So it doesn't happen again. What was it? Were you mugged?'

'In a manner of speaking.'

'You don't sound very sure.'

He laughed. 'All these questions. Where's Donna?'

Gayle sat very still. 'Would you mind,' she said, pressing her thumbs together in her lap, 'telling me how you know about my sister?'

*

After the funeral, they put on a spectacle for Lola at the Pentecostal Christian Centre. He's barred of course – yes, barred from his own wife's memorial.

They haven't let him in since February 1984, when he interrupted their so-called service with the Good News. It was after his dream of Brother Vernon – January 12 of the same year to be exact – when the Word bubbled up out of Brother V's bosom and landed splat at his feet. As soon as Frank woke up he placed an order for five hundred tracts from the Bible Truth Depot.

He waited three weeks for them to arrive and then nipped into the hall just as those false preachers were singing and rolling their eyes into their heads and clasping hands. He threw a swarm of tracts in the air, told them they would all roast in the fires of hell, every last one of them, man, woman and child, a very barbecue of sinners, if they did not let him baptize them with the Word. Jesus was the only path to Redemption. The only Saviour. Not their Jesus, but his Jesus.

The pastor put two of his mindless bouncers on the door and told him he was barred. Instructed the congregation to slam the door in his face if he came near them or their families. 'Sister Lola doesn't want you here.' (As if he, Frank Chapman, didn't know what his own wife wanted!) 'She wants fellowship and peace!'

'Go on, then,' and he'd kicked the wall, 'persecute me! Cast me down! It wouldn't be the first time! You'll answer for it on Judgement Day! Sin don't come free of charge, you know!'

'We're not interested in doing anything to you,' said the

pastor, cracking open the door, sticking out his white fuzz-ball of a chin, 'do whatever you like, Mr Chapman, but don't do it here.'

Sister Lola, indeed! The Church says its false, hollow prayers for her when she has her first angina attack, but still lets her go on pouring her baking down its throat. When he tries to stop her, she tells him the gas and flour come straight out of her pension and are hers to do with as she likes. At the Church, she says, her hesitant, ungrammatical English don't matter, she's welcomed in. There's always so much singing and rejoicing, so much fellowship.

She hides her Last Will and Testament from him, of course she does. Leaves everything (eight hundred pounds he could have done with) to the Church. She begs that she be buried with a Polaroid of Bunty (the poodle) – diabetic and blind. And she wants the dog put down after she's gone. As if he can't even look after a dog – as if the animal would be better off dead!

So, after thirty-six years of marriage, she finally lets him know what she thinks of him; he finally knows exactly where he stands.

So after her funeral, whilst they rant and wail in their makeshift place of worship, he catches the number 57 home and finds some meatballs she made, at the back of the fridge. Working back from the day of her death, he calculates them to be less than ten days old, so he heats them up and has them with cream crackers and margarine.

It's unexpectedly comforting, to eat food cooked by his wife. Afterwards, much revived, he spends two hours stamping the Good News onto envelopes. Malachi 4:5 and

Revelation 10:7. Feels less sorry for himself. Sleeps like a log, a lamb.

*

Things had changed in the five years Donna had worked in Serendipity. They'd gone from a tiny shop on a Battersea backstreet to a great site on Lavender Hill, dead opposite the Arts Centre. Lavender Hill was definitely on the up, Sarka said.

Sarka had started Serendipity as a gift shop almost ten years ago (Gifts for All Ages and All Occasions, the flyer had said), but they got so many mums coming in and the Ambi and Brio toys did so well that they'd eventually started doing kids' clothes too – Absorba, Osh-Kosh, Petit Bateau – all that top-of-the-range stuff, which you'd otherwise have had to go over the river for.

Sarka had never really said it, but the fact was that Donna was a kind of unofficial partner. All the running was more or less left to her. She controlled stock and did most of the buying. Sarka said Donna had such a flair for identifying gaps in the market. It had been her idea to start children's hairdressing on Saturday mornings, and she thought up the nanny-share noticeboard too, which brought a million extra people into the shop. When the local paper came and did a piece on them, Sarka made sure they took a photo of Donna, too.

In the last five years, Sarka had divorced her accountant husband and remarried a sculptor. Her heart wasn't really in the shop any more. 'I've just lost interest,' she said, 'I want excitement. Maybe I should be a travel agent.'

So every day Donna was surrounded by baby clothes. It was all right for Sarka, who'd never wanted kids and had three teenaged stepsons now anyway. But for Donna, just being in the shop increased her longing for a baby by about one hundred per cent.

Perhaps it should have helped. Perhaps the contact with babies – holding them, the downy hair teasing her upper lip, rocking them whilst their mothers browsed through clothes – should have worked the problem out of her system. But the fact was that every pushchair that came through that door, every perspiring woman squatting to sort through the drawer of pink-striped bodysuits with poppers, every gasping, screaming red face, every tale of a sleepless night, reminded her of what she could not have.

Sometimes she wept in the back room.

'Just let it go,' Sarka said, 'there's more to life than kids, for Christ's sake. Borrow mine sometime.' But Donna didn't want to borrow, she wanted to have. And she wanted it so much that, when it happened at Christmas – miraculous, incredible, significant – she wondered whether perhaps she, too, had been visited by an angel.

They were doing the Christmas window, pine cones and fir cones and holly sprays – no tinsel, Sarka said. She wanted countrified, natural, she said as she stepped back and lit a cigarette. The smoke – which had never bothered her before – suddenly made Donna's throat tighten. She rushed to the small loo which doubled as an extra stockroom and immediately threw up.

The man rang up the Clear Blue Kit without a second glance, as if it was just any old bottle of shampoo, slipped it in a white paper bag, where it danced in her hands. She crept out past the rubber-tipped weaning spoons and teething gels and chubby jars of chicken and carrot.

When the blue line appeared, she knelt on the bath mat and held her breath. 'You can't have it,' Will said immediately, 'think of what it would do to you.'

Don't worry, she told the liquid beginnings of her baby, you're in there and I won't let anything happen to you. Will sat watching *NYPD Blue*, biting his nails. She walked around upstairs, singing. 'OK,' he said finally, 'we'll talk to Gruber before we decide.'

Dr Gruber didn't smile any congratulations. Instead he calmly explained the facts – that she would be in pain and hugely incapacitated by the growing weight of the baby, that the birth would have to be early by Caesarean section, and that she might not be able to walk for some time after. How she'd be affected in the long term, he really couldn't say.

'Maybe it would cure me?' Donna joked. She felt zany, light-hearted, dizzy with desire.

The doctor didn't laugh. 'I can see you want a baby very much,' he said.

'Not at the expense of her health,' Will said quickly. As if he could mould her verbally into submission.

'But you don't know that I'll necessarily be worse?' Donna asked, fingering the knob of her stick, the loveheart's symmetrical, curled outline.

'We don't really know anything,' the doctor agreed, 'but I'm not going to lie to you and say it will be all right.'

Donna wanted to be lied to.

She pretended to think it through. She frowned. She pretended she hadn't already made up her mind. 'All sorts of bad things can happen to anyone,' she told Will in the freezing car park, 'anyone could go under a bus tomorrow. You can't live your life on that basis.'

'That's no comparison,' said Will abruptly.

'For me it is.'

'So what are you saying?'

'Please can we let this baby be born?'

He hesitated, frowning, and then he squeezed her shoulders. They didn't speak about it again. Slowly, the question mark left her face.

They lived off the news all Christmas. She stopped feeling sick, the dragging tiredness seemed to lift. Her mother went on about a wedding but they stalled. 'I've never been so happy,' Donna told Will truthfully, 'never.'

Then, in the third week of January, she woke in the night to feel wetness all around her. At first she thought she must have peed, but when she turned on the light she saw the black glisten of blood.

Will held her on the lavatory for an hour as she sweated and sobbed, as with each spasm her body rejected her child, spat it out and forced it off its lifeline. Levered its knuckles off the edge.

'I can't sustain life,' she gasped to Will at some point in the long violence of that night, and he shushed her and stroked the wet hair from her face. He tried to stop her seeing the pale mass which was clearly the foetus – a terrible, shadowy human shape on the wad of lavatory paper – but she made sure she drank it in, locked the picture into her memory before he flushed it down.

Dr Gruber sent her for a D&C and remarked gently that, though he well understood that she didn't want to hear this, it really probably was for the best. For the best. Everyone repeated the phrase to her. Only she knew the truth – that the damage was all inside.

Previously, her womb had been an unknown space, clear and curved, forged of air. Now it was a wedge of knitted flesh – a grave, a scab.

*

'I have the healing touch,' Frank Chapman told Gayle, 'handed down from Christ, Amen. Believe me. I want to help Donna.' He spread his hands, palms up, childlike.

'But how do you know there's anything wrong with her?' Gayle said. She glanced down at her watch. She knew she must get back to the ward.

He eased himself up on the pillows. 'That was a mistake, to look at your watch,' he said. 'In a hurry are you?'

'I have to get back to work, yes,' she told him.

'You spend time healing others, but turn a blind eye to your own sister.'

'I find that remark incredibly offensive,' she said quietly.

He ignored her. 'She is a distressed person. She's so young, isn't she? You wouldn't wish pain on her?'

'Oh, for Heaven's sake,' Gayle began, then added, realizing he was leading her away from the main issue, 'I would like to know when you've seen her.'

'Maybe you would.' Frank Chapman grabbed her hand. His grip was hard, horny, the skin rough with neglect. 'Maybe you would. But His powers are hidden. And Donna's had enough.'

Gayle pulled away, full of anger. 'Get off me. Shut up about my sister.'

He sighed, softened, closed his eyes. 'Does it matter, how I know?'

'Yes it does. To me. If you want me to listen to all this stuff.' She stood up because she'd had enough. Five minutes ago she'd had enough. He followed with his eyes.

'Jesus Christ tells me things. Things which will benefit you.'

'Oh yes? Such as?'

'If you don't wish to heed what I say, that's your business.' He shut his eyes. His eyelids were pure white, smooth as eggs.

'Why should I trust you? You never answer any of my questions.'

He opened one eye. 'Oh, well, the love of Christ has no whys and wherefores.'

'That,' she told him, 'is a meaningless thing to say. If you really want to know, I don't like you very much – not from what I've seen so far. I don't like your aggression.'

'So far!' He smashed his fists together and laughed.

'Yes,' she put the plastic chair back on a stack, 'your aggressive tone of voice. It puts me right off.'

'Fine.' He closed his eyes, but he was smiling and she didn't like it. 'Have it your way.'

'Thanks,' she said, 'I will,' and walked off quickly before he could steal the last word.

three

Will's father was killed on a perfect summer's afternoon, during a heatwave, whilst Evonne Goolagong took the Ladies' Singles title at Wimbledon in straight sets.

Will had a folder full of cuttings from his father's showbiz column days, and a photo of him in Luigi's, his face eroded by cigarette smoke. He didn't remember him as a journalist – only afterwards, the lighting business at Virginia Water. And Terri.

When his father lost his job on the paper, he set up Evison Lighting in the garage. Fewer overheads, he said. He put in a carpet and a phone line, and got a secretary. Terri was nice. She gave Will Milky Ways when he came in from school: dark blue waxy crackle, shower of white stars. 'To keep the wolf from the door,' she winked. He felt guilty, didn't know why.

She wore jeans and skinny-ribs and eyeliner. Her sheepskin coat reeked of animal and a perfume she said was Coty's White Musk. The smell floated out behind her when she walked past, clung to the air like the end of a shout. You could tell she'd arrived in the morning just by opening the office door and breathing in.

Terri's dad had a carpet shop, the biggest in Hayward's

Heath. 'Worth a fortune, but common as muck,' his mum would announce as they drove past.

Every morning Terri flung her car keys on the kitchen table, made coffee for herself and his father and picked her way across the paved area to the garage. Sometimes the key-ring – wet-look red with a bitten apple motif on – was still there at midnight. Will came down once and saw his Mum standing there next to the kettle and the mug-tree, just staring at Terri's keys and breathing.

Will knew something was going on. Often his dad didn't come to bed. He knew because he'd creep into his mum's bed in the middle of the night and sleep there, his stomach all knotted up, his face pressed into the foetal curl of her brushed nylon back.

A year later, Terri's car just veered off the road in the middle of the fierce heat of a July afternoon and overturned three times down the steep embankment. She was at the wheel.

They weren't found until dusk. Terri had chipped her collarbone and fractured her jaw and three ribs, but she lived; Will's father had sustained a single blow to his skull and died instantly. His body was perfect, intact, his mum said – even his shoes still on, the laces tied with double knots.

Will was eleven.

Straight away, his mum sold the business – 'For peanuts,' she told Will, 'because your father and that woman weren't making a bean, only pissing around' – and got things in order. She only gave in to grief on Sunday nights when she watched *The Onedin Line* on TV, her stockinged feet tucked under her on the sofa and a stiff gin in her hand. Once she tried to cry all over Will, but he pulled away from her alcohol breath and sat on another chair.

In September, she suddenly decided to send him away to school – just like that, with barely time to buy name tapes. 'We'll look forward to the holidays,' she said.

But he didn't look forward to anything ever again. Sometimes he felt he too had died that summer and, like his father, he'd hardly a mark to show for it, no chance to get used to it.

At school, he told a teacher that he wanted to die. The teacher called his mum in, said they could arrange for him to see a counsellor. She said no thanks. 'What a cheek,' she stopped in the school car park to prise the gravel from under the toe of her strappy sandals. 'Who the hell do they think they are?'

She signed a note releasing him from games. 'I hope you'd never take drugs,' she remarked.

Nothing more was ever said.

Gradually, he lost the impulse to die.

*

Donna lay on the floor.

She was dressing for work and she'd pulled her leggings on, but the pain through her hip had suddenly become too much and she'd had to lie down. She reached for a paperback to put under her head, tried to relax. She'd have been tempted to take a couple of Diazepam, but Will had hidden them. So she took two Nurofen and lay there half-dressed, waiting for her pelvis to straighten and drop.

Down the street a dog was barking – short, incessant yaps. On the TV breakfast news a man had accidentally crushed his six-year-old daughter to death when he backed his lorry up. Sometimes it seemed to Donna that the world was full of nothing but people crushing one another, killing each other because they hadn't bothered to look.

*

Dan Mintoe stood just outside the doorway of Will's office. He took his hands from his pockets and offered Will a piece of Stimorol. Will declined.

'Chemistry,' Dan said, separating the gum from the foil, 'that's what we're thinking about – vital at the presentation stage. Got to kick off on the right foot before you get anything in place. You're good with clients, they like you, you know what I mean.'

The last part was not a question. When Dan said things a sufficient number of times, they became true.

'Yeah?' Will said. He never knew where Dan was leading – never knew what to think about him.

Dan's wife had just given birth prematurely to their first child, Genevieve, who was in a Special Baby Unit and – in the Polaroid on Dan's desk – had a shadowy, old lady's face. Will didn't know why he found that elderly face in the white cotton cap so disturbing. If Dan felt any worry or grief he hid it well. He was the sharpest of the three partners – quick and so incisive it was almost sad. At thirty-eight or so, his hair was already entirely silver, lending him gravity. He almost always chewed gum.

'Yes,' he said (and here it was, what he'd come to say), 'it's you. They really like you. It's within our control, so to speak, that they like you. A carrot, so to speak.' He grinned in a showman way and showed the shadowy black of his fillings.

'I'm flattered.' Will smiled. He still had his head in the ideas for the commercial. John had said that Snake Williams could direct it and he really respected Snake's work with Eslo Butter and BL. John had said he just knew Will and Snake would click.

'John and I have discussed it,' Dan said, 'we'd like you to head the presentation.' He watched Will's face. 'It's the right thing,' he added.

Will said carefully, 'Well, that's great. I'm delighted.'

Dan, who'd kept his distance all through this conversation, now looked away. Will had huge admiration for Dan. He was one of the cleverest in the business. Everyone knew he'd started by sweeping the pavement outside Saatchi's when he was seventeen.

'Oh, good,' said Dan.

'How's the baby?' Will asked him.

Dan grimaced. 'Bearing up. How's your girlfriend?'

'Oh, much the same,' said Will but Dan had already moved away and he was talking to the open door.

*

Frank's the same but different. He's feeling better; everything is going according to plan.

When the bobby asks if he wants to make a statement – because no one can act if he doesn't press charges – he replies, 'I'm too busy to start casting stones.'

He means it. He knows they will bring Donna to him pretty soon. His healing hands are anointed magnets, drawn stealthily along the route picked out by Jesus.

He remembers how the girl stood over him at last on the frozen ground, leaning on her stick, holding her twisted frame tense with concern for him. For him! He remembers the sallow curve of her jaw and her short mop of hair and her dark, long-lashed eyes and her loose dark clothes – browns and greys. Out of all of that darkness, only two things shone: eyes and earrings.

His wife Lola stopped bothering with earrings when she was forty. 'I'm not going to deck myself out like a Christmas tree,' she said. 'Who's going to look?'

He knew this was a direct reference to his withdrawal from her, but he pretended not to hear. She wore overalls and slippers, but it was always noticeable that long after she'd stopped putting earrings in, and her hair had greyed and her face retracted into a mass of lines, her lobes remained stretched – distorted with the memory of all those jewels.

*

'He's a complete fucking waste of time,' Gayle told Annie, 'I don't know why I bothered to go and see him.'

'Well, you weren't to know,' said Annie.

'No, I wasn't, was I?' Gayle toyed with telling Annie the other part of the story, this extra knowledge Frank Chapman appeared to have, then decided against it. Outside, the threat of rain discoloured the sky.

'Maybe you should have just left him where he was?' Annie said and laughed. She flicked on the overhead light and the room grew whiter, uglier.

Lucy Henson slid down in her chair. 'I'm burning to death,' she yelled, her arms stiff and straight. 'Fetch Roger!'

She'd burned her leg a week ago sitting too close to the gas fire – riveted, laughing in a panicky way as the skin turned a crazy molten colour.

Gayle got the trolley and prepared to change Lucy's catheter, whilst Annie held her still. Fingers snapping into surgical gloves. 'My head's throbbing,' Annie said, and her black plait swung and brushed Lucy's face, 'I think I'm allergic to this building.' The urine danced choppily in its polythene bag as Lucy kicked and twisted.

'I'm not going to see him again, anyway,' Gayle told Annie, 'he's not worth the trouble. I'm just leaving him to it, now.' She placed the full bag, which was amber coloured and strong smelling, in a tray and clipped on the new one, pulled off the gloves and stood up, blowing a strand of hair off her mouth.

'I don't know why you went in the first place,' Annie smiled, 'he's not your concern. I don't know how you find the time.'

*

That evening, Donna phoned Gayle. 'Don't tell Will I said this,' she whispered between sobs. 'I'm going crazy. I can't manage any more.'

'It's bad?'

Donna said nothing.

'Has it got worse? Has it changed?'

'Maybe. I don't know.'

'Donna, has it? Do you feel that it has?'

'Oh, well,' Donna swallowed, 'I may just be imagining things.'

'Don't be silly. It was bad enough for you to phone.'

'I shouldn't have phoned. I just found myself doing it. It's all down my left side. My leg too. I'm just very down about it right now.'

'Why can't you tell Will? What's the matter with you two? Is he giving you a hard time?'

'Oh, no,' Donna gave a little sob, 'no. It's just so hard for him. We're so bored of this – this—'

'What are you taking?' Gayle asked her.

'Well, he's hidden the Diazepam.'

'Yes, but have you got strong painkillers? Paramax?'

'Oh, yeah, but they don't touch it. Anyway, it's not just the pain. It's the not being able to move. It rules our lives.'

'Oh, sweetheart,' said Gayle, 'I'm so sorry. Do you want me to talk to him about the Diazepam? One or two ought to be all right when it's this bad.'

'No,' said Donna, 'it's me. I made him hide them. I don't want to take them. I'm sick of pills. I want to be better, not just on some fucking floppy drug.'

*

When the other girl, Gayle, comes back to see him, he pretends to be asleep.

But he watches her through his eyelids, notices her thick dark wavy hair, her long, serious face and the way her hands move. The patch of freckles on her nose. The full, childish lips and the nervous habit of chewing the inside of her cheek.

'That's cannibalism,' he tells her, snapping his eyes open, making her jump. He feels exactly what he expects to feel: a light tightness in his bones, in his head. An unwanted thwack of tension, pushing his blood to one side. She ignores him – well, he'll give her credit for that.

'OK,' she says, seating herself by his bed, 'your last chance. Tell me what it is you'd do for Donna. I'm prepared to listen if you'll talk sensibly.'

But he'll tease her a little longer. Punish her for doubting. 'You remind me of my son,' he says.

'Your son?'

'Tommy. Doubting Tommy.'

He shouldn't have said it – the word, To-mee. Tommy. Like letting loose a beakerful of devils. Black tails flicking against the glass, drowning mouths pressing, roving tongues. A pressure on the back of the skull. Funny, but he could weep at that word sometimes even now.

'You didn't say you had a son,' she says and he can see her eyes getting all excited.

'I'm saying now.'

'Well, where is he?' she asks. 'Do you want me to contact him?' He'd like to see her do that. What would Tommy say to that?

'When am I out of this place?' he asks her.

'Friday,' she tells him, 'maybe Thursday.'

'If you bring her to see me, I'll lay hands on her. It'll take less than ten minutes. In my house.'

'What if she doesn't want it?'

'She'll want it when she sees what I can do. Commit thy way unto the Lord, trust also in Him and He shall bring it to pass.'

'You're barking.'

'But I'm a good dog.' He grins and shows his teeth,

white as white, straighter than straight. 'Hallelujah.' He ate no sweets at all until he was forty-two.

'I'm not scared of you,' she says, and he can see she means it.

'I know,' he says, 'of course you're not. I'm an old man.'

She looks exasperated, but he lies very still, hands by his sides (resisting the urge to cross them over his breast), because he is. An old man who's been mugged and is recovering, praise the Lord. But very slowly. Bow wow.

*

Gayle and Donna were watching Kitty tie two chairs together with string.

'How would you feel about seeing a faith healer?' Gayle asked her.

'What?'

'I mean, you've tried everything else. Why not a faith healer?'

Donna leaned back and pushed the hair out of her eyes and laughed. 'Give me a break. What made you think of that?'

Gayle shrugged. 'Oh, nothing. Just a thought.'

'Well, no thanks.'

Kitty came up, frowning. 'Move,' she said to Gayle. Gayle moved into another chair. Kitty began to tie the chair she'd vacated.

'Do you want to get better?' Gayle asked Donna.

Donna gave her a look. 'What a stupid question.'

'Not at all – sometimes I really wonder,' Gayle said. 'I mean, I thought the other day you were so desperate?'

Donna stood up, limped over to the sink without her

stick, ran the tap. 'That's a bit rough,' she said, 'using that against me. Just because I turn to you when I'm low—' She diluted some apple juice for Kitty.

'Well, I'm sorry—' Gayle began.

'Anyway, I'm much better today.'

'Oh. Good.'

'Move,' said Kitty again.

She moved out of her chair so Kitty could tie it to the others, and leaned against the counter.

'I wish you wouldn't always cross-question me,' Donna said suddenly.

'I'm sorry if I took you seriously the other day,' Gayle said, 'I'll try not to in future. God, you're difficult to talk to these days. I'm not going to apologize for caring about you. Either your back bloody well hurts or it doesn't.'

'Not at all,' Donna said, 'it's not as simple as that. There are good days and bad days.'

'You want to have your cake and eat it,' Gayle said, 'and then throw it up.'

Donna sat back down on one of the tied-up chairs. 'What an absolutely horrible thing to say.'

'Oh, well,' said Gayle, 'I have my bad days too.'

'Look!' Kitty shouted. 'A train!'

*

In the bunch of January days following Lola's death, Frank gets himself up in the black winter dawn, pulls his pants up with an energy he never knew he had. Sometimes he pulls them up so hard that the distressed grey elastic of his pants hangs over the top of his trousers, where the belt should be only he doesn't have one. He doesn't see this, because he has no mirror either. Nor a wife to tell him any more.

There's a lot he doesn't have – doesn't see – only who's counting now?

When Lola's Church banned him, he went and preached at the Church of the Seven Thunders in Balham, until they kicked him out, too. That's when he gets to it – realizes it'll have to be a one-man show. So he goes round the parks tacking the Good News to trees: Wandsworth Common, Wimbledon Common, Brockwell Park, Clapham, according to how he feels and what he fancies. He likes to be out in the fresh air and see the Good News dotted across these public areas, flapping like so many surprised birds and all his doing. One day a young black-haired bobby tells him he'll be summonsed if he keeps it up. 'Go in peace, young man!' Frank retorts and he can't remember but he might have gnashed his teeth. Either way, the man went.

On Thursday afternoons, he and Lola splash out on a mini-cab to Tesco's. She shops whilst he saves souls – chucks leaflets into trolleys if they won't take them from his hand. He sticks the rest under windscreen wipers in the car park. When the manager threatens to call the police, Frank says, 'Hallelujah! Jesus don't shop at your outfit, no, sir!' And he marches away with Lola, who's not at all pleased.

He grabs the handle of her shopper, swings a carrier bag.

'Watch it,' she says, 'there's Harpic in one of them bags.'

He laughs. If she could only see what he can see. The world spread before him like a dance floor. The sky's lit up pink and the clouds are parting. White light pours down onto the precinct. Jesus is in charge of the weather all right; the air throbs.

'I'm getting such a headache,' she says (always the moaner) as they round the corner by Iceland and hail a mini-cab. And meanwhile, he glows inside as he works. Hums softly under his breath. He's a hot-shot. All he has to do is pass on the Good News. Jesus organizes everything – the Great Organizer, the Fixer. You could say Jesus is his boss.

In the tangled weeks since Lola went to Heaven, he's stepped it up, working from eight in the morning, often not stopping till dusk – walking home in the dark, singing. Free at last, he's followers of his own now, too. Disciples – they turn to him, all of them. Love without reserve.

It's all there – it's all there in the plan, if you just bother to look.

*

Will was not expecting to pick up the phone and hear Gayle. She'd never called him at work before – never called him at all except to get hold of Donna.

'I'm sorry' – she sounded defensive, tired – 'you're busy.'

'No, no, it's OK. How are things?' He leaned back, waiting.

'Fine.' She paused. 'I wanted to talk to you.'

'Yeah?' He stared into the foyer where he could see Betty talking to John Beanie. Betty had one hand on the photocopier and the other at her throat, fingering a bead she always wore on a thong. John threw his head back and laughed at something she said. Betty was incredibly witty sometimes; wasted fucking a PE teacher.

'Frank Chapman,' Gayle said, 'look, he's saying he wants to see Donna.'

'What?' Will had virtually forgotten him. Two days had passed. He had enough to do. Now he wondered what she was on about. 'What do you mean, see Donna?' He heard Gayle take a breath.

'Well, he says he's a healer. You know – I told you.'

Will laughed loudly. Betty was now bending to reload the machine. John handed her the wad of paper. For God's sake.

'You're not taking him seriously?' he said to Gayle. 'I can't believe you're listening to him. You said yourself he was just some fucking weirdo. When have you spoken to him?'

'I'm sorry,' her voice tightened, 'I can tell it's a bad time. You're busy.'

'I just didn't think you were taking any notice of this – this character. You got him to the hospital and that's that.'

'Well, it isn't quite.' She sounded close to tears.

'Hey, are you all right?' he asked.

'Yes. No. I'm worried about Donna. And I'm having a shitty week.'

'Really?' Despite himself he was interested.

'I just wondered whether he actually might be able to do something, that's all.'

He laughed again. 'I can't believe you're serious.'

'Forget it, just don't say anything to Donna,' was all she said before she rang off.

Shit. He couldn't ring her back. He didn't have a number for her – Christ, maybe she didn't even have an office.

Maybe it was a payphone. He realized he had no visual sense whatsoever of where she worked.

*

Next time she visits, she starts to wheedle his life story out of him. Frank gives her just enough, not too much.

'I was born above an ironmonger's on Silver Street,' he says. 'It backed onto the wharf, you see.'

'Yes?' She was frowning, tensed.

'We had a dinghy called the *Jean Sweet*. You could see the whole river from my bed – small ships from the Baltic bringing timber. Humber keels and steam tugs. A tidal river, it was.'

Lincolnshire. A land so flat you can't get away with much. Him and Arthur and Merle playing where they weren't allowed on the steep bank. Tender spines and brains, soft hair, wet eyes. The children of Annie Chapman, née East. Annie who lies leaking into the soil, murdered by a baby, chewing on a mouthful of worms.

'I had a big sister and a little brother,' he says.

'Are they alive?'

'No, dead. Both of them.'

Children so pure and transparent you can see straight through 'em. No tumours, no poisons in their systems, no devils drumming their fists for access. A wind flattens the grass for a moment, lifting Merle's hair, flapping Arthur's little jacket. Was it a jacket?

'My brother and sister were not saved. My conversion came too late for them and they missed out on the Good News. Our father was a violinist – could have been in an orchestra, oh yes. Studied at the conservatoire in Berlin. But the family business swallowed him up. Him and his music.'

He allows himself a glance. She's still listening. Her eyes are fixed on his. He likes it. Her heart is opening to him and he likes it.

'He married my mother just like that, out of nowhere. She'd a tattoo on her thigh, rumour had it. Yes, really! On my fifth birthday, she killed a mouse with a single crack shot from an air pistol. What do you make of that?'

The girl laughs, fiddles with her hair. He continues, 'Merle came first, then me. Arthur was an afterthought and it was too bad because something of him got left inside our ma and she died. Tore the room apart – smashing up vases, tearing curtains – she died in a rage, my mother, her jaw wide open. Cheated of her life. They stood her coffin on six chairs, two rows of three facing each other, and I ran around them and I knew what I had lost.

'Father gave up the violin, sat alone in rooms, meals on a tray. Then, one afternoon in the middle of winter, he walks into the music room and sees a ball of fire – a great scorching knob of flame – hurtling towards him. About the size of a dinner plate, he says later.

'He slams the big oak doors and has the room sealed off. Forbids anyone to go in there again in his lifetime. Which turns out to be long – ha!'

She's silent. He makes a little sad movement with his hands to show there's no more. 'How's Donna?' he says. 'Have you put it to her?'

'She's thinking about it.'

'Ah.'

'No, I mean it, she is.'

'I believe you, young lady. We're on the same side, you and me.'

*

There had been nothing obvious in Donna's growing-up to cause her to develop a hysterical illness. Gayle and Simon had, after all, had identical upbringings. OK, so maybe you couldn't call Simon – twenty-five and still homeless, mostly jobless – a success, but still both he and Gayle enjoyed the full range of physical movement, woke each morning and leapt out of bed to confront their various problems.

Their mum and dad had been happily married right through until their father's sudden death a few years ago, and she still lived in the house where they'd all been born – with its red roof and rows of wellington boots in the outhouse, the games and puzzles in the sideboard, the thirty-year-old painted macaroni necklaces still hanging in the downstairs loo. A rusty swing still hung in the garden, but Kitty refused to go on it because the seat was rough and slimy. When Donna or Gayle or Simon visited the house, they wandered aimlessly from room to room, unsure of how to exist among all those ghosts and tattered objects, unable to think or settle. They had to push past their adolescent selves in order to be there at all.

Their dad had had his own hot-foil-blocking business. His machines swallowed black cigarette packets, spat them out with gold bits on. A girl called Myra had worked the machines, and two Asian boys did the packing. Myra kept cough sweets in the gritty nylon pockets of her overall.

Raj and Ali – barely older than Gayle – had black fluff

on their upper lips and never spoke. 'That's Pakis for you,' their dad said, 'work hard because they know what's what. Worth their bloody weight in gold, those two.'

He couldn't say the same for Myra and he sacked her one Friday afternoon because her hourly output had decreased. She wept and begged and said she had a heart complaint, but he wasn't going to fall for that one. He told this to the family as he ate his pork pie and salad, as the birds tweeted outside. Bits of pastry flaked from his mouth as he spoke.

'Don't look away when your father talks about work,' Donna's mother told her, 'it bloody well puts the food in your mouths.' She'd climbed the business ladder with only a shorthand and typing course to her name. Now she was a big success in frozen foods.

Groomed for work in her dark suit, her face disturbingly beige, her lips dark brown, she always seemed to Donna a predatory thing, a bird of prey. Area Sales Manager – promoted over the heads of three men: Graham this, and Geoff that – and company cars and so many thou' a year. 'Well, I took them apart,' she'd exclaim when she got home, pouring herself a drink, kicking off her high heels, 'wiped the floor with them. You should have seen their faces.'

Their father would bend to light her cigarette with his own, pat her on the bottom, call her a helluva woman, a go-getter. 'Some men would find your mother's success threatening,' he commented as he chucked handfuls of Winalot into a tin bowl for the dog, 'but not me.'

Next to her mother, Donna felt like nothing. 'Don't hold your mouth that way,' she would be told in a shopping mall, or on the way to school, 'it looks ridiculous.'

'What way?' Donna's hand would fly to her face.

'In a pout like that,' her mum said. 'I don't know who you're trying to be, but if you think it looks appealing you're wrong – it just looks put-on.'

Gayle and Simon were never around, of course. Gayle got a Saturday job as soon as she could; Simon hung around with the dope smokers. Donna was stuck in a place she sometimes felt was of her own making, her own desiring. 'Thank God one of you's amenable,' her mother said, as she took Donna for a haircut, or to buy a denim skirt at TopShop or to help with the shopping at Asda.

'I think we'd better put you on the pill,' she announced one day, just like that, when Donna had still not been within six feet of a boy. But they went off to the doctor's. And as she dutifully pressed the little white pills from their curling blister pack, swallowed them down, she realized here was another conversation she would never have to have.

For her mother pre-empted everything, took control. Nothing ever took her by surprise. These days, when Donna visited, she stood in that same bathroom with the frosted glass windows where her father had finally had an embolism and died, and looked out at the wintry garden and the rusty swing which even Kitty at three years old knew how to spurn, and the misery just sprang back at her. 'I had a happy childhood,' she told Will.

Told everyone. But doubted it.

*

When Will got home, Donna was standing in the kitchen pushing carrots into the Magimix.

'Have you spoken to Gayle?' he asked.

She looked at him. 'Not since last night – why?'

'No reason. I just wondered.'

Her stick was leaning against the dishwasher. She took it and limped across the room, grabbing stuff for a dressing. He tried to touch her as she walked past, but she looked like she didn't want it. There was a smudge of grey under each eye, a balled-up piece of kitchen towel on the table.

'What's the matter?'

'Nothing. I've made a salad but I don't know what else we can eat. There's no bread.' She sat down heavily. He got a beer from the fridge.

'You're in pain.'

'No,' she said, 'I'm fine.'

'What is it, then?' He watched as she stared around at everything in the room but him. 'I just wondered,' he said, 'if Gayle had been to see that old man?'

'She hasn't told me,' Donna said. 'Why should she go and see him? Anyway, don't ask me, ask her, if you care so much.'

*

Frank seemed almost pleased to see her. 'It's you.' He licked his lips.

'It's me.' Gayle put a bottle of Lucozade and a Mars bar on his table. 'I haven't got long,' she said.

'Sit down.' He indicated the chair which someone had pulled away from the bed. 'What did you say your name was?'

'Gayle.' She wondered whether he could really have forgotten.

'I wanted to say a proper goodbye,' she said, 'I'm glad you'll be home on Friday.'

She looked at the chair and finally pulled it up and sat down. He looked different. She realized it was the glasses – the hospital had give him some new ones, whose thick black frames had a calming effect on his big face. A piece of sticking plaster on the hinge said *Frank Chapman* in messy, slanty capitals. 'Temporary ones,' he said, touching the frame. 'Anyway, it's not goodbye. What about Donna?'

'I can't really say,' she told him, 'she's still thinking. I have your address.'

'I could talk her round,' he said suddenly, and she saw him stiffen.

'I'm sure.'

'I'm a powerful persuader. My wife wasn't a wishy-washy sort of woman. She was a mighty strong character, yes, sir, and some of it rubbed off on me. I tamed her. I brought her to the Love of the Lord Jesus Christ and it wasn't an easy job – it was a job for heroes. Frank the Fearless, they called me in Arizona, Frank the Fearless! They may have been kidding of course, but if not, it's quite a compliment, that.'

Gayle smiled.

'Anyway, Gayle,' he licked his lips, 'I had this one hundred per cent Roman Catholic bride and I brought her to Jesus. A daughter of Tartars. I tamed her as they used to tame horses on the Hungarian plains. And thanks to Jesus, she was a sweeter person for the last thirty years of her life, though at times it wasn't easy. The greater the battle, the greater the victory.'

'Really,' she said. Once he'd started, he was impossible to stop. She hadn't any more time to listen to Jesus stuff.

'Of course,' he went on, 'I never fully tamed her or she would have gone on with Malachi 4 chapter 5 and taken the Seven Thunders – the very same which I saw coming out of his bosom in my dream at 3 a.m. on September 17th 1964.' His eyes glittered. Polka dots of spit patterned his lips.

'Look,' said Gayle, 'it's nice to hear about your wife, but do you mind if we don't talk about religion?'

'Your sister, then?'

'No,' she said, 'tell me about your son.'

He blinked.

'Come on,' she said gently.

'You need to watch the army, you know,' he said, 'soldiers pick up demons from all those dead bodies lying around. We purged a few at our Glory meetings – ha! – you should've seen.'

'Where does he live?' She asked again, 'Is he in London?'

'Why? What's it to you?' He pulled the cuffs of his pyjamas down over his big purplish hands.

'I just want to help you if I can.' It was true, she did, though maybe she'd only just that moment realized it.

'He was born in the summer of '58,' Frank said. 'Lola nearly died of complications.'

'Complications?'

'Very tight across the hips, you see' – indicating his own girth with his big hands – 'very small and tight. But Jesus saw to it that she got better.'

Gayle was quiet. 'So don't you see him now?' Something awful sprang into view, and she ignored it. 'Couldn't I at least contact him for you? I'd like to do that. Surely he'd want to know you're in here?'

Frank Chapman didn't move, not at all, save for a snake flicker of his eyelids. He opened his mouth to speak and then shut it again. He looked at his hands, spread his fingers on the cotton cover, and then he said something, and what he said was: 'Isn't it obvious to you yet young lady that my son is dead?'

*

'I'll be straight with you,' John Beanie stretched out his legs, nudged a Carlucci's bag which leant up against his desk, 'I never thought we'd get this far. I never thought we'd make the shortlist. We're a small, young company but maybe that's our strength. Anyway, the acid test is now. The acid test is doing it – what we can come up with.'

'There's been a bust-up at Hyatt Barly Cormack,' said Dave Durlitt. 'They won't contain it. They'll go right down the list once it hits the press.' Durlitt's hair was so black it seemed colourful. Short, dark hairs grew up from under his shirt. His stubble spread like a bruise.

One of the designers made a noise of surprise. Dan Mintoe just stared at Durlitt and sipped a glass of Volvic and said nothing. Just then Betty tapped on the glass.

'Excuse me.' Will jumped up and opened the door a crack.

'Sorry,' she said, 'can I put a quick call through?'

'No,' he said, 'not right now. Give me ten minutes, fifteen max.'

'It's a friend of Donna's,' Betty whispered, 'I think it's urgent.'

'I can't,' said Will. 'This is important. What's the matter? Can't you find out?' Betty shrugged that she didn't know, but she looked pissed off. Will turned back to the meeting. 'Sorry,' he told them, 'can you give me a second?'

He stood at Betty's desk, annoyed. She passed him the phone. It was Sarka from the shop. 'Will,' she said, 'I wasn't sure I should say it to your secretary. I think you need to come home. Something's wrong with Donna.'

'What do you mean, wrong?' He always found Sarka's manner irritating – her flowery vagueness. 'I'm in a very important meeting. I'll be out in twenty minutes. Tell her I'll call her then.'

'No,' Sarka said, 'it's worse than that.'

'Meaning?'

'I don't know. She's going crazy.'

'For Christ's sake,' he said.

He saw through the glass partition that John and Dan were looking at him, waiting. Dave had lit a cigarette, stood up to pull the blind. 'Look, I'm sorry, I have to go. I'll try and leave early. Tell her an hour at the most.'

'I don't think you understand,' Sarka said.

'As I said, I'm really sorry.' He cut her off. He turned to Betty, who just looked at him.

'Problems?' Dan asked him.

'No, it's fine,' Will told them, 'sorry.'

'Can we get on?' Dave Durlitt moved his jacket just enough to see his watch.

Will apologized again.

*

So, he uses Tommy's death as bait – a fat, white thing, it hangs there, tempting with its shock.

'I'm so sorry,' and she's rightly cut up and torn apart by his revelation, 'I'm so sorry, I never thought—'

He presses his lips together, 'Yes, leukaemia. At the age of fourteen. Easter '73. I'm sorry, too.'

She is doing it, she is taking it between her teeth! What a bite! What a marvellous big bite! Well done, Frank. Just when he thought he might be losing her. 'I'm so sorry,' she says again. He feels the gift of her embarrassment – such a warm, unexpected bonus.

He punches and shoves at the heavy hospital pillows, crackle of polythene and rough, laundered linen. Outside, a helicopter's circling. He can detect the cold cup of tea on his locker top. When he squeezes his eyelids shut, he sees a crimson light: blood.

'I'd like to be left alone now.'

'Of course.' She stands up. 'Will you be all right?' She picks up her bag, adjusts the belt of her uniform – moving her hands over herself because there's nothing else she can do.

'There's nothing you can do for me, young woman.' He says it aloud. 'Go away, please.'

Such daring! He keeps his eyes shut tight throughout.

All babies are born with a devil in them and soon Tommy has Lola at his beck and call, using his powerful tongue and gums to drain her dry, drinking her up to gasping point. Finally, thank the Lord Jesus Christ for powdered milk.

As the girl hesitates a moment and then walks away

between the beds and screens, Frank turns to spy on her through the curtain, then flicks it shut and bites thoughtfully at the skin on the sides of his fingers. He doesn't allow himself a moment of doubt that she'll be back.

Finally, he zaps on the TV.

*

Donna was on the bathroom floor when Will got back. He couldn't see her face. She sat, hunched forward, in her dressing gown. Sarka had gone and Gayle was with her.

'Will. You missed all the fun,' Gayle said as the door swung on its hinges. She didn't look up from where she held Donna tight. He noticed that the bath tap was running – a wasteful trickle flooding around the neck of the hot tap – and he longed to turn it off, but stopped himself.

'I'm sorry.' He stood there, sensing Gayle's disapproval. Then he laid his coat across the laundry basket and got down on his knees. There was a roughly made bandage on Donna's thumb. Her eyes were shut. Her stick winked at him from the floor, its knob split into stars by the bright light. Through the door, he glimpsed Kitty on their bed, wading on her knees, singing, oblivious, moving the pillows around.

'What happened?' He couldn't see Donna's face, she was hanging her head so low. Was she asleep? He felt a drag of fear in his chest. Looking up, he noticed traces of blood in the basin, flecks and spots down the side of the bath.

'We don't know, she won't talk. A locum came and bandaged her, sedated her a bit, but she won't move out of here. Sarka rushed round when she didn't turn up at work.

She went crazy or something, I'm afraid she's made a mess of your bedroom walls.'

'Is that blood?' He swallowed.

'She used a pair of scissors on the walls, ripped the paper. Then she snipped the top off her thumb – didn't you?' Gayle almost laughed, then kissed the side of Donna's head, where an ear showed through the fine dark hair.

'Sweetie, I wish you'd check with me before you do these things,' he joked shakily, but no one laughed. He was suddenly strangely glad Gayle was there. 'What did the doctor say to do?'

Gayle shrugged. 'Lots of rest. Lots of these.' She shook a bottle of pills.

'Christ,' said Will as it sank in. He wondered whether Donna had had what might be termed a breakdown.

'Don't ask me,' Gayle said somewhat uncannily, 'I don't understand either.'

*

Miss Freeman is the most regular visitor at his flat – more regular now since Lola's out of the picture.

'That woman's lusting after you, you blind old man,' Lola would complain, 'and look at you, you can't even see it.'

A diabetic from Worksop, Miss F. worked all her life in a chocolate factory – harsh, phlegmy breath, cheeks furred and rouged as old cinema seats.

Lola always gave a put-on shudder when she heard those nails rap on the window. Trampling her sweet williams. 'Can't you use the bloody damn door bell like everyone else?' she'd yell. 'She's using you, can't you see it?' Lola would go on at him. Sometimes she said he needed his head examined – called him a nut, but he had his reply ready: 'A nut's useful, in't it? Holds things together. Any engineer'll tell you that.'

He wouldn't give in to her fiery Tartar temper.

Miss Freeman comes for the Good News and the Good News alone. He preaches, she listens. Sometimes her breathing grows heavier and he wonders whether she might go into a trance and be delivered of a demon, but more often than not she just sits there sucking her toffees and boiled sweets. Waiting to be baptized in the love of the Lord Jesus Christ.

One chilly, dark day, as they're kneeling at the side of the settee praying together, she falls against him. He feels the shock of her bulk – the folds of skin at her neck, the thick elastic strap of her brassiere.

He catches and holds her, easing the passage of Satan. 'That's right,' he says, 'that's right.'

'Frank,' she murmurs and her eye flickers open with reptilian rapidity, 'oh boy, Frank.'

He wonders if he should fetch a bowl in case she's going to vomit, but he doesn't want to hold up the exorcism. He stretches out his right hand, extends a finger up towards the Lord. 'Hallelujah! Praise Jesus! Deliver this woman, Thy servant, from sin!'

She's writhing against him now. He tries to hold her, calm her, till it's over. The Prince of Darkness strips you of your dignity – part of the process, of course. As her blouse slips, he catches sight of the stiff grey cup of her brassiere.

'Frank,' she strains in his arms, 'bed. Bed. Pull down my panties please, Frank.'

Her breath's a mix of gases: onions and parma violets.

'Miss Freeman,' he pushes her away now because she's clutching at his privates, 'you're being delivered of a demon. Let it out.'

But she clings on as hard as he tries to push her off, hitching up her skirt, revealing a tang of fishy nylons, and more. 'Just once,' she begs him, 'do us a favour. Stick it in, lovey. Just quickly.'

Then she parts her legs and her body is limp, amazed. Her mouth opens and her lips are wet. He removes her carefully and drags her to a chair, purged – he supposes – of her sins.

'I'll make some tea,' he whispers.

As the kettle screams to the boil, he kneels at the small Formica table in the kitchen and starts to pray. He doesn't know what to pray for. His hands are trembling. He would like Lola back right now, to make the tea.

'Your kettle's boiling,' Miss Freeman calls.

He is still praying and the kettle still screaming when Miss Freeman walks stiffly out of the flat.

*

Even when pressed, Donna couldn't say what exactly had made her do it. 'I was hurting,' she told Will, 'everywhere – hips, back, neck, down my legs. I was worn out and so fucking sick of it. The pain was all over so I couldn't function. I couldn't go to work, I couldn't even clean my teeth. I mean it, it hurt to walk even with my stick.'

'Why didn't you tell me?' Will asked her. He said it in a monotone, the way you'd speak to a very uncooperative person.

'Well, you weren't there. You're always at the office when I wake up.'

He didn't argue with that. 'Was it worse than usual?'

She considered this. Was it worse? Or had she just had enough? Somehow, she'd lost all track of pain, run out of ways of measuring it. The panic, the rebellion, had come suddenly. One moment she'd been lying there on her ice-pack, doing her relaxation and visualization exercises, breathing deeply – in, out – telling herself it did not matter, that she'd just phone Sarka and go in late. And then she'd found herself up at the wall, head against the papered plaster, tears dropping down her neck, taking great chunks out with her haircutting scissors.

'I was driven up the wall,' she said and it suddenly seemed incredibly funny, but he just looked at her harder, dropped his chin and sighed. 'It was a rage,' she told him, trying to come back, making a big effort to use words he'd understand, 'a great fucking rage. I didn't want to hurt myself. I just wanted to do damage.'

She smiled again. That was exactly it, she was right. It was almost a pleasure, to articulate her anger so assiduously. To lie there on the bed and have him listen, to be scrupulously careful in her search for the right words. She almost wanted to write them down, like homework – get them absolutely right. She wanted to sit back and say, I've expressed it all.

Now that it was over, she felt incredibly calm.

'And your thumb?' he said, still frowning even though she'd been so lucid and conscientious.

She looked at the bandage, almost surprised by the evidence. 'It didn't hurt at all.'

'Yes, but why did you do it? I don't understand. It's not like you.'

'I don't know. What am I like? What is like me?' Why didn't she feel like helping him? She wanted to laugh at his put-on gravity, but found instead her nose was stinging with tears. She looked away.

'What is it, Donna?' he said, and she blinked. 'What?' He didn't move from his chair. 'Are you depressed?'

She shrugged. The ears of the armchair framed his face in a peculiar way. If she tried to focus on any one feature of his, he went blurred and slipped away. In fact he kept slipping away from her, like the flashes of red which move away from you when you close your eyes.

'Is it the miscarriage still?'

She shook her head, blinked him back into focus. This was how he referred to the death of their unborn child and she knew she would have to put up with it. Even Gayle had tried to emphasize that it hadn't been a child at all but just an unformed embryo – a fertilized egg which failed to get a hold. Not even the beginnings of a baby.

'But something?' Donna had insisted greedily.

OK, something, but nothing that the heart could properly mourn, nothing viable, not even a foetus.

This was supposed to make it easier. Lots of people went through this.

She remembered the tiny, transparent blood-mass of flesh

on the wad of lavatory paper. Sometimes she thought she remembered seeing a small bowed head and four jutting limb buds. Was that possible? Privately, she thought of it as a girl – a paler, sadder version of Kitty. Privately, she called the little girl baby Harriet.

She shouldn't have let Will flush her away. It wasn't his fault, but sometimes she couldn't stand to think that her Harriet slid down the loo. Maybe it was that fact alone that made her go for the wall with the scissors. And then her thumb. The snip had been so neat – held out over the basin to minimize the mess. The cap of flesh had detached itself and swung loose immediately, viciously, as if on a hinge, and there'd been a perfect amount of blood. She'd thought of her child flushed away down those dark, filthy pipes. She had passed out cold, next to the avocado-coloured lavatory where she last saw Harriet.

Will said he'd Polyfilla the holes in the wall as soon as he had time and she had a stitch in her thumb now, and a great dressing which Kitty said made it look like a microphone. She was feeling better. The spasm in her back had subsided a little because of the Diazepam.

In bed, she and Will kissed. She felt a lot closer to him now, a lot calmer about everything. Or a lot further away, which amounted to the same. In bed, they touched each other. He rolled towards her and sighed. They did things with their hands which signalled that they might make love. But each time she stopped, he stopped. She knew that if she kept still long enough, left her hand exactly where it was, he'd just drift off to sleep.

four

Sometimes Gayle loved Kitty so hard she wanted to turn away, she wanted to run. Sometimes she just wanted to be free of the feeling she sometimes imagined she'd spent her entire life trying to avoid.

'Just trust me,' Harry Skeat had said, four years ago, staring into her through the hard, round windows of his glasses, telling her to relax and that it would be OK. Binding her wrists with his bright orange nylon chandler's cord, his eyes exact with concentration. Relax and trust – and look what had happened. Her life pulled from under her, given back to her enlarged, sublimely different.

If she had ever told a girlfriend about it – which she had not, because she had no friends of that sort – the friend would most probably have said, 'You were raped.' But that wouldn't have been true. It would not have expressed it. It would not have become true either, however long she waited for her perceptions to change.

That first evening, Gayle had brought the baby home from the hospital and laid her on the wide, crumpled landscape of her unmade bed. In the cut-off darkness of the taxi, she'd named her Kitty. Now she made a space for her on the stained bedspread and inspected the folded-up crimson face and tight-curled fists, the soft, translucent shreds of her fingernails. She smoothed the white blanket and sat there, staring, hypnotized by the sound of three-day-old breath.

When she went to draw the curtains and glanced back, it was the first time she'd seen her child from across a room, with all that space between them, and it wasn't as she thought it would be. The distance was a shock; the air was fizzy with the fact of her baby. And the front of her T-shirt was suddenly wet, just from looking.

*

Now, the phone rang and after getting on for five years it was Harry. 'Hiya' – it was as if he'd just popped to Vinegar Joe's for cigarettes – 'it's me.'

She said, 'It's better that we leave it as it is.'

'She's my flesh and blood,' he replied.

She laughed. 'Cut the clichés. You've got a nerve, haven't you?' It occurred to her that she was good at this.

'I miss you.' He said it in a surprisingly small voice, but she was ready, she girded herself against it. She knew Harry. She knew he'd get her if she wasn't careful, so she set the phone down gently in its cradle – click – then lifted it off the hook. Her hand was trembling. She left it off the hook all evening.

Kitty had been felt-tipping in the kitchen, ominously quiet. Now she came in and her face and hands were black, her lips turquoise. 'Kitty! That had better come off,' Gayle took her on her lap.

Kitty just looked at her, and her silence made Gayle feel exhausted.

She remembered how sex with Harry had turned her inside out, made her cry.

*

In his hospital bed at 5 a.m., Frank Chapman is dreaming he's a life peer.

'You're a life peer,' they tell him, 'lucky you. Something in the region of fifty thousand pounds, that's what you'll get. World's your oyster now.'

In the dream, he relishes the idea – not the money of course, but to be carried through London on a sedan chair. Through Spitalfields, past the meat market, up to London Bridge, where Jesus sits on his throne all lamb 'n' lettuce. Grinning like a baby. Jerusalem. My Fair Lady. London Pride. Crowds cheering.

When he wakes it's still with him, cheers still pumping in his ears. His life would have amounted to something had it not been for Lola holding him back, all the time preventing him. Wouldn't even leave the house. Not even five days in Majorca. But Lola's in the ground – Lola's lowered into a dark shaft, daylight narrowing, one last fluorescent sky-fleck then all eaten up, devoured and gone. He's mourning her, if that's what mourning is. But – sorry – he doesn't feel bereaved. He's raring to go. His finger's right there, on the button.

And Jesus has reassured him, told him he doesn't have to be sorry for anything. That's the beauty of TLJC (The Lord Jesus Christ); Jesus has promised him he'll never have to pay. The clock says five fifteen. Jesus says: I love you, Frank. I love you as a lover loves – unthinking, right up close, closing my eyes.

Closing his eyes. He thought he was awake just then but now he wakes again, struggling to the surface, hands clasping his knees. Limbs glued to the sheets by his sweat. Only five o'clock. Hum of monitors or generators, constant dim white lighting.

Lola has no light in the ground.

He pushes up on his elbows and gulps water from the plastic bedside beaker. His eyes fix on a yellow plastic bin. Contaminated sharps. He concentrates on these words in order to stay awake. Just these two words: 'contaminated' and 'sharps'. His brain stiffens in response; the exact opposite of counting sheep.

'No, I don't know when she's coming,' says the nurse when she hands him his breakfast tray two hours later, 'but she only works over in Thompson, I can get a message to her if you want.'

It is not like Frank to be filled with doubt. But the plan is vital to him. He obtains a scrappy bit of paper and a biro and sits for a long time staring at nothing, thinking about what to write. And finally it comes.

*

Gayle rang Will from the payphone outside the canteen. 'I wondered how she was.'

'Odd.' He gave a short laugh.

'Odd? What do you mean?'

'I don't know. According to her she's all right.'

'Great. Should I come over?'

'No, don't worry.'

'It's no trouble, Will.'

'I know, I know. I don't think it's necessary. I wondered, have you been to see the old man?'

'Frank? Yes. He's out tomorrow. Why?'

'Oh, it's "Frank" now, is it?'

'Yes. Why not?'

'Look, sorry, I'd better go.'

'Of course you must. Bye.'

And she did it. She got the phone down first. Bastard. Her cheeks felt hot. He was a loathsome individual – no warmth at all and arrogant as hell. Sometimes she thought he was the source of all Donna's troubles.

'You've got a letter,' Annie said when she went back, 'internal.'

'What?'

Annie pressed a piece of paper into her hand. Gayle sat down next to Florrie Pykett's chair, unfolded it. There was no envelope and it was folded tight, several times.

'Have you any children, love?' Florrie asked in a whisper. Gayle read the note. Spidery writing, crossings out.

'Yes,' she said absently.

'She's got a little girl, Florrie,' said Annie.

'A girl? May I ask how old?'

'Three,' said Annie.

'Almost four,' Gayle added, then looked up, refolding the note. 'Frank Chapman.' She laughed.

'Got a love letter, has she?' Florrie said, looking away, jerking her chin up as her wrist hit the side of the chair.

Annie tucked the crocheted blanket around Florrie's knees. 'Mind your own business, Florrie. What's he sending you letters for?'

'I don't know.' Gayle got up. 'Well, actually, it's a kind of an apology.'

'Apology? What's he done?'

'I wouldn't know where to begin,' Gayle said.

She pocketed the note, where it stayed all day, crisp and unlikely against the nylon of her uniform.

*

'Is Donna all right?' Betty looked up from her screen. 'Is she better now?'

Will went to the window and parted the blinds and looked out, then walked back to his desk without knowing what he'd seen. 'I think so,' he said, 'I don't know.'

'God, it must be such a drag,' Betty said, 'to have a thing like that. The pain. I don't know how I'd cope. She's amazing.'

'She doesn't always cope,' he said abruptly, surprising himself. Why not tell Betty the truth?

'Oh,' said Betty, unmoved. 'Well, I don't blame her.' She tapped the keys. Rain battered the window. He said nothing, sat down again. 'If she ever wants to give it a try,' Betty said then without taking her eyes off the screen, 'I know a wonderful healer.'

'Healer?'

'Yeah, yeah, I know. This isn't like that. It's a fact that faith healing works for some people. I promise you. No one knows why.'

He laughed. Betty had a chunk of crystal in her desk drawer, Rescue Remedy, aromatherapy oils, the lot – read Tarot cards at office parties. 'I mean it,' she said, 'two of my mum's friends. They got better instantly.'

'Oh well, then,' he said, 'it must be true.'

'She wouldn't lie,' she said quickly.

'So how's it supposed to work?'

'I don't know, but does that matter, if it does work?'

'Oh Christ,' Will said, before he even suspected he was going to, 'maybe she should try it. Why not? For fuck's sake, she's tried everything else.' He wondered if he could get Donna to a faith healer. Then Gayle crossed his mind.

'You think I'm a crank,' Betty said.

'No,' he said, 'you're nice. You do your best.' She made a face.

'What time's this meeting?' he asked her.

'Are you OK?' she said. 'You've gone white as a sheet. D'you want a painkiller or something?'

'No, it's all right.' He went over to the window, looked out at the wet grey peaks and troughs of Golden Square, the iron rail daubed with starling droppings. He filled a paper cone with iced water from the dispenser. 'Wish I could have a cigarette, that's all.' He was giving up again. He'd promised Donna. It had been two days.

'You're so good,' Betty said, tapping her biro on her perfect straight little teeth, 'you really are. I'd have cracked by now, I know I would.'

But I have, he thought, minutes later, leaning on the white curl of the basin in the men's lavatory, gazing at the wreck of his face in the mirror. I have. I've cracked, and there are two pieces of me, and I don't know what I should fucking well be doing with either of them.

*

19 November 1990

Dear Tommy

I have to tell you your mother consorted with that Great Whore, the Roman Catholic Church, seated on the Seven Hills of Rome.

Kings and Queens all bow down before her – our supposed protestant Queen has done it and so have Princess Diana Spencer and Mrs Thatcher, so I suppose we can forgive poor L. But you'll see what I was up against?

Hope this postcard reaches you in the back of beyond. I'm in Cleethorpes, in bracing wind, in a twenty-two foot caravan, view over the sea – quite choppy out there, big breakers. Have given out more than three hundred pamphlets, but they prefer fish and chips so as ever it's an uphill struggle,

Your loving father,

Frank Chapman (who probably gave you too much too young but there we are. Amen.)

PS I haven't left your mother. This is a holiday.

PPS Tommy, where are you?

*

Donna knelt and leaned forward over her knees so her face and arms touched the carpet. 'Rub me,' she said, 'just there, please. Massage it.'

He bent over and kissed her neck as he rubbed, allowing his fingers to dip a little lower, to touch her bottom.

'No,' she said, nudging him off, 'please do it properly.'

He laughed.

'What's funny?'

'I am,' he said, 'I'm falling apart.'

'Why do you say that?'

He didn't know. He honestly had no idea why.

When he'd finished, he brought her up level with his face and kissed her, rubbed her sharp boy's hair between his fingers. Her skin was flawless – even and taut and the same colour all over. Even Betty's face had a few marks, a few shadows. 'Donna,' he said. She was so light, so fierce.

'Thanks,' she said, flexing forward, testing, 'that's a little bit better.'

'Come on,' he pulled at her hand, 'bed.'

'I can't have sex,' she told him, letting her arm hang by her side, 'I can barely move. Look at me.'

*

'It was a nice note and I appreciate it,' Gayle told Frank, 'but you didn't have to apologize.'

He shrugged. He had his glasses on slightly crooked and he looked weary – wearier. He was watching some soap or other on the TV. He kept one eye on it. A young boy in a T-shirt was shouting.

'Look,' she said, 'I want to know, what sort of a healer are you? Have you actually healed anyone?'

Straight away, he zapped off the TV and turned to her and said yes. He smiled, pushed his glasses up his nose till they were straight.

He said he had been at regular prayer meetings at the Gospel Hall in Surrey, where young mothers had brought their children, professional men their ailing mothers. He described how minor ailments – verrucas, sinus problems, lumbago, common colds – had been relieved immediately. How with three or four sessions of prayer even a case of TB was found to have disappeared.

'The hospital was baffled,' he said. 'Not a cloud on the X-ray, not a shadow, not a thing.' He laughed to himself.

'And what else?' Gayle demanded.

He told her how a woman who'd been paralysed from the waist down when she contracted polio as a teenager was pulled from her wheelchair and bathed with the Holy Spirit and compelled to walk. 'She fell at first. Tottered to the ground weeping – said she'd never do it. But Brother Piggott pulled her to her feet, drove the Prince of Darkness out.' Frank straightened himself in the bed, raised his arm in a straight salute. Gayle drew back.

'She renounced in our sight the Devil and all his works. Her ankles were like cottage loaves, all puffed out with sitting in that chair. She walked out of that hall and to the local swimming baths where she was baptized with fire and water. Swam five lengths. Yes, sir!' He relaxed against the pillows, a bubble on his lip.

Gayle stared at him. 'And all this just with prayer?'

'That and the laying on of hands, yes.'

He looked sad, modest almost. What had she expected? To find him out clearly in a lie? To be ranted at? She did not know what to think – did not know what to feel about Frank Chapman. She thought about what Will would no doubt say if she so much as raised the subject again. Did she care? Did she need to involve him?

She looked again into Frank's face, into his eyes which were – despite the trace of sadness – clear and grey and eternally, disconcertingly watchful. She wanted answers, she knew that; so why was it that when she looked into that big, pale face – looked properly at what was going on in there – the only thing she really saw was herself?

*

As soon as he got to the office the next day, Will rang Gayle. It was seven forty. He'd no idea how her shifts worked and he hoped she'd be at home still. She answered straight away.

'I'm sorry,' he said, 'it was difficult the other day.'

'How is she?' Her voice sounded like she'd just woken up.

'Fine.' He leaned back in his chair. 'Look, is this a bad time? Did I wake you?'

'Christ, no,' she said, 'Kitty's up at six.' She laughed.

'Actually she's not fine. I was wondering,' he said, and stopped.

'Yes? What?'

'I don't know – superficially, she is better, but the problem isn't going to go away.'

Gayle seemed to be about to say something, then stopped. He heard Kitty complaining in the background and then Gayle cupped her hand over the phone and said something. 'Sorry,' she came back to him, 'you think she'd do something similar again?'

'Yeah, I suppose I do.'

'I'm sure she will,' Gayle said, surprising him.

'So, this Chapman man, what sort of a healer does he say he is?'

'Frank?' Gayle sounded incredulous. 'Sorry – you're saying you're interested?'

'I don't know.' He was unwilling to pander to her. 'I don't know what I'm saying. Like you, I just don't want to pass up any opportunities.'

'Well,' she gave a quick little laugh, 'you do surprise me.'

'So?' He waited.

'I don't know. He's not very straightforward. I'm still finding him out. He's had a few tragedies.'

'Oh?'

'Well, his son died when he was a teenager.' She paused. 'I can't believe you, Will. You're saying you want her to see him? The laying on of hands?'

'I have no faith in it at all,' he said, 'but I'm desperate.' He stopped, unwilling to confide this far in Gayle. 'And Donna's highly suggestible.'

'He has healed people,' she said carefully, 'or at least he's told me some pretty weird stories. It's hard to know how to take him. But she'd never see him. You'd never persuade her – you know that?'

'I can but try.'

'Well,' she said again, 'I am surprised.'

'It's ruining our lives, Gayle. We've nothing to lose. If it works, great. If it doesn't, no harm done. But I ought to meet him at least.'

'Well, he's coming out today. I've said I'll go and see him at home. He lives in Brixton.'

'So I'll come?'

'I thought you'd got such a lot on?'

'I'll fit it in.'

*

Frank Chapman was always wanting to gather disciples unto him, but he never made a proper start whilst Lola was alive and kicking. Now she's up there with that nice girl the Queen of Heaven, Christ's mother, drinking Babycham. The coast is clear – clearer than it's ever been.

Boxing Day – barely a week after they'd laid her cast-off flesh in the ground. A warmish, windy afternoon. He exits the flat with a wad of the Truth in a carrier bag, strides up Acre Lane to the Common.

'Hallelujah!' No one around – just a few dog walkers, hands in pockets. Getting back to warmed-over turkey and the TV. Near the bandstand, a boy sidles up. The First. It is after three and the wide arms of trees filter out the light. He's maybe sixteen: fattish lips, freckles, cropped reddish hair. A flat green bottle of Gordon's gin under his arm.

He comes right over, Frank doesn't have to move a muscle. Settles like a rare butterfly, delicate, dark and bright. 'This in't gin, old man,' he exclaims, waving the bottle around, 'it's not wha' you think.' He laughs loudly and he's not moving away. His skin's so white you can detect the workings of his body, the schemings of his heart, beneath.

'No?' Frank holds his breath, careful to make no sudden movements, taps in a tack with his hammer. The tract panics against the tree. He rejoices silently. Good News, he wants to say, but he doesn't, not yet. He stops himself.

Trust me, little boy.

'Nah.' The boy laughs again, looks away, sits down at his feet. ''S water in 'ere.' A true disciple. Tame as your breath. Gin into water.

'Heard the Good News?' Frank asks him then, softly,

picking his moment, squatting down beside him, smelling the fumes from his mouth, so close he can see his lashes tremble, one pimply eyelid begin to tick. He lays his hammer and the carrier bag down, next to a large whitening dog turd.

'You wha'?'

'The Good News, boy. Have you heard it?'

'News?' The youth giggles doubtfully, gazes up at him. 'Whatcha doin' wi' them things anyway?'

In the sky, a plane is moving silently, discharging a soft rope of white. 'That Jesus Christ died at Calvary for your sins. That he loved you so much.' Frank feels his whole body grow and fill as he preaches. It is always like this. He trembles as Jesus passes him his weapons.

Holy Saviour enter here!

'Ah, fuck off.' The boy tips back his head, exposes his pale and spotty throat, swigs at his bottle, but Frank Chapman reaches out and grabs it from him and casts it away, dashing it against the nearest tree. Into a thousand pieces.

'Thank you, Holy Angels, Amen, Hallelujah.'

'Oi, you bleedin' old fucker.' The boy goes for him now, but Frank moves his own body right, perfectly on top, and pins him to the ground.

Time to act. He smacks the boy hard on the face – a preventative measure only – extracting a cry, surprisingly frail and pained. The hopeless weakness of flesh. Too small and breakable – Frank can feel the stick body giving beneath his own weight, the devils bunching up inside him – snapping sparrow bones. Was his Tommy once this frail?

And now he's trembling with the ache of exorcism – the

effort of making something happen. A light is shining at Calvary. The boy wants to shout – oh yes – but Frank lays a hand over his mouth, his soft chin, reduces him.

It's a shame to see the blood flowing from his nose – now a spiked black line, now a flat slapping pool.

'He . . . so . . . loved . . . you.' Frank knocks the small, pale head back against the ground with each word. 'Thank you, Lord, thank you' – with each skull-crack, emphasis – 'Amen.' The boy stops crying, closes his eyes, seems to relax.

When the moment comes, Frank's glad to release him. 'I tell you now, you can be born again – I can lead you to Him.' He smiles up at the sky, panting. 'You may find you vomit now as the devils tumble forth – don't be alarmed, this is quite normal.'

But this last is shouted, for the boy's already on his feet and gone from him – his devil half in, half hanging out – one moment staggering, one moment running in the fading, agitating light.

*

In the canteen, they warmed their hands on the sickly green radiator and peeled foil off fingers of Kit-Kat. 'I haven't told you,' Annie said, 'I've got a new boyfriend.'

'Really?' said Gayle. 'That's great.' She meant it. She had thought Annie seemed happier.

'Mm,' Annie said, 'met him at church.'

'I didn't think you went to church?'

'Well, I don't. Just now and then.'

'So? What does he do? What's he called?'

'Geoff. He manages a video shop.'

'Manager, huh?' Gayle was only half concentrating. She was wondering how Frank would take a visit from Will. It might be a good thing – might take the load off her. Somewhere, somehow, she could feel emotional dependence entering her relationship with Frank. He'd told her too much.

'Trouble is,' Annie leaned forward, 'he's married. His wife's expecting a baby. He's devastated. He didn't want to start a family. He's not even sure it's his. They don't sleep together any more, you see.'

'That's what he told you, is it?'

'Fuck off,' said Annie.

And Gayle looked at her and didn't say anything. The fact that she said nothing proved she'd finally grown up, and that she should suddenly have such vivid proof seemed gross and shocking.

*

Harry Skeat didn't beat about the bush. This was the quality which had initially attracted her.

'I don't under any circumstances want a child,' he said, 'and neither do you – we didn't get into this for that. The fucking thing broke – it's as simple as that. It's not an emotional issue, it's an accident. A mess which can be sorted.'

'Do you mean the "fucking thing"?' she asked. 'Or the thing we used for fucking?'

'Don't be so fucking facetious,' he said.

Harry Skeat – the acid-blue spots of his eyes, his gelled blond hair. She'd never had a boyfriend other women looked at before. 'I'll come along with you, of course,' he continued, 'no one says it's going to be nice, but you're a big girl, you'll handle it.'

As he spoke, a light came on and Gayle saw him clearly. She saw where she'd gone wrong. 'You ought to get out in the open more, Harry,' she told him, 'you could do with more fresh air '

They met at a party in Southampton when she was training. She was struck by his edginess – by the way he blinked all the time and licked his lips. Increasingly dry, that was Harry. She wondered why he flew out of his skin when someone dropped a wineglass near him.

'I'm shy with you,' he lied, grasping her shoulder bones, grazing with his lips on her neck. 'Look at me – really shy.'

He took a Polaroid of her lying naked on his bed. She was very drunk, very uncaring. She couldn't count the number of times her legs slid apart. As the Polaroid developed, he squashed it with his fingers, blurring the edges, so that the pale photographed flesh bled onto the maroon sheets.

'We'll have sex in the morning,' he said, 'more fun when you're sober.'

He knew all about fun. The huge four-bedroomed flat belonged to his father, who worked abroad. Estate agents pushed leaflets through his door begging to be allowed to sell it for him. Despite everything, it still whispered the presence of his dead mother – rich brown and mauve Liberty fabrics and gilt mirrors, endless rows of dry-cleaned polythened dresses in the built-in wardrobes. 'It feels as if she might come back at any moment,' Gayle observed, 'as if a babysitter's here.'

'You're my babysitter,' he said, pulling her knickers down with one hand, 'and Mummy's not coming back.'

His mother had died of a brain haemorrhage. Harry was a slut. He never emptied the vacuum cleaner. There were hair pins and pale, crusty bath salts and an almost-empty bottle of Arpège in the bathroom cupboard; talc trodden into the pale green carpet at the foot of the basin.

Harry'd pared his own room down to a drawing board and a low, hard futon, next to which there was a lacquered Chinese cabinet in whose shiny drawers he kept film magazines and lubricants and condoms in Dolly Mixture colours.

He had a twin sister, who came and went, took drugs with him, shopped, clubbed and then went back to Milan where she studied History of Art. 'Which one are you,' she asked when she and Gayle met half-clothed, in the tiny aspirin-white kitchen, 'the nurse or the potter?'

Gayle always meant to break it off with Harry, but she waited too long for the right moment. One afternoon when the city was subdued with heat, he took her by the hand and showed her a coil of rope lying next to the low bed. 'Know what I'd like to do?' he asked, a private expression spreading over his baby face.

'No,' she shook her head, 'I don't want to.'

'Yes, you do.'

'No, I mean it, Harry. I don't.'

He sulked for a moment, sitting on the edge of the bed, lit a cigarette. There were white and yellow stains on the sheet – remains of their breakfasts and bodily fluids. He yawned and she could see all the dark caves of his fillings. They kissed, emptily. 'I'm not going to, Harry,' she whispered through their embrace, 'you can't force me.'

But he pulled her onto his lap, kissed her cheek – a little chaste smoke-scented peck. It was boiling hot. Outside there were workmen and stray notes of soul music detached themselves from a nearby scaffold. Gotta . . . getcha . . . hold on, baby . . . he pushed her back on the bed, pinned her wrists till the blood began to jump.

She closed her eyes. She was exhausted. She'd spent the last two weeks on the Special Care baby unit – moving all night between the glass tanks, checking monitors, watching the voiceless babies who were born too early to cry.

As Harry reached for the rope she felt the chill of sweat between her breasts. 'Just this once,' he whispered, and the odd thing was he trembled. It was him who held his breath.

Whilst he tied her, he was very loving.

But once he'd begun to lose himself she noticed the slick of hatred in his eyes and felt ashamed. Black knots and lines floated and uncoiled in her heart. She moved against him as he wanted and dug down and found the part of herself which enjoyed it – and then the condom broke.

So her baby was conceived not only without love, but in bondage.

*

'I don't believe what I'm hearing,' Donna said, 'I can't believe you're saying I should go to some religious creep!'

'Donna, all I'm saying is I can't go on like this.'

'You can't go on like this?' she snorted from where she lay on the floor, her spine pressed on the carpet, silver bangles slipping down her arm. 'You can't go on!'

'All I want,' he put his forehead in his hands, 'is to find a cure, a solution for this . . .' – he hesitated because he didn't want to seem to make it all her fault – 'this thing which dogs our lives.'

'Through Jesus Christ?' She almost spat.

'If you tense up,' he said, 'you'll hurt more.'

'I was like this when we moved in together,' she said, 'I was often in pain. I told you about it, I let you know what it would be like. I've never hidden it from you.'

'I just want to find out what sort of a healer he is. Gayle agrees with me. That's all we want to do.'

'It is extraordinary,' she said as she stood up with the help of her stick, 'that you and Gayle should agree about something, I will give you that. That fact alone totally knocks me out.'

And she towered above him for a moment – an illusion of perfect grace and strength – before she left the room.

*

Their younger brother Simon turned up in the middle of the night, using the spare key Gayle let him keep. He always just turned up, never let her know what he was doing from one day to the next. She hadn't seen or heard from him for a while until his phone call last week. Kitty went crazy with excitement at finding him asleep on the sofa.

'I thought you were coming tomorrow?' Gayle said. She shook Rice Pops into a bowl, lifted Kitty onto her seat, filled the kettle. She sneaked a glance at Simon over her shoulder. He was using her only good coat as a blanket.

'Shoog, shoog, shoogar . . .' sang Kitty.

'Oh, yeah, well it was never definite,' he muttered, blinking at her, his hair all crazy with sleep.

'Got a job, then?'

He yawned. 'Maybe. I've got to go talk to someone.'

'Oh, really?'

He rolled over and closed his eyes.

Si. Little brother. The room smelt of him already – of his dope and his lack of plans and his aimless, unwashed limbs.

*

He sits there on the edge of his hospital bed, the curtains drawn, the clothes he arrived in washed and folded on the chair.

He dresses slowly, startled by the forgotten elastic grip of his underpants, suspicious of the artificial nylon warmth of socks, stiffened with the neatness of Lola's darns. His coat lies over the chair and in its pocket is Miss Gayle Dermondy's telephone number.

'So,' she says, 'you're off. How're you feeling?'

'Oh, I'm not bad.'

'Well, we're going to try and bring Donna to you.'

He rubs his hands together.

'But Will wants to meet you first.'

He nods consent. Then he sighs.

'What is it, Frank?'

'I'll miss this place.'

'The hospital? No, you won't, what a thing to say.'

'You won't come and see me. You've got better things to do than visit an old man. There's no one left now that Lola's gone.' He holds her eyes for a moment. 'You see, I've no one to talk to.'

'I promise you've got me,' she says, and he sucks the phrase from her like food.

At the desk they discharge him and he collects his painkillers from the pharmacy and walks down the long concrete ramp to catch the bus. London lies spread out, waiting for him, all spit and dust and solid cold.

At the bus stop, people stare at him and he stares back, encouraged.

*

When he agrees to marry Lola, it's the purest pink spring evening. He leaves her at her hostel and walks west towards Bayswater.

A man is standing under an awning of blossom in Hyde Park. 'This planet is ruled by the Prince of Darkness,' shouts the man, 'Judgement Day will come, and I tell you this: if you are not saved, you will burn. Man, woman and child. All the fires of Hell will roast you alive!'

A shower of petals floats down and sticks in his oiled hair. Frank stops in his tracks and cannot budge. He sees clearly for the first time that he is veering out of control – his life a skidding, dangerous thing. His shoulders ache with the force of his sins.

Looking back, that was his first step away from the vortex.

*

Gayle didn't know when the thing with Simon had started.

Thing was of course the wrong word for it – made it sound like something, which it most definitely wasn't. It wasn't anything at all, just a feeling. A prickle on her flesh when he was near. Sometimes she was ashamed of herself, even for suspecting.

He had never said anything to her – obviously he had no idea that she guessed. He would die if she knew. Or would he? Did he want to be found out? The only way forward was to ignore it – hope that it would go away – and meanwhile treat him normally. She couldn't cut him out of her life, after all. Instinctively she knew that would be wrong. He was her brother. He could not hang onto anything and he most definitely had no staying power. A key to her flat was the very least she could do. Let the thing – whatever it was – run its course.

All his life, everything – exam results, friends, jobs, flats – had slipped out of his grasp. 'That boy's too reliant on you,' their mother told Gayle – all the while ruthlessly pumping Si's account with money in a way she'd never done for either of them.

'He's not,' said Gayle, 'I wouldn't let him be,' but she knew at heart he was and it was her fault. She could not reject him. She closed her eyes to the situation, gave it no thought. It had to run its course.

It had been ten years now.

*

Donna lay on the bed.

After a while, as she knew he would, Will came up the stairs and into the room. He seemed even larger than usual – the room barely containing him. 'Hey,' he said, and sat down.

'If you think about it,' she said, aloud but somehow to herself, 'it really is a most peculiar idea. We find an injured man on Clapham Common and get him to hospital. My sister, whom you have always despised, starts to visit him and he turns out, frankly, to be a religious nut. Together – and suddenly, oh so miraculously seeing eye to eye – you and my sister plot that he should lay hands on me. And all because I damaged your bloody wall with a pair of bloody scissors.'

Will smiled. 'I know how it must look to you,' he said, and he gazed into her eyes with an understanding she loathed.

*

Gayle got home to find a chain letter on the mat.

'This letter has been sent to you for good luck. It has been around the world nine times – the original is in New England.'

She threw it on the table among the bills and the circles of milk from Kitty's breakfast and didn't give it a second look until she was clearing up an hour later. 'Do not keep this letter,' – the words were distorted by a bad typewriter – 'it must leave your hands within 96 hours. After a few days you will get a surprise, even if you are not superstitious.'

She forgot about it as soon as she opened the next letter – a thin brown one which informed her that Kitty had a nursery place at the local primary starting at the end of April. That was what she called good luck. She tore off the acceptance slip and put it to one side. Then she gathered the rest of the papers up and put them on top of the washing machine and wiped the table down.

The phone rang. It was Harry. She threw the cloth into the sink. She still had a handful of crumbs from the table top. 'All I want to do is see you both – say hello.'

'I know your hellos, Harry,' she said.

'Look,' he said and his voice faltered wonderfully, 'I'm sorry and all that. What more can I say?'

'God knows,' she said, her finger already poised to cut him off, 'I'll have a think.'

Much later, when Kitty was in bed, she stuffed a load of washing in the machine and the letter caught her eye again:

'Do not ignore this letter. In 1953, Constance Lanar sent out 20 copies and a few days later won a lottery for 2 million dollars. Janni Dallit, an office worker, forgot to send it out and lost his job. The next day he found the letter and sent it out and, two days after that, got a new and better job. Pestya Iguya received the letter and not believing it threw it away. Nine days later he died.'

She swept it, along with several circulars, into the bin. 'This is no joke. You will receive good luck in the mail. Send no money as fate has no price.'

She'd no wish to separate a child from its father, but Harry was less than useless to anyone. As she bent to pick up her book and her shoes and Kitty's doll, she fished the letter out of the bin and put it back on the table, where its white face was the last thing she saw as she climbed the stairs.

*

That evening, Donna phoned. 'What's going on?' she demanded.

'What?' Gayle had just come out of the shower. With one hand she tried to drag a towel over her wet hair.

'This idea I should go and see some born-again weirdo healer?'

'Well—' Gayle wondered how much Will had said.

'Look, I really appreciate all the concern, believe me I do, but right now the last thing I need is praying over. Really, I can't believe you two.'

'It's not quite praying,' Gayle said. Just then, Simon came in. 'Do you want to talk to your brother?' she asked Donna.

'He's there?'

'Right here in front of me.'

'Well, thanks a lot for telling me.'

'He came last night,' Gayle said, 'he only just fucking well turned up. He didn't tell me either.'

'Not right now, thanks. I'll call him later.'

Simon just stood there with his hand held out for the phone. 'She's gone,' Gayle said, 'too pissed off to talk.' She realized she was only wearing a towel. 'Can I just get dressed please, Simon?'

A little too slowly, he left the room.

*

Deciding to have the baby was relatively easy – the only totally straightforward thing she'd ever done.

She simply cancelled the abortion: one phone call, that was all. Said no thanks to more counselling. And that was it. There was nothing else to do except sit back and wait. The baby would grow, her body would make room. Everything – including the mess in her head – would settle gently into place.

She didn't bother to tell Harry she'd cancelled. She thought she'd let him go through the hassle – turn up at the clinic, find a parking place, ask self-consciously at the desk, failing to conceal his irritation as he registered the NO SMOKING signs. Let him be told. Get back in his car. Fume and rant and be frightened because she'd chosen to have his child.

He came straight round as she knew he would, real anxiety tearing through his face. She was peeling an orange very carefully, keeping the fragrant spiral of skin whole.

'Go away,' she said, 'I'm busy.'

Later that night, he reappeared, with his chequebook. 'This is what it would have cost if you'd gone through with it, plus a bit,' he said, pen between his teeth, tearing off the rectangle of paper and chucking it down on the table, 'but you have to understand I want nothing more to do with this, Gayle. I respect your decision and now I have to think of myself.'

Gone through with it? she thought. I am going through with it. 'I've spoken to friends,' he added, 'I've taken advice.'

She smiled, genuinely amused. After a moment's thought, she sacrificed the brilliantly tempting gesture of tearing up the cheque and distributing the pieces in the air around his face, because she'd done her sums and she wasn't going to refuse money. She knew what the baby would cost. She nodded and hoped he'd go. 'OK, Harry.'

He must have misunderstood because he came across and put his arms around her, tried to nudge a space in her chair for himself. 'Oh, Gayle, Gayle,' he began.

'Are you for real?' she whispered, as he reached over and put her fingers on his erection. He tried to put his hands down between her secret, pregnant thighs.

'Once more,' he whinged, 'for the hell of it?'

She couldn't speak. Her thoughts were flying all over the place like bullets.

'I can't think why I ever bothered with you,' she told him as he staggered to the door. She felt euphoric, blameless. She felt just like him.

'Just tell me,' he wailed, pulling at his car keys with both hands, 'who the fuck talked you into this, who, who?'

She laughed, she couldn't stop herself, and then she said very softly, 'You did, Harry.'

*

'What's this?' Simon asked, holding it up. 'A chain letter?'

'Give it to me,' Gayle said, and she pulled it from his fingers and screwed it up and tossed it in the bin. Her aim was perfect but the bin was full so the ball bounced out again and rolled on the carpet where it sat, the tight knot of paper relaxing very slowly.

He slumped down, rolled a cigarette. Outside the sky was windy, haywire. Car doors slammed up and down the street. Kitty came out from behind the sofa chewing a piece of bread. She wore her doll in a pink plastic heart-shaped locket around her neck. 'This Polly Pocket is smaller than a pea,' she told Simon.

'Yeah?' His eyes were closed but he reached out and nipped her nose with his fingers.

'Is that all you're going to do?' Gayle said. 'Lie there and smoke?'

'I thought I'd go and see Donna.'

'Good luck.'

'This man you're going to see,' Simon said.

'Frank Chapman, Frank Chapman,' said Kitty.

'You're going to get him to lay hands on Donna?'

Gayle came up and sat down. 'You won't believe this,' she said, 'but it was Will's idea.'

'Why will the man put his hand on Donna?' Kitty asked.

*

Because the bus doesn't look like it's coming, he sets off on foot and ends up going past Lambeth Walk and all the way down Kennington Lane. He picks out a café with steamed-up windows and a youthful clientele. Here he'll pick out a new disciple.

Peter (he'll name him Peter) is sitting with his head on the greasy table, hair falling in crumbs and ketchup. Frank buys him a tea – heaping loose change from his trouser pockets on the Formica.

'That one's a dosser,' the man at the till says, 'I want him out.' He shoves a pile of sandwiches behind the perspex screen, and turns to pull the switch on the hot water – passes Frank the tea in a cracked mug, milk slopping.

'You want to be careful who you call a dosser,' says Frank, 'you really want to watch out. All accountable to Jesus.'

'Oh boy, dearie me,' the man stands, feet apart, and gawps into the till, 'look what we got now. Bleedin' religious crank.'

'Customer's always right,' says Frank – he won't like that. He picks up the tea.

Peter doesn't look up. 'I'll tell you something interesting,' Frank begins, sliding into the seat opposite, 'Jesus was no wimp. Knew what He was doing when He stayed a bachelor. People get that wrong, you know.'

The disciple-to-be nods. His face is a mess of scabs and torn-up eczema. 'Don't shit me,' he says, 'I done nothing.'

'Yes,' Frank drops two lumps in his own tea, stirs, 'I thought I knew all about Jesus, thought I'd had all my spiritual teaching, but the first time I heard the Good News of the Gospel, I knew I'd been entirely ignorant of it! I did not know a verse of scripture! I realized then that I was depending on the church to save me, instead of depending on Jesus Christ.'

He watches the disciple for signs of recognition – the nod, the blink, the opened eye.

'I was amazed,' he goes on, more certain of his audience. 'There was no mention of good works, penance et cetera – it was just a plain invitation to come to Jesus and accept Him as Saviour and Lord. Commit thy way unto the Lord, trust also in Him and He shall bring it to pass!

'It's a remarkable thing, how the love of Jesus sustains. If you follow the Word of Christ. Shuffle free of your sins, young man.'

Someone smashes a plate behind the counter. Dance music plays on the radio. 'Yes.' Frank looks at Peter, and his breath's pumping freely now, his mind lit and warmed by his own words. It's a long time since he's preached this freely. Beneath his coat he can feel his shirt cool and sticky with sweat – the familiar flush of perspiration which comes when he preaches.

'Don' stare at me like that,' Peter grumbles.

'For instance,' Frank says, 'I knew an upstanding man, in the Guards and the SAS and a Falklands veteran – an heroic type of man, hallelujah, Amen. Married and a grandfather twice over and with a holiday caravanette in Skegness. Yes. And yet,' he lowers his voice, 'his heart was empty – yes, there was a veil over his eyes.'

Peter blinks.

'Yes, a veil of tears. Well, I led him to the Lord,' Frank says, 'it was a marvellous thing – him with his grief and his tears and all that. He went home to his wife reborn, I tell you.

'"Darling," he said, "I've been saved." "You've been what?" she says. "I've been saved," he says. In a short space of time she, too, came to know the Lord. Sadly, they didn't have a lot of time to enjoy it. A week later, the Lord saw fit to take her. Polio on the brain.'

Peter stared without flinching now.

'I think I shall call you Peter,' Frank tells him with a smile. 'OK with you, Peter?'

It's all as it should be. When Frank gets up to leave, Peter follows, moving after him through the Lambeth streets like a shadow and only finally disappearing from sight somewhere around The Cut. But Frank is confident.

He's already given him his name and address – scribbled in ballpoint, on a piece of paper stamped with the words Good News.

*

'You must come and say hello to Geoff sometime,' Annie said, as they went for their break, 'he'd really like you.'

'Well,' Gayle said, 'I'd like to, yes.'

'We should all go for a drink or a pizza or something.'

'It's a bit difficult after work,' said Gayle, 'with Kitty.'

'Do you never leave her, never go out?'

'No, no, it's not that. I mean, yes, I do.'

'Well, then, what's the problem? You ought to have a social life,' Annie said.

'I do,' said Gayle.

'I know what you're thinking,' Annie went on. 'He must be a shit because he cheats on his wife and there's nothing to say he wouldn't cheat on me too.'

'It hadn't even crossed my mind. Has it crossed yours?'

'Oh, spare me the agony aunt bit.'

Gayle said nothing. They squelched down the corridor in their nurse's shoes. 'What about you, anyway?' Annie said.

'What about me?'

'Don't you get sick of being alone?'

'Not right now,' said Gayle, truthfully.

But all morning she gave it thought. She began to wonder why she wasn't lonely and then to wonder whether in fact she was. It began to disturb her that she couldn't remember the state sufficiently well to detect the symptoms in herself. She knew she'd been lonely at some time in her life, but when she thought back she couldn't recall it. Great wads of years, huge areas which must have contained time and events, were blank. Sometimes, she woke up in the morning and couldn't piece the rhythm of her life together – couldn't remember what to do first. Was that loneliness?

On the way home she thought for a terrible moment she saw Harry standing there in the road by the skip, but when the man turned he was older, sallower. Something about him was similar, but she couldn't have said what it was.

Anyway, it wasn't him; that was the point.

*

'Si's back,' Donna said, flopping down and chucking her stick on the sofa where it bounced and then rolled to the floor.

'I know.'

'How do you know?'

'Gayle said.'

'When did you speak to her?'

'Just now.' Will hesitated. Why hide the truth? 'We made a plan for the weekend. To see this guy.'

Donna looked at him.

'I have to check,' he said, 'I have to.'

She kept her head, her eyes, very still. 'Of course you do.'

'That's right,' he said, 'you just carry on being angry.'

'I don't enjoy being angry,' she said, turning on him. 'Is that what you think, that I enjoy it?'

He tried to listen to her, struggled to work out the meaning of the things she said. 'I don't know what you enjoy any more,' he said.

She was silent.

'I'm sorry,' he said.

'Don't be,' she said.

'Well, I am anyway.'

He wondered whether he was lying. He tried to examine himself, but could only answer questions with questions. Why was he doing this? What had he come here for?

*

'Look.' Kitty showed Gayle her drawing – a human figure with insect legs and beady, wide-apart eyes. 'It's a mum.'

'Your mum?' said Simon.

'No, just a mum.'

'It's lovely,' Gayle kissed the top of her head. The paper was wrinkled and she turned it over. '. . . round the world nine times . . . do not ignore this letter.' Oh shit, she thought.

Kitty wouldn't give the picture up, so Gayle had to resort to stealing it back later when it was forgotten. She tore it in small pieces and actually took it out to the dustbin.

'What's come over you?' Simon laughed. 'What's that letter going to do to you?'

She laughed back, answerless.

*

He marries Lola on St Swithin's Day. His sister Merle leaps up and catches the bouquet, much good it does her.

'Look,' she says, pulling her frock down at the back, 'baby's breath.'

'Baby's what?'

'Baby's breath – the white ones.'

Merle is dead within the year of cancer of the womb.

He's almost put off by the puny, pale fragility of his bride. Undressed at last, she is the Real Thing. Forbidden, goose-bump flesh, sharp knees, nipples he used to dream about. He frets briefly about crushing her with his weight, but the worry passes with the night and with her barely noticeable virginity.

*

Kitty climbed into bed with Gayle at six fifteen in the morning wearing nothing but a red sou'wester, the chinstrap flapping. 'Rabbits are awful jumpy,' she said and snuggled down, pushing the chilly moons of her bottom into Gayle's belly.

And Gayle, from the depths of her sleep, agreed.

five

Will stood in Gayle's doorway at ten o'clock on Saturday morning, wishing he was somewhere else, preferably in bed. He kept his coat on, held his car keys, waited. Kitty ran up and wrapped herself around his leg, tried to climb him.

'Get off him, Kitty.' Gayle marched up and down the room, lifted her arms and fixed her frizz of dark hair back with a clip, pulled on a cardigan, frowning.

'No,' he let Kitty turn a somersault with her feet on his chest, 'it's OK.'

Simon walked past them into the kitchen, half-asleep, squatted down and looked in the fridge. 'Hiya,' he said without looking at Will.

'Hi, how're you?'

'How cold is it?' Gayle asked Will. He knew she was trying to be friendly, asking him these everyday questions. A sister-in-law. He tried to reciprocate.

'Cold,' he said. 'Well, coldish,' he added brightly.

Kitty shouted various unintelligible words and flung her head backwards, laughing. He let her climb him again – the buckles of her sandals catching on his combed cotton trousers. He said nothing, ran his fingers over afterwards to check they had not snagged.

'OK.' Gayle turned Kitty the right way up, shoved her

arms into a cardigan, then a coat. 'Let's go.' She picked up her bag.

He gave Kitty a piggyback down the steep, shabby lino stairs to the street. 'I get the feeling you'd rather be going alone,' he said. The trick with Gayle was to be straight.

'Nonsense,' she replied without looking at him. He got in and pushed open the car door for her.

The sky was chalky, thick with impending rain. They didn't have to talk in the car because Kitty sang. 'Ye-llow bi-ird, up high in banana tree . . .' She twiddled a paper party decoration in her hand, occasionally letting it fall between the seats so Gayle had to keep on twisting around to pick it up.

'You may find him a bit strange,' Gayle said suddenly, 'I mean, he seems to trust me, but he may be different with you. I can't guarantee what he'll be like.'

'I know,' he said, 'I don't expect you to.'

'OK,' she said, 'fine.'

They sat – in silence again – in the traffic on Clapham Park Road, then sped, relieved, into Brixton.

*

At first, without Lola, the flat on St Saviour's Road falls apart. Or, rather, it knits together – its dirt finally unites and congeals.

The kettle scales up all the time, there are brown rims around the taps and black growths in the grouting, and the tea towels infest Frank's fingers with a bad smell at one touch. He knows where the launderette is, but has no idea what you press or where to put the soap.

The lavatory grows fur on its bend and the seat is

splashed with whatever you care to mention, and everything in the kitchen cupboards is stale. Crackers fold like cardboard at the touch of a knife and when he forgets to use a clean one in the margarine, next day there's a clump of green spores to mark the spot. Eventually, he's forced to dig down under in order to find anything to put on his bread.

He finally makes it to the Co-op – careful at first, then bolder as a new world opens up. He takes his pick. Yoghurts with little punnets of cereal on the side; pizzas the size of a Sellotape roll; tarts you pop in the toaster. All in all, Lola kept him on a very plain diet, didn't she? Most of all, he likes the children's food. The small, wrapped portions and the squeaky colours and the cartoon characters on the side. You couldn't get anything like that in Tommy's day. He often has a bowl of Coco Pops for supper now.

He's not entirely above board; he still makes mistakes. One day, an assistant points out that he's using a disabled trolley. 'Oh heck,' he says, 'I knew it felt funny.' But it's a scream. He is a camper in a foreign region, exploring the lingo. He enjoys the touch and go of it.

He stamps his tracts at the small oak table with the barley-sugar legs, where Lola so often sat with her reading glasses on and her ankles crossed, stuck into her Church magazines and Friendship books.

Sometimes he turns his head sharply, thinking he hears her key in the door, her zip-front boots on the mat, her accusing sigh, the bump of the red and white check nylon shopping bag on the step. But the only ghost in this flat is the Holy Ghost and He's welcome.

Now he piles his papers and tracts wherever he likes,

does not have to clear away for meals. He can eat standing up, with the TV on, if the fancy takes him. Though he forbade Lola a TV in her lifetime, he recently found a good 'un – too good a bargain to miss – at a car boot sale. The picture's good, though the sound comes and goes.

He has it on its side by the bed, so he can watch it lying down, though this means lying always on one side and his limbs go to sleep. Soon he'll change it round.

He watches anything – tunes in whenever he feels like it. News, comedies, dating programmes, recipes, *Gladiators*. Lola will be looking down from her place at His feet, going crazy, seeing what she's missing!

*

Frank's basement flat was almost at the end of St Saviour's Road, by the boarded-up, derelict church where the early lilac was in bud. A car on the road outside had had its window smashed and pale blue crumbs of glass lay heaped on the pavement. Will, Gayle and Kitty crunched over the glass and into a tiny, filthy garden, half-cemented over, with narrow steps down to his door.

As they went down, Will caught a whiff of the dustbin whose black rubber lid was flung down on the dead grass. The bin hadn't been emptied for some time and household muck spewed out all over the place. Plastic bottles, cartons, empty tins. Weeds clogged the paving stones, circulars lifted in the breeze. One dust-blackened daffodil stood alone, still straight and alive.

'Look!' said Kitty, picking a used tea bag off the step.

'Put it down,' said Gayle, 'it's dirty, leave it.'

They rang the bell several times. No reply.

'Out?' Will put a foot back on the step, ready to walk up.

'Or not answering.' Gayle tried to peer through the glass.

'Pick me up!' said Kitty, holding up her arms, but they shushed her.

They pressed up against the windows, which were opaque and filmy with dirt. The wind blew above them, a patter of rain. Gayle rang again, tried the door handle, then banged on the door.

'Oh, damn.' She looked at him. 'He was sort of expecting us. I suppose I didn't fix a time.' Kitty was kicking bits of broken glass. Will pulled her up into his arms. She rested her elbow comfortably on his shoulder, looked around, tipped her head and gazed at the darkening sky. It was raining properly now.

'Shit,' Gayle said, 'shit. It's my fault.' She bit her lip and looked irritated and tired.

'We'll go away for a bit and come back,' Will said, suddenly inexplicably anxious for her sake that the plan shouldn't fail. 'Come on, I'll buy you a coffee.'

As they walked back up Station Road in the pissing rain he felt beneficent, almost elated, as if he'd taken charge.

*

When Donna came back from the bathroom, Simon was watching her.

'What do you do in there?' he said. 'You've been ages. Are you taking something? Can I have some? What's that smell?'

He had his feet on the table and he was smoking. There

were great holes in his socks and one of his toenails was black with dye from his shoe.

'You're such a schlock,' she said, 'look at you.'

'Tell me what you were doing.'

'I squat down for a few minutes to stretch out my spine,' she told him. 'It looks stupid or I'd do it here. And, yes I just swallowed two Panadol. But I don't use them every day, or I try not to. And what you can smell is bergamot and marjoram. Aromatherapy oil.'

It was her private routine. Every couple of hours, if she could, she'd sidle off and do it: the bathroom, the little room at the back of the shop, department store loos – anywhere she could shut the door. She rubbed the muscles in her buttocks and the small of her back with oils from a small brown glass bottle. Then she leaned forward till she felt the joint facets separate and click. Just like that – click click click. Her osteopath said it released an artificial rush of endorphins and warned her that she ought not to do it too often, but that didn't put her off. She didn't see herself as having much choice. Who was to judge what was artificial and what was real?

Simon's spliff had gone out. He laid it carefully on one of Kitty's picture books.

'Why aren't you working at the moment?' she asked him. 'What happened with the bike job?'

He shrugged. 'Bike got written off. I'm thinking of doing a course. A degree.'

Donna looked at him, surprised. 'In what?'

'Physics.'

'You'd never get a grant,' she told him. Simon had had a

place to read physics somewhere once and had pissed off to Mexico.

'Gayle thinks I would.' He looked out of the window.

'I shouldn't think so. You haven't worked for long enough.' She didn't know why Gayle put up with Simon as she did. She was a saint of a sister. The carer of the family.

Donna hadn't been at all close to Gayle until she had Kitty. She'd gone off to work at a hospital in Southampton and for more than a year she hadn't come home. There were postcards and brief phone calls. Their mother was frantic. 'What's she playing at? She should bloody well just get on a train.'

'She'll come when she's ready,' Donna loyally said, 'she's thirty-four years old.'

But when Gayle finally stepped off the train with a bag in each hand and a seven-week-old baby in a sling on her breast, Donna fell instantly in love. With the baby, and with her sister – so altered, so shocking: such a picture of quiet beauty and fragility.

'Do you think you could hold her?' Gayle said, flushed and tired. 'I'm desperate for a pee.' Donna stood in the ladies' lavatory at Waterloo and held her niece in her arms. She stirred at one point and looked up. The sensation was unbelievable. By the time Donna gave her back, her shoulders ached with the shock.

Simon changed the subject. 'She's very worried about you,' he said, 'do you know that?' Donna shrugged assent. 'You really freaked, didn't you?' he said. 'With those scissors.'

'I know.'

'So, are you going to see the preacher chap?'

'He isn't a preacher.'

'What is he, then?'

'Just an ordinary man. An arsehole.'

'Are you going to see him?'

'What is this?'

'I just want to know. I'm your brother.'

'Almost certainly not.'

*

'I'm sorry,' Gayle unbuttoned her cardigan and slumped back on the plastic bench, 'I'm just so tired.'

They sat in McDonald's on the corner of Brixton High Street. A panorama of lorries and traffic lights changing. A sky full of flux blowing blue then grey again. The deathly, acid light before heavy rain.

'How's the hospital?' he said.

'Much the same. What about you, how's your work?'

'The same,' he said, 'but you don't want to know.'

She looked at him sharply. 'I do.'

He said, as reasonably as he could, 'All I mean is, don't feel you have to ask me.'

'I don't feel I have to, actually.'

Silence whilst Kitty licked her milkshake off the straw, then said she didn't like it, pushed it away.

'OK, leave it, but don't tell me you're hungry.' Gayle lit a cigarette, offered one to Will, then remembered he'd given up. 'Do you mind?' she said, tucking the packet away in her bag. He shook his head. Kitty struggled in Gayle's lap. Gayle passed her a sachet of sugar.

'So the pitch is going well?' she went on.

He smiled at hearing her say it. 'Fine. Well, as far as anyone can tell at this stage.'

'You like pitching?'

He thought about it. 'It's part of the fun, yes. Why?'

'I don't know. I don't think I see you as one of life's pitchers.'

'I'm not sure how to take that,' he said.

How mealy-mouthed he sounded! He wanted to be able to lighten up, to tell her he didn't take his own job very seriously either, that he'd always meant to do something better with his life, that she was welcome to criticize it to his face. But he couldn't. Everything he planned to say went exactly the opposite way. It was her. She always had this cloying effect on him – made him serious and unresponsive and dull.

'We don't really know each other,' was what she said then and somehow it was supposed to be a criticism of him. 'He'd better be in when we go back,' she added, 'I don't want to have made you come for nothing.' She sucked on her cigarette and her eyes crinkled with anxiety all over again.

'Calm down,' he told her, 'he'll be in. And if he's not, it's not your responsibility.'

He'd never spoken to her like that before and she glanced at him again with a look of what he imagined was pure surprise.

*

They sat there for about half an hour.

Gayle asked him about Donna, whether he thought the

scissors episode was just delayed grief about the loss of the baby. He tried to answer in a considered and tactful way, but found himself admitting that he'd barely discussed the miscarriage with Donna, because every time he'd tried to she'd just jumped down his throat. In fact the more he thought about it, the more certain he was that Donna had lost control on purpose. That this was pure and simple anger at not being allowed – so to speak – to try again for a baby.

'It was your baby, too,' Gayle said gently.

He said of course he knew that, but that most of the time it didn't feel that way – that it felt like Donna's wish and Donna's loss and Donna's sadness. A small part of him was actually running scared of the strength of her wish for a child. He felt it had caused everything to shift – had altered their relationship somehow irretrievably.

He tried to explain this without being disloyal to Donna, though he was sure he could trust Gayle when it came to her sister. It was the first time he'd spoken to anyone like this about the whole business and he was surprised at himself. Some of what he said he hadn't known was true until he heard himself saying it, and he wondered whether Gayle knew how upfront he was being.

He had never found her especially easy to talk to, and he realized that this was the first time they'd ever spoken to each other properly, truthfully, without rancour or sarcasm. The seats around them were emptying as sun flashed briefly in the darkening sky. He noticed that objects around them – the hard plastic table, the maroon plastic bench, the orange swing bin – suddenly seemed brighter, darker, as if everything had moved into focus. Finally, he said, 'If you don't mind, I'll have a cigarette.'

'Oh dear,' she said, 'you shouldn't. It's my fault. Now I've made you smoke.' He didn't say anything, but of course she was right, she had. She'd put him on edge with all these questions and he needed a hit of nicotine to get over the shock of it, and when he got it, he felt better.

He stretched out his legs and asked her what he'd never asked her – how she managed alone with Kitty, whether everything was OK – and she suddenly said, 'Actually, it's been hard lately because Harry's around. Trying to get back on the scene and I don't know what to do.'

'Harry?' He'd never known the names of any of her boyfriends – if indeed there were any.

'Harry Skeat. *Son père.*' She indicated Kitty, then looked away. To hide his surprise, he picked up a sachet of sugar, flicked the creased corner of it back and forward with his fingers.

'I didn't know . . .'

'No,' she said quickly, 'no, Donna doesn't even know. Simon knew once, a long time ago, but I think he's forgotten. He never refers to it, anyway.'

'So who is he?'

'Just someone I knew in Southampton.'

'And back in London now?'

She nodded in a matter-of-fact way, stubbed out her cigarette. He didn't know what he should ask next.

They looked at Kitty, sitting on the shiny floor, pushing herself along with her feet, the skirt of her dress riding up to show her knickers. Gayle called her over, pulled her onto her knee. 'Grubby girl,' she said and kissed her.

'Can we go?' said Kitty. 'I want to go.'

'Is it amicable?' Will asked.

'Yes and no. Not really.' Gayle put her lips on Kitty's hair again and then inspected her scalp. Kitty tried to wriggle off her lap. Outside the sky had brightened a little. Lorry tyres sent sprays of black water into the air.

'Can we go now?' Kitty said again.

'I'm surprised you're telling me this,' Will said.

'So am I.'

*

Frank opened the door instantly. They didn't tell him anything – didn't say they'd already been there once. 'Well, how's that for timing?' he said, looking at all of them at once. 'I popped out and I only just got back.'

'You look terrific,' Gayle said and meant it, because his powerful frame seemed suddenly abnormal and extraordinary in the small, tight doorway. Was this the first time she'd seen him standing up? He was taller than Will by a fraction, and Will was tall. 'I bet you don't remember Will?'

'I do, I do,' he said, though it had, of course, to be a lie. He led them in.

He went in and out of the small kitchen, putting the kettle on, moving the armchairs in the tiny living room. The house smelled horrible – of sourish milk and of urine – the washing-up was stacked in the sink and the carpet was filthier than the pavement outside. They made faces to each other each time he disappeared to the kitchen.

'So,' he called to them, 'how am I doing so far?' There was no laughter in his voice.

'We'll let you know,' Gayle said and she felt Will glance across at her in surprise. She knew he'd already made up his mind about Frank – he wouldn't be able to stomach the dirt and the uncertainty. She pulled Kitty to sit beside her on a narrow single bed in front of the window. Next to the pillow was a cheap soft toy – a monkey with big flat stuck-on eyes and long neon-blue hair. Kitty grabbed at it immediately. 'Is it OK for her to play with this monkey thing?' Gayle called.

'It was Lola's,' Frank said, coming in with the tea, 'she's with the ancient saints and the holy angels, little girl, so it's all yours.' He set down the tray and his arm shot into the air. 'Hallelujah! Praise Jesus!'

Gayle looked at Will, whose face gave nothing away. She did not want to sit on Lola's bed, but it was too late to move. She glanced a couple of times at the pillow, which still had a faded, striped pillowcase on.

'We want to talk about healing,' Will said, as soon as Frank was sitting down.

'Good,' said Frank, looking at Kitty.

'Yes,' said Will. 'But we need to know a lot more.'

'Can we go now?' Kitty tossed Lola's monkey back on the bed.

'Soon,' Gayle said, 'but not yet.' The teacups still had tea bags floating in them as Frank poured in the milk.

Gayle looked around the room. Every surface, every inch of wall, every area of carpet, had something on it. There were mirrors and pendants and pictures in cheap plastic frames, some of them of biblical scenes. There was *The Light of the World* picture of Jesus, and there were scenes of bearded men on mountains holding staffs – purplish skies, tiny woollen clouds. She didn't recognize the scenes.

There were clocks and paperweights and doilies and

photographs – crocheted cushions all over the armchairs, a piece of sheepskin on the floor by the bed. She noticed, with a shiver, a grubby white candlewick dressing gown and a plastic bottle of magnolia handcream by the head of the bed.

'I've had enough,' Kitty said, throwing herself against Gayle's knees.

'Would she like a boiled sweetie?' Frank asked and Kitty jumped up.

Gayle hesitated. 'Oh, why not?' she said and then worried because she dreaded to think what they were. 'If you suck it very slowly,' she told Kitty. They had to talk properly to Frank or there was no point in coming. Kitty put the sweet in her mouth.

'It's simple,' Frank said. 'Several years ago, I was given a plain invitation – nothing fancy – an invitation to come to Jesus. Commit thy way unto the Lord, trust also in Him and He shall bring it to pass.'

Will smiled and looked down at the carpet.

'He invested my hands with powers. Simple as that. Singled me out from the crowd. When I lay my hands on your sister, the pain shall cease. Praise Jesus. Would she like that?'

'Of course she would,' Gayle said, impatient with the jargon, the gestures.

'But have you ever actually healed anyone?' Will wanted to know. Neither of them had touched their tea. There was solid yellow milk on the surface.

'Yes,' Frank said, 'there was my son, Tommy. Praise the Lord.' He looked at them steadily. Kitty began to crunch her sweet, a mix of bliss and anxiety on her face.

'But . . .' Gayle hesitated. 'I thought he died?' She wondered whether he hadn't. Whether Frank didn't mean it literally when he spoke of him dying.

'No, no, I healed him,' Frank's eyes shone, 'he walked from his bed.'

'And where is he now?' asked Will, somewhat over-aggressively, Gayle thought.

'Oh, I don't want to talk about Tommy.'

'It's all right,' she said quickly, 'we don't need to.'

Will sighed and stuck his hands in his pockets. 'I want to go,' moaned Kitty.

'OK, then,' Frank said, 'OK, put me on the spot. I can give you a list. I can supply names and addresses. The brothers and sisters who can testify. Skin complaints, heart murmurs, rheumatism – I'm particularly good at muscles – possibly your sister's trouble. You can write off, for confirmation.' He was shuffling in a drawer and now held up a piece of paper.

'How do we know these people are telling the truth?' said Will.

Frank gave a little jump away from him. 'How do you know?'

'Oh, for God's sake,' Gayle said to Will. 'Of course we don't need to ring people. It either works or it doesn't, no harm done.' She turned to Frank. 'We'll get Donna here. How long would it take?'

He smiled at her. 'I place my hands on her bare back and say a prayer. Hey presto! Ten minutes at the most.'

'That's all?' said Gayle.

Now Will laughed out loud. 'I'm sorry,' he said, 'it just sounds so ludicrous. OK, so what does it cost?'

'Oh,' Frank nodded emphatically, 'it costs her, that's for sure. She puts her faith in Jesus Christ. Amen. We're talking souls – that's our currency, yes, sir.'

'Great value, then,' said Will.

'If you like,' said Frank. Gayle saw something in his eyes when he looked at Will – a flash of something like anger, only it wasn't anger. It made her uncomfortable for a moment – guilty almost.

'I'll tell you a story,' Frank said then. 'A woman was married to a white American Air Force officer and she went and had twins – a black one and a white one, just like that: piano keys. Bit of a shock.

'"How come?" says the officer. "That black one's never mine – there's no Negro blood in our family." And finally she confessed she'd had intercourse with his pal, a black man in the American Army, at the same time, and ended up with one of each. Found her out, eh?'

Will was speechless. He stood up. 'Must go,' Gayle said, moving between him and Frank. But Frank came up close to Will and said, 'You want to know how I know about Donna? Is that it? Well, I'll tell you, it's nothing – there's no great mystery. I saw her pain – it's a small planet. Does she ever get on the number 87 bus?'

'I don't think so,' Will said tersely.

'Ah!' Frank lifted a finger. 'But can you be sure?' They all moved toward the door. 'Does the little girl want to keep the monkey?' he asked.

'No!' Kitty shouted rudely.

'No thank you.' Gayle put her hand on Kitty's head. 'That's very kind, but she's got more than enough at home.'

They climbed the steps and got to the car and he was

still standing down there as Will pulled out. They could see the top of his head, the silvery helmet of hair, motionless against the brick.

*

Will said it straight away, as soon as he slammed the door of the car. 'He's barking. A basket case. How could you fail to see it?'

'I told you what to expect,' she said quietly, 'I said. How did you think he'd be?'

'Well, not like that. Not quite so mad.'

'He's not a balanced person,' she said tightly, obviously objecting to his terminology.

'You're telling me he's not.'

'OK,' she said, 'calm down.'

He ignored her. 'No way,' he said, 'no way am I going to waste Donna's time by sending her there, no fucking way.'

'Really?' She looked at him. 'I don't see what she has to lose. OK, it probably won't work, yes I know that. And it's impossible to know whether these stories of his are true. But what if they were? It's no different from any of these things she's tried. Most of these therapies aren't backed up by orthodox medicine, you know.'

Will laughed bitterly. 'That story about the black and white twins, it was repulsive, offensive. Weren't you offended?'

She shrugged. 'It was naïve. He's naïve. But it's not malice. It's because he gets the tone so wrong, keeps messing up so drastically, that I'm inclined to trust him.'

'I wouldn't leave him alone with Donna for one moment.'

'Oh,' she said, 'so what's he going to do? He's harmless, Will, I assure you. I've seen him a few times, remember.'

'He's latched onto you and he's using you. He knows you feel sorry for him. I'm surprised you can't see it.'

'How is it you suddenly know so much about everyone's motives? Tell me that.'

'There are people far worse off than Frank Chapman,' he remarked, suddenly fed up with her fucking liberal piety.

She frowned and fiddled with a strand of hair. 'I think he scared you, Will. I wonder why.'

He laughed. 'Come off it.'

'No, ' she said, 'I mean it. You seem scared.'

'OK,' he said, 'OK, yes, if you want to know, I experience a degree of fear when I come across such hideous fanaticism. He's a nutter, a liar. He makes it up as he goes along. And what frightens me most of all is that you're so taken in by him.'

'You don't like him at all.' But she was talking almost to herself.

He said nothing.

'What's a nutter?' Kitty asked from the back.

'Come back to the real world, Gayle,' he said after a moment. He remembered why they didn't get on. Suddenly, he regretted confiding in her in McDonald's; he tried to remember what he'd said.

'She doesn't have to like it or take it seriously,' Gayle said, 'she just has to do it.'

'What's a nutter?' Kitty wailed.

'I thought you were desperate,' Gayle turned to him, 'I really thought you were at the end of your tether. I thought anything was worth a try?'

'There are limits.' He was still trying to remember what he'd said to her about Donna and the miscarriage.

'Oh, really, are there? Well, I wish you'd said. I wish you'd told me before we wasted our time. I've got better things to do too, you know, than hang around whilst you define your limits.' She pulled a tissue from her bag and turned to wipe Kitty's nose. 'A nutter's just a silly, grown-up word for someone people don't understand,' she told her.

*

He sits still for a long time after they've gone, just listening to the sound of them disappear. Sometimes it feels like he's spent his whole life listening to people walk away from him. If only they'd allowed him to roam free, do as he pleased. He'd have gone hot-foot to the US of A to preach with Brother Gisborne years ago. Arizona, Texas, Kentucky. Preaching the Gospel and healing.

He purified himself all those years ago. Sanctified his head, defied the enemy. Spat the bile into a bowl. All things work together for good for them that love the Lord.

This time he knows they'll be back.

He turns on the TV and it's all sport. He used to have a soft spot for soccer, but now he can't understand what they get so excited about – all those legs tearing down a muddy field.

Eventually, though, he drops off to it, comforted by the greenish light in the dull room and the persistent roar of the crowd.

*

They came in and Will sat in his coat on the arm of the sofa next to Donna. Gayle took Kitty up to the loo.

'Well?' Simon looked at him and laughed. 'How did the healing powers shape up?'

Will said nothing. He didn't know what to say to Donna, where to start. He hadn't had time to decide what he thought. As if she knew, Donna fitted her hand over his, carefully, like a child testing for size, and said nothing.

'Well?' Simon said again.

Gayle came down the stairs, followed by Kitty, who was pulling up her tights. 'I need to feed Kitty,' she said. She didn't look at Will.

'There's cheese in the fridge,' said Donna, getting up.

'He made us the most repulsive tea,' Gayle laughed, 'we couldn't touch it.' She and Donna and Kitty went into the kitchen.

'Not egg,' he heard Kitty say.

'So?' Simon turned to him. 'Did you pray?'

'It wasn't a fucking prayer meeting.'

'Were there crucifixes all over the walls?'

'It's easy to send it up,' Will said, feeling dislike of Simon forcing him over onto Gayle's side.

'Just a joke,' said Simon. He kept his eyes on Will. Will got up and went into the kitchen.

*

They sat around the table, ate bread and cheese, drank beer. Donna poured Kitty a glass of milk. 'Don't want that cup,' Kitty said, shoving it away.

'You'll have the cup you're given,' Gayle said and pushed it back.

'Didn't you hear me?' Kitty said, in a high, cross voice, and she swiped with the back of her hand and the milk went over the table and mostly into Donna's lap. Simon laughed.

'You naughty girl!' Gayle pulled Kitty from her seat and carried her into the sitting room. Kitty began to scream. Donna was dabbing at her jeans with kitchen towel.

'Poor old Kitty,' she said.

'You haven't told us anything.' Simon wasn't going to let it go. Will was sick of him, wished he'd leave.

'I don't want to talk about it,' Donna said quickly, 'don't want to hear about it. Will can tell me later.'

Will got up and took his beer into the sitting room and turned on the TV. Gayle was sitting in the armchair with Kitty almost asleep in her lap. 'Worn out,' she said, looking down at Kitty.

'You or her?'

She smiled suddenly. 'Both.'

*

'Is something wrong?' Donna asked him later.

'Wrong?'

'You seem fed up, depressed.'

He shook his head. 'I'm fine.'

'OK,' she said, oddly serene, 'tell me what Frank Chapman said. You're going to make me do it, right?'

He looked at her. 'No one's going to make you do anything.'

'You've changed your tune.'

'To be honest,' he said, 'I'm not sure about him. He's worse than Gayle said. He's raving.'

'Oh?' She perked up. 'How?'

He shrugged. 'I don't know. Unpleasant, unhinged, very fanatical. Dangerous, almost. I don't know why Gayle doesn't see it.'

'Well,' Donna said, 'she likes people to be dependent on her. She collects people who're damaged in some way.'

He laughed, because he could see the truth of it. 'What a horrible idea.'

*

Later, he and Donna shared a bath. He lay back at the tap end, trying to find a comfortable position, and she sat up and wiped the make-up off her eyes and washed her face with some pink gel in a bottle. When she'd finished splashing her face, he saw that she was crying.

'What is it?'

She was crying with her mouth tight shut and without moving her face – but her breasts and shoulders were shaking and the tears were streaming down her face. 'What is it?' he asked her again, moving forward to touch any part of her.

'Leave me,' she said, angrily jerking her naked arms away from him. Her fingers sought her palms and made fists. 'Leave me,' she said again.

She stood up and let the water run off her and reached for her towel, stepped out and wrapped it round her, and took her stick from where she'd left it on the laundry basket. She did not look at him, and as she turned and left the room, he felt blindly sorry for her.

*

Annie was in love with the video shop manager whose wife was expecting twins at the end of May.

'Twins now?' Gayle said. 'I didn't know it was twins.'

'What am I to do?' said Annie. 'I love him. I just do. I'd do anything for him.'

They sorted stockings from the laundry – tried to match them, tan for tan, mink for mink, beige for beige.

'Jesus has got the hots for me!' Peggy Tyler shouted. 'Jesus loves me.' She scattered the crusts from her breakfast tray on the floor around her feet. Oh no, thought Gayle, not Him again.

*

On Monday morning, Gayle phoned Will at the office. 'I just wanted to say sorry, about Simon.'

He was surprised. 'You don't have to apologize for him.'

'I feel I do,' she said, 'I feel responsible. He does it as a way of getting at me.'

'Does he?' This had never occurred to Will.

She hesitated. 'Brother–sister dynamics – I can't explain and it's not very interesting. But I could see you were angry.'

'Look,' he said, 'it's not your responsibility, what Simon does.'

She paused. 'I feel it. I can't help it.'

'Why?' he asked. 'Why?'

But she changed the subject. 'How's Donna?'

'Terrible. But I think she'll go.'

'Really? I thought you'd have persuaded her against it.'

'No,' he said, 'I wouldn't do that.'

*

Donna still wanted to cut things, only the desire was no longer driven by rage, it was something else.

She wanted to snip and halve things and make them useless. Scissors or a knife (or small scalpel such as Will kept upstairs) would do – only it had to be a blade, a length of metal sharpened for the purpose of incision. She hadn't told anyone about this – this craving of hers. 'When I was pregnant,' Gayle told her once, 'I wanted to sniff exhaust fumes. Towards the end I had to avoid walking in traffic – I was worried I was going to get down on my knees and breathe it straight from the pipe.'

Donna had laughed and so had Gayle. A craving was a physical thing beyond someone's control – neither logical nor desirable, but forgivable because of its strength. Usually temporary, a craving was bigger than you. That's why it was funny.

Donna's thing about cutting was a craving. That's what she told herself.

She knew Will was worrying about her, and that was why she thought she'd go and see this man – to appease the gods, a sacrifice to make up for the unnatural things she was doing behind his back.

Only yesterday, she'd chopped a pair of thick rubber gloves into small pieces with their only sharp vegetable knife – a bad thing to do because it might blunt the knife, as well as wasting the gloves. And just now, she'd gone and taken her best pair of Marie-Jo knickers – charcoal grey with a lace trim – from her drawer and cut them into eight long strips with the now infamous haircutting scissors. The elastic had been tough to get through, but the stretch satin had crunched open, relaxed in an even, satisfying way.

Afterwards, she hadn't known where to put the pieces so Will wouldn't find them, so she'd had to get up off the bed and find an old plastic carrier bag, tie it up and take it down to the dustbin. By the time she'd done all this, she was in such pain that she'd come back upstairs and lain down on the carpet and wept.

*

In the supermarket, Kitty made a big fuss about Batman pasta and Gayle had to pull right out of the tinned food aisle, and into detergents. 'Next time,' she said.

'Want so-ome!' Kitty arched back to throw herself out of the trolley and reached out with her hand and swiped at a row of fabric conditioners. Nine or ten of them rolled on the floor.

'Now look, you bloody girl!' Gayle shouted. Kitty began to cry – a routine, tearless, testing cry. Gayle felt herself begin to perspire all over. She wanted to grab the soft tops of Kitty's arms and shake her, leave little bruisy fingerprints. She had to grip the trolley and breathe.

Then she picked up the plastic bottles.

She made herself check along the list Frank Chapman had given her. Baked beans, HP Sauce, matches, toilet roll, Spam. Donna would take it all when she went on Wednesday.

The girl at the checkout was just a teenager – black, plump and assured, her hair intricately twisted and pinned with pastel-coloured children's slides. Fish and boats and yellow stars. Gayle found herself staring at the girl, using her as a fixed point. She had once meditated with a candle flame.

The girl sat still and straight and did not seem to hear Kitty, who was now shouting monstrosities. She smiled and kept her eyes on the conveyor belt, slid Frank's things over the green flash. 'Trust in the Lord,' she sang, 'do not dismay. Trust Him, praise Him, trust in the Lord . . .'

*

After their wedding in '57, they lease a small edge-of-the-water café on the Broads and Frank steers *The Princessita* up and down that stretch, trippers' litter bobbing in the shallows.

Lola works in the café, doling ice cream, washing pots in a porcelain sink up to her elbows, scrubbing the floors with Vim. She loses two babies that first summer, screaming the place down each time she begins to bleed.

There's no midwife, only Mrs Warsop. Mrs Warsop says Lola is too weak and should never have children, that they should get an indoor toilet. Mrs W. is in league with the Devil, Frank discovers later. It is proven when she later bleeds to death after a seemingly minor operation.

But before she dies, she puts her hex on Tommy, whom Lola manages to carry almost full-term. At thirty-seven weeks, he shoots out screaming, purple faced, with brown, animal hair and an extra toe on each foot (which they lop off in the hospital, before it can be produced as evidence). He's not small or premature looking, not at all. He has his full quota of everything. Had he lived he would have been bigger even than Frank. Jesus keeps the keys of death and Hell, but the Devil borrows them under a different name: Mrs Warsop.

After Tommy's born, Frank gets himself out as much as

possible. He spots an old BSA motorcycle advertised in the *Swaffham Echo*, buys it on the hire purchase, polishes it up. It's a beauty – black tank, gold lettering. Each evening, as the air cools and the roads give up their smells, he rides it into Lowestoft and back – wind thudding in his ears.

*

'She'll do it,' Will told Gayle over the phone, 'she's said she'll go.'

'When?'

'Day after tomorrow.'

'Great. Well done. I'll tell Frank.'

'I don't think she'll change her mind, but maybe you should warn him that she's reluctant.'

'Oh? Why?'

'Well, in case she's difficult.'

'Donna's never difficult. I'm the difficult one.'

He laughed. 'Is that what they say?'

'It is.'

He laughed again.

*

Out of season, they close up the café and live on the boat. Nappies flying in the rigging – petrol coating the water, lilac, oily blue.

Tommy turns one, then two. One spring morning, he's being bathed up on deck when the water turns red. Lola screams the place down, the kiddy just standing there rigid and naked and up to his knees in the colour of blood. People come running, jump aboard. They discover that a pack of henna powder has been tipped in accidentally. Lola is handed a cup of strong tea. 'I felt my heart turn over,' she says.

The dye takes months to come out of the cuticles of Tommy's finger- and toenails.

This is his life. There is no more than this. There will never be any more. Once, he had plans. He wanted to buy a schooner or ketch and sail to the West Indies, make a living trading between the islands.

But he married a Catholic. The Pope has a lot to answer for. Oh, he's a clever chap all right – pretends to be so humble, but he heads the Vatican, which is full of computers, fax machines, office staff, secret plots. They are taking over the world by stealth; the Bible declares it.

Sometimes, Frank stands by the rails, watching his own, powerful golden arc and he thinks, That's what I'm doing – pissing it all away.

'Don't blame me for all your bad luck,' Lola retorts before he's even opened his mouth, 'all I want is to live like a normal person.'

She complains it's too dark on the river, goes on about wanting to live in a street with electric lights. Every night when they go to bed she complains of the blackness pressing on her face. 'So much bloody dark,' she whispers, 'it'll kill me.'

He lies there and says nothing. What can he say? That he thrives on it? That he's got used to having his eyes wide open and seeing nothing at all?

SIX

On the day Donna was to go and visit Frank Chapman, she woke early. The light through the curtains was sharply acidic, yellow-green. 'It's like spring,' she said to Will, 'look.' But she knew before she spoke that he was still asleep.

She got out of bed and stretched her back, pulling her knees to her on the floor, feeling each knot of muscle give and, as it gave, sensing a corresponding pain somewhere else. When she got back into bed, Will sighed and pulled her to him and started to touch her.

'Tell me I don't have to do this,' she said, but when she looked for a response his face was blank.

She took two Nurofen and he rubbed her back for her and then he pushed her over and they made love quickly, holding their breath and concentrating – as if they were on top of a cliff and the slightest fault in their synchronicity might send them to their deaths.

She had insisted she would go alone. 'I can't bear you all watching me,' she said, 'I won't be a spectator sport.' She looked on her visit to Frank Chapman as a duty, a sacrifice – the one thing she would do so that they'd leave her alone. Once she had done it, she didn't want any more discussions. She looked forward to being back, safely alone with her pain – snug in the knowledge that no one else was involved.

'Does he really not want any money?' she asked Gayle, who'd dropped by with the shopping she'd done for him.

'No, none. Just this.'

'Look,' said Will, 'if he tries anything funny, you walk out, right?'

'What do you class as funny?'

'You know what I mean.'

She did, but she felt flippant, disengaged – faintly, rebelliously angry. She took a minicab to St Saviour's Road and as soon as she had paid the driver, Frank Chapman was out of the flat and helping her down the dirty, uneven steps.

*

At last, she stands there, half in, half out of the room with one hand in her coat pocket and the other resting on the silver knob of her stick. 'Posh walking stick,' he says, 'not that you'll be wanting it any more.' He smiles but she resists him. Her face is stiff.

Donna.

'I ought to say,' she begins and he can see just exactly how bad she feels, how much in need of the living power of the Lord Jesus Christ, 'I didn't want to come. I'm doing it for them. I don't believe in God or anything. I'm an atheist.'

'Better that than a Roman Catholic,' he says.

And just look at her. Donna. Hair cut short like a boy's – a steep incline at the back, a flop of fringe in front. Delicate features with thin lines of colour painted on – red, black and white, like a foreign flag. And earrings – always earrings – little droopy things which shudder against her little-boy's jaw. She's thin. Young and frail and thin.

'Donna' – her name rolls in his mouth – 'Donna, God is neither here nor there.' He takes her coat – the softest black wool, so soft you can't feel it on your finger ends – lays it as carefully as he can over the bed. 'It's the Son of God you want to worry about.'

'Or Him,' she says and juts out her boy's chin so far that he can see clearly how needy she is. 'What I mean is I don't believe in anything.'

*

When Tommy's seven, he fixes up a swing for him round the back of the boatyard near his office. From his desk, if he tips his chair right back, he can see a flash of movement as the lean and bendy body rocks the rope through its metal loops. Sometimes he can catch the brown bubbles of Tommy's curls. Down to his shoulders. Lola still can't bring herself to cut his hair.

Now and then, strangers walk past: 'Hello, little girl,' they say, 'and where do you live, then?'

'Sheffield.' Tommy does not flinch, he swings higher and higher, so his feet fly over their heads. 'I live in Sheffield, it never rains there.'

Such a little fibber. He floats there in the air, lying.

When he's dead and Lola tidies him up in his coffin, she still manages to find a curl to cry over even on his clammy, fourteen-year-old head. Frank catches her coaxing it and stroking it – having one last go at teasing it to a perfect circle – before getting the bacon scissors from the kitchen drawer and shearing it off.

She has it buried with her, coiled in a locket, a hard, cold jewel against the dissolving flesh of her ribs.

*

He brings Donna a cup of tea. She sits in the chair at the table with the barley-sugar legs and looks all around her. She looks like butter wouldn't melt in her mouth, a proper madam. She looks like Tommy.

The first time he saw her, by the bus stop outside Kwik-Fit on Acre Lane, with her plastic carriers and her tasselled shoulder bag, the resemblance hit him so hard it was almost unpleasant – knocked him sideways. He got on and sat behind her, watching the back of her neck, trying to calm down. It was on impulse, that he got on that bus – but then so is everything he does, one way or another. Obeying the voice of Jesus.

He thinks he'll give her tea in Tommy's mug, the one that Lola kept, the black one with a gold line sketch of Elton John.

'Do you take sugar?' He reaches for the mug at the back of the cupboard. It's dusty and there's a dead something in it so he tips it out and wipes it off with a dishcloth. Tommy was mad about all that pop music – especially a band called Mud.

'No thanks, just milk.'

'The thing is,' he says as he places the mug of tea down on the table, 'a band of devils have gotten hold of your body.'

'That's disgusting,' she says, and the look in her eyes is so cool and barmily righteous, 'I don't believe that for one moment. What devils?'

On the bus a woman had got on and said, 'Hey, Donna, hi!' and they'd turned their heads together and all the way up Acre Lane, he'd listened in – taken the facts for himself.

He'd stayed on all the way to the terminus, where she got off, but he didn't follow her home. Instead, he turned and walked back onto the Common, giving thanks to the Lord Jesus Christ as he walked. He stretched his arm out in a cheery salute, just like that: 'Thank you, Lord! Thank you, Holy Angels!' – and anyone else up there he could think of.

On days like this, life was his to do as he liked with – a gift-wrapped luxury expressed from Heaven.

He bought a scotch egg from the 7-Eleven, ate it under the trees. He had so much energy he didn't know what to do with it. He wished he was in better shape so he could jog. Seventy-one years old and wanting to run!

But Donna. Now Donna.

Now he inclines his head and spreads his hands. 'Purging isn't what you think,' he says, 'it will take less than five minutes and you won't feel a thing. It involves only one simple prayer.'

'Is that so?' She doesn't look at him but examines her teaspoon. The teaspoon is silver with a man's head and shoulders on the tip of the handle.

'I pinched that,' he tells her.

'Yeah?' A flicker of interest. As she looks up, he notices she's drawn around her eyes with a black pencil.

'You shouldn't draw on your face,' he says, 'I pinched it from an hôtel on the Isle of Man.'

She puts the spoon on the table. 'Really.' And he thinks, Yes, that's exactly how Tommy would've reacted – a shrug, head down. Maybe nicking from a hotel is not so bad. Maybe everyone does it. Or maybe, just like Tommy, she is too bloody-minded to let him surprise her. To let him have an effect.

'There's a demon trapped,' he tells her again, working on the phrases, tinkering for her benefit, 'I release demons.'

'I'm sorry,' she says, her lips on Elton John's scanty head, 'I'm not into demons, OK?'

*

She knew his game, trying to distract her with his sorry little stories. All these lies. The tea was disgusting. So was the talk of demons. Why had she bothered to come here? Why didn't she just go straight home?

'I don't know why I took it,' he said, 'I just did. Jesus has forgiven me.' His eyes were chalky, blue-green as the mould on bread.

'How convenient for you,' she said.

She wasn't going to spend much time listening to his prayers. Ten more minutes she'd give him. Ten more and that was it – anecdotes, healing and all. The one thing chronic pain had taught her was to be less tolerant. 'Could we get on,' she said, 'I've got to be somewhere else, so could you just get on and do it?'

The funny thing was, she felt able to be rude to him. She felt powerful. She felt released in his presence.

*

He's all at sea because it's like having Tommy in his flat – disorientating, harsh. He'll have to be quick, though he'd like to keep her close for a long time, bury his face in her, keep her for nourishment like a tin of emergency food.

'If you don't mind standing up,' he says. She stands. 'I'm going to come behind and place my hands on your back,' he tells her. 'Can you just show me exactly where it hurts.'

'A lot of different places.' She looks momentarily embarrassed. 'Here.' She puts her hands in the dip, the small of her back. 'But also down here, particularly on the left, and into this leg. It varies from day to day, but basically, the more I twist over, the worse it is.'

She keeps looking around at him, so gently he turns her chin back and touches her, feels the compliant buzz of her flesh, the clock ticking, her breath. A bus rolls by, shakes the houses. Someone walks up and shoves a pizza delivery leaflet through the door. Steps recede obediently on the path.

'Holy Angels,' he makes room for his body to receive the Holy Spirit, 'Holy Jesus, deliver this woman from pain and let her put her faith in You.'

He invokes the Spirit of the Holy Ghost and recites a couple of very short prayers because he thinks that may be all he's allowed. TLJC will have to understand that this one's a difficult customer and he doesn't know how long she'll give him. No worry, Jesus can work to deadlines. When he's done, he steps back.

'Is that it?' She turns her head again, surprised.

'I felt something,' he says, 'there was an energy shift. I can't say any more than that.'

She stares at him, and then laughs. 'Well, I'm afraid it

doesn't feel any different. Exactly the same, in fact.' She bends, testing. 'The pain's still there.'

'This isn't magic,' he says, 'this is healing from the Lord Jesus Christ. There's no abracadabra involved. Have faith, little lady.'

'Easy for you to say,' she says, looking around for her bag.

'Not yet,' he puts his hand on her arm, 'I've something to show you.'

'I want to go.' She's beginning to flap and flutter.

He holds up a finger. 'One minute, that's all.'

She says nothing, sighs. He opens the middle drawer of the dresser and takes out the photo of Tommy in the red Boots frame. It's not a good photo really – slightly out of focus – but it's Tommy in jeans and a white jacket, standing in front of a Christmas tree, pushing out his bottom lip, looking fed up. Hair touching his collar. Crimson light-spots in his eyes. The year before he got ill.

'Who is it?' She tenses, looks scared. Good.

'My boy Tommy.'

She says nothing. She must know.

'Do you notice anything?' He holds his breath.

'What?'

'He's the spit of you. The spit.'

She's in a hurry, putting her bag on her shoulder, picking up her stick. 'No,' she says, 'no, I can't see that.'

'Don't worry.' He holds the picture for a moment, then puts it back in the dresser, shoves the drawer (which is stiff and packed with papers, rubbish) shut. 'It's all right,' he tells her.

She looks at him. 'Why do you keep it in there?'

'Because I can't bear to have my failures staring me in the face.'

She's trembling as he helps her on with her coat. 'See how you feel later,' he says, 'Remember the Lord Jesus Christ died on the cross at Golgotha so you could be saved. How're you getting back?'

'Don't worry, I'll pick up a cab.'

'Watch yourself, it's cold. Not spring yet.'

She goes without thanking him. What does he expect? 'Let me know how you get on,' he calls after her up the steps and she raises a tiny bangled wrist to show she's heard.

*

2 January 1994

Dear Tommy (in the name of The Lord Jesus Christ)

I married a real 100% Hungarian Tartar whose ancestors came galloping from the North East conquering and to conquer – her features and build declared it. If they were short of nourishment and in a hurry they would nick a vein in their horses' necks, have a drink of horse blood and gallop on. Eventually they were all conned by the Pope into the Church of Rome.

Lola was a dyed-in-the-wool true Roman Catholic – sorry, that's a contradiction: they are not true to the Lord Jesus Christ, they don't worry about The Word, they pretend to worship a baby on his Mum's knee and a dead man on a cross. They love Baby Jesus and think they can talk to his Mother but she can't hear 'em – she is with you and Lola having a good time.

I ought to tell you that your mother was predestined to meet me and become a born again Christian, which she finally did. We were remarried in '78, in the name of the Lord Jesus Christ. I wanted her buried in that name too. At the grave I felt like nudging that old boy (with the white fuzzball on his chin) into Lola's grave and taking over his job.

In all modesty, I could have done it better.

Anyway, living with that Hungarian Tartar for thirty-six years and getting her converted to North Sea Gas was a Big Job and it has given me character. The hard way.

I'd like to see someone else take on a Tartar-Catholic and do what I did (in all modesty!). It was a job for heroes.

Your loving father,

Frank Chapman

*

He was right, it was cold. The day had begun with the right kind of light but had turned shrill and cold.

Donna went straight in to work. She'd told Sarka she had a dental appointment. There was no one in – just Sarka, wearing her reading glasses, gloves and a wrap. 'Heating's fucked again, and I can't find the electric one.' She looked up from the local magazine. 'Did you have anything done?'

'Nothing.' Donna kept her coat on and sorted out some piles of moccasins which had just come in – striped socks with suede soles for the newly toddling. Then she went and found the small electric bar heater which at least warmed the area by the till. After that she made them both some coffee and went to lie down in the back for five minutes.

'Don't get too cold,' Sarka called to her, 'you'll really seize up.' A woman had come in and was talking to Sarka about a documentary they'd both seen about the drawbacks of immunization for children.

Donna lay there on the mat she kept in the back room and did her stretches and the base of her spine felt just as tight and stiff as ever. If anything, the pain down her left side was slightly worse, the joint a bit inflamed, but then that could have been the weather. Sarka came in to get something. 'Where has spring gone?' she said, and walked out again.

Donna shut her eyes and tried to relax. Felt the ladder of her spine sink into the ground. The room was freezing, the tap dripped. Tommy's face swam in and out of the space behind her eyes – the shock, the stab of fear when she'd had the photo thrust under her nose by Frank. The frisson of familiarity when she'd looked into those eyes, made red by the camera.

She sat up. I've done it now, she thought. At least they can't say I haven't tried everything. You name it, I've tried it. Thinking about everything she'd tried, she almost laughed.

*

'Well?' After the meeting with Snake Williams, Will phoned Donna.

'Nothing. It didn't work,' she said, with perfect equanimity. He supposed because she'd been proved right.

'What did he do?'

'Put his hands on my bum. Muttered some religious crap.'

'How long did it take?'

'About five minutes. Less.'

'Did you tell him it hadn't worked?'

She gave a short laugh. 'Yes, of course I did. He said I should wait and see. He didn't say how long.'

He sighed. 'Well, it was worth a try.'

'Yes,' she said, more gently, 'it was worth a try.'

As he put the phone down, Dan Mintoe's head appeared round the door. 'So?' he said. 'Did you click? With Snake?'

Will stared at him, for a moment unable to fix the context of the words. He fumbled for a cigarette. He'd gone back to smoking properly now. 'Yeah,' he said, 'he's great.'

'Goodie,' said Mintoe, 'he's just a babe, you know.'

'A babe?'

'Twenty-six. Makes even you seem old. Just out of film school. Supposed to be hot. But I think he's a genuinely nice person, I really do.'

Will nodded. Everyone was probably genuinely nice, he thought, depending upon where you stood.

*

Gayle phoned Donna in her break. Her period had just started and it felt like her insides were falling out.

'I don't suppose it worked,' she said.

'No.'

'I'm sorry. Thanks for giving it a go. Was it awful?'

'No,' Donna said, 'it was OK.'

Gayle said, 'I'm sorry we pushed you into it.'

'You didn't.'

'Yes we did.'

'All right, you did. But it was worth a try.'

'Thanks,' Gayle said, 'thanks for seeing it that way.'

*

'Frank Chapman's son,' Donna said to Will later.

'Tommy.'

'That's right. Is he dead?'

'Gayle told me he was,' Will said, 'Frank denied it – well, he was deliberately vague. Which version did he give you?'

'No. He didn't.'

'So, why—?'

'I don't know. But he is dead. He died a long time ago and it was in the spring.'

'In the spring?' Will laughed.

'Don't laugh,' Donna said, 'it's not funny. It's awful. I can't remember why I know about Tommy.'

'What?'

'He was fourteen. Nothing in the world could save him.'

Donna tensed. Will put his arms around her. She looked up at his face and saw he felt sorry for her and she was angry with him for it. 'Don't be spooked by any rubbish he told you,' he said slowly, 'remember he's a nut.'

'Yes, but he showed me this photo.' Donna felt she might as well say it. 'It was horrible.' She sat down, suddenly weightless. She felt the heat of misery flow through her – as though hatred and grief had loosened her up – across her shoulders, in her teeth, her hips, her legs.

'Why? What photo?'

'Of Tommy. I look just like him.' Somehow sorry, she took both Will's hands in her own. Big hands, ten half-moons staring at her. She felt if she let go of him she might just float away.

'Like who?'

'Like Tommy.'

'How can you? You're a girl.'

'Oh, well, but he was that kind of boy. You know, a bit like a girl.'

*

Donna woke sometime in the night, certain she'd heard someone calling her name. She sat up for a moment, rigid, listening, trying to decide whether it was just a noise from the street. But the world was oddly quiet, not even the sound of a car. Someone had said Donna, she knew it. It had so definitely been her name. It had pulled her from sleep – loud and definite and urgent enough to open her eyes.

She lay down again, intending to keep listening, but was instantly gone – scooped straight back into the oblivion of sleep.

*

In the morning she woke very early and lay still for a while, more than usually aware of the length of her limbs and the tick of her heart. Confused, she put her hands up and felt her breasts, the hard, definite slope of her ribs.

The red eye of the digital clock said 6:09. She got up, naked, to go to the loo and bumped right into the corner of the chest of drawers as she passed it – even though she could see it quite clearly, even though she'd always known it was there. What was the matter? She felt light and shaky, unpredictable – what was it? Was she ill? Was she going to be sick?

She saw the tray on the dressing table where they'd left it the night before – two wineglasses, a jar of pickle, the butter dish. A bottle of paracetamol, the lid off. Her earrings, her watch. A half-empty bottle of mineral water. On the floor, her brown boots with the buckle around the ankle. Will's black jeans.

Donna, someone had cried in the night, Donna.

'Will?' she said. It didn't sound as it normally did, the name, so she tried it again. Nothing felt right. Will? Will? Something was missing, even though he was there – she knew it because she could see him right there in front of her sleeping, waking. What was wrong with him? She said his name again. 'Will?'

Soon, she began to cry and to shake. She sat down on the bed. It was so strong it had woken her. She stood up again, certain she must be wrong. She walked around. She bent over. She was covered in goose pimples, shivering, every inch of her, but she didn't care. Will, Will, Will!

'What?' He shot up on his elbows, eyes still half-closed, still in sleep. He looked scared.

She didn't want him to be afraid, but she couldn't bring herself to tell him what she knew. She tried to speak, but what had begun as a shout had lost faith in itself and tapered into a whisper. 'What?' he said. 'Donna, what?'

Yes, he was scared. How could she help him?

Her face was wet, her eyes streaming and she was wiping her nose on her naked arms. 'It's gone,' she held her bare body out in front of him – a sign, a gift – 'the pain has completely gone. Look. Look at me, I'm totally straight.'

PART TWO

one

They rang Gayle – they had to – even though it was still only six fifteen. She said nothing for a moment and then she said, 'I can't believe it. Oh, Christ, are you sure? Don't get excited – it could be a false alarm. Could it just be a better day?'

In the background, Kitty was crying. 'Shut up,' Donna heard Gayle say, 'shush.' Then Donna began to weep again – she couldn't stop – so Will took the phone.

'The change is fucking unbelievable,' was all she heard him say, 'I've never seen her like this, never. Come and have breakfast, see for yourself.'

'Yes, yes.' Donna struck her knees with her fists, lifted her legs off the ground and felt no snag of pain low in her pelvis. 'Do,' she said, 'do.'

'Well, come over later then.' Will took Donna's hand, squeezed it hard, ran his fingers over her knees. 'We'll be here. We're both taking the day off. We're in shock. We need to celebrate.'

*

They phoned work. Donna said she couldn't tell Sarka over the phone, would have to save it for face to face.

'No one will believe it anyway,' Will told her, 'you'd better get ready for that.'

Donna had a bath and Will sat and watched her. She couldn't stop laughing. 'It's amazing, when pain stops,' she said, 'it's like a drug. I mean it. I'm sort of high.'

Then they went back and had breakfast in bed and she put on the TV and lay there zapping between morning magazine programmes – sometimes sitting up, sometimes stretched out on her stomach. Will understood what she was doing: she was trying out all sorts of mundane everyday activities without pain. She was trying out being a normal person, enjoying dull things, just being OK. Once she turned and smiled at him and he'd never seen her smile like that.

Finally, he could bear it no longer and he pulled her into his arms and fucked her new-made body, enjoying the way she moved and turned and wriggled against him. He'd made her put her diaphragm in. 'We could think about a baby now,' she'd said, turning to him as she held the tube of spermicide.

'Don't let's rush it,' he'd replied, 'let's get used to this. Let's check it's all real.'

When they'd finished and she'd come – her orgasm oddly more subdued than the rest of her – she said again, 'It would be nice, to do it with nothing, see what happens.' She was desperate for a baby, desperate to begin.

'All in good time,' he said and hated himself for the flare of fear he felt. Was he so scared? Donna's disability had held things up. He was used to being held up.

They drifted back to sleep.

He woke first and tried to read the paper but the news

seemed unreal and irrelevant. He wondered how long this paralysis would last. His happiness seemed numbing. He just lay there staring at the front page, unable to think.

He looked at Donna asleep with her mouth open and her hair sticking up like a young boy's hair and thought with pleasure of how he loved her. He tried to imagine back to the day before, as if it hadn't happened, then allowed himself to remember it all over again. It had happened. What did he feel? Excitement? Amazement? Disbelief.

What would the doctors make of it? What would they tell her mother? He could imagine Betty's reaction. And Gayle. It was Kitty's first day at nursery school, but Gayle was coming over after lunch, as soon as she'd dropped her off.

'We must tell Frank,' he said at last when Donna sighed and opened her eyes. Neither of them had mentioned Frank until now – the heat of the moment. Donna stretched carefully, testing her body all over again, tentative and afraid after waking.

'Was it definitely him?' she said, and she sounded almost sad.

Will was shocked. 'Yes, of course. He's somehow managed to heal you. How can it not be him?'

'Well, it didn't happen instantly.' She sat up and curled over in a perfect, supple curl and picked at her toenails, her face tight and sulky.

'Donna,' he said, 'the coincidence is too overwhelming, too extraordinary. I'm sorry but, painful though it may be to you, this is Frank Chapman.'

'OK, OK,' she said, slipping off the bed, 'but let's not spoil today.'

'You owe him – he deserves at least to know—' Will hesitated. The idea of going round to see Frank on this particular perfect day was faintly depressing. Donna stood there, all naked and straight, and looked at him.

'I don't owe anyone anything,' she said, 'I deserve this. I've been down there too long to care whom I owe.' She turned and looked at herself in the long mirror, at the perfect symmetry of her limbs – placed her hands on her hip bones and measured. She laughed. 'I'm level, Will, look. I'm level and I don't hurt and I don't give a fuck how it happened.'

He looked at her and said nothing.

'I feel selfish,' she said, as if it needed saying. Then she added, 'Anyway, why would God cure me? Tell me that.'

'Jesus,' said Will before he could stop himself.

'Jesus then. Why?'

Suddenly she began to cry again. She pushed her wrists in her eyes to stop the tears. He didn't go to her. 'So-called miracle healing,' he said, 'presumably works entirely psychosomatically.'

'It was all in my mind?'

He shrugged.

'That's what you think?' she said. 'That he just made me pull myself together? After all these years?'

'I didn't say that.'

'You did. You implied it.' She had stopped crying.

'No, Donna, just that you probably cured yourself,' he said, 'with Frank somehow acting as intermediary. I don't believe in all that Jesus crap, for Christ's sake. You don't either. What's your explanation?'

'I don't know.' She went into the bathroom and turned on the shower. Water crashing on tiles.

'There is no explanation,' he called out over the noise of the water. She came back in the room but didn't come near him.

'He'll try and force his religion on us,' she said, 'and I just don't want it, not today – not any day. I can't deal with it. I can't deal with anything. I need to be left to breathe.'

'Like a good wine,' he said, but she didn't smile.

*

Gayle said to Annie, 'My sister's been healed. After all these years, she just woke up this morning and was better.'

'I can't believe it,' said Annie, when Gayle had told her the whole story. 'Just like that? Just get up and walk like the Bible? Are you sure?'

'Pretty sure. I'm going to see her later. Frank doesn't even know. I'm dying to tell him but he's not on the phone.'

'It's a real miracle,' Annie said, unable to make sense of it, 'it really is. What about if he could do something about my face?'

*

Eleven thirty. The light outside was hot and glittery. Next door's magnolia was in bloom, pushing over the fence like a massive and subdued candelabra.

Donna dressed and ran around the house, hardly stopping, letting her body take her where it wanted to go. She was out of breath already – winded by the ease, the symmetry, the comfort.

Will said they should sit down and at least have a talk about Frank, but she told him it could wait. She'd been talking all her life – weighing up, working out – and now she just wanted to keep going. She didn't want explanations. She didn't want to think about that man, or about Jesus, or about how they had both connected themselves to her by making her look at that photo of Tommy in the red frame.

*

Simon came over. He walked straight past Will, flopped down on the sofa in his jacket. 'OK, let's see,' he said.

Donna stood up. Opened her cardigan to show her straight, level hips. She walked, touched the mantelpiece, came back. Then she jumped around, like a dancer. 'I can really see the difference when you walk,' Simon said, 'fucking hell. Without a stick. You just woke up and that was it?'

She laughed and sat down.

'And you think it was what he did?'

She shrugged. 'Will thinks it's all in my head.'

'Rubbish,' Will said.

Simon was still staring. 'I can't believe it. All those doctors you saw.' He sat back and lifted his hips, fumbling in his pockets for a cigarette. 'You know you should try and get some publicity for this – go on TV. There might be money in it. I could be your manager.'

'Fuck off, Si,' she said.

*

Later in the morning, Will's racing euphoria suddenly swerved and came to a standstill. He felt inexplicably depressed, panicky – his throat full of tears.

'What is it?' Donna came and bent over him. 'Is it that you can't quite believe in it?'

'Yes,' he said, 'it's probably that.'

'I know, I feel it too,' she agreed, 'but then I remember it's real because of how I am inside. You haven't got that.'

'Maybe.'

'Look at me.' She threw herself back in a chair and laughed.

'Yes,' he laughed back, 'look at you.'

For several hours now she had not stopped. He was exhausted by her motion – dipping and ducking and bending and stretching. Unloading the dishwasher and getting things from the bottom of the fridge. All the things she'd barely been able to do before. He felt he couldn't get close to her for a moment, couldn't take her in properly, pin her down. And then he said to himself, why should he? They went for a walk, to buy some things for lunch, and she skipped and danced across the road. A man in an Audi whistled.

'Be careful,' he said, 'don't overdo it. Your body isn't used to it, remember.'

Which was true. Her body was a new toy to her. He watched as she played and the more he watched and the more she moved, the farther away from him she seemed to go. It must be for the best, he told himself. The whole thing was good. He was glad for her. He loved her so much.

*

Gayle and Kitty stood in the main playground holding hands and looked through the green mesh at the nursery: the wooden house, the Noah's Ark mural, the plastic trough of water and the worktable with blocks of wood. 'There's a hammer!' Kitty strained to go in.

The sky was filling, black clouds leaking into one another. 'You'll ask if you need a wee,' Gayle said, pulling Kitty's rucked-up skirt down over her tights.

'Lift your hand up,' said Kitty and Gayle did and Kitty broke away to chase a pigeon across the playground. 'Runnin' at the chickens!' she screamed, such a small, lonely figure in her red check anorak, scooting across the expanse of tarmac. Love ends, thought Gayle, we all die.

They went inside and Kitty accepted half a breadstick and was shown the row of tiny lavatories. 'Do you call her Kitty or Katherine?' the teacher asked, her pen poised over the form.

'Well, Kitty,' Gayle wavered for a moment. Now it was happening. Kitty was joining the world.

'You can stay if you want,' the teacher said.

'Go, go!' Kitty shouted.

'She'll be fine,' said the teacher. 'If you could bring in a photo next time for her peg—'

The window was painted all over with large red and yellow flowers. Back in the main playground, Gayle peered in between the petals and saw that Kitty was playing with dinosaurs in a tray of sand. It was obvious just from the way she held herself – the set of her mouth – that already she was telling other kids what to do.

Walking away, Gayle thought of Kitty and of Donna and all the good things and she just wanted to lie down and go to sleep. She was the lonely one – her life bereft and dark and hard. It was loneliness, that was all. Why had a miracle had to happen, before she could see it for what it was?

*

Donna said, 'Poor old stick, I don't need you any more.'

Will said, 'What are you going to do with it? Have it silver plated? Send it to the British Museum?'

'I don't know. Maybe I'll give it to Frank Chapman.'

'Quirky but apt,' he agreed.

*

So Jesus has done it, He's pulled it off.

In the morning post, Frank gets a letter with a first-class stamp on – her Majesty all hoity-toity in red – from big sis Gayle: 'We can't tell you what this means to us . . . Donna would write herself but she hasn't the words right now . . . You must believe me when I tell you you have quite simply changed her life . . . Hoping to see you before long, with best wishes,' etc. etc.

Of course, there's a bit more than that – it's so long he has to read it through a couple of times. There are sentences about how it took a night before it could happen – how they admit they all doubted initially – how she just woke next morning to feel the pain gone, how thrilled they all are and so on. Thrilled! Well, the Lord is seeking hearts that will receive Him who is the Word.

Nice one, Frank! Well, Lola, what do you say now? That ought to wipe the smile off your face. This isn't the sort of thing you can wangle, no, sir!

He stands there in his flat for a long time just looking at the walls, wondering what to do next, then he puts on his hat and coat and goes out. He pulls the door shut behind him and remembers he's left his keys inside. Never mind, he can push the sash window up later – it's never locked, Praise the Lord.

Praise the Lord indeed! As he walks down the street and into the park, he spots a grey and threadbare tennis ball on a bench and he takes it and chucks it overarm and it hits a small kiddy. 'Hey!' the mother says. The kiddy takes a breath whilst it grasps what has happened, then screams blue murder (why is it always blue?).

He laughs. 'Sorry about that. No harm done, I hope?' And runs.

The screams ring in his ears, live and painful. Must be the anger surfacing at last.

*

Donna just would not come with them to see Frank Chapman, she flatly refused, so Gayle and Will went instead. Will felt cheated somehow – felt Donna was behaving like a child. 'Don't imagine I want to go,' he told her, 'but even I don't feel it would be right just to drop him.'

'Even you?' she repeated to no particular purpose. 'Even you?'

'We shouldn't judge her,' Gayle said to him later, 'it's been a tremendous shock for her. A good shock, but a shock all the same.'

'She seems happy enough,' Will said. Gayle as usual was understanding beyond belief, beyond sense.

In fact Donna seemed ecstatic most of the time, touched with health, with life. She seemed almost to have lost her memory – forgotten the problem, demolished that part of herself and turned her face forwards. She talked about opening her own shop. Or doing a degree. 'Like Simon,' she said.

'Simon's only talking about it,' Will muttered as disparagingly as he could, 'he'll never get off his ass and do it. Just you watch.'

Some days she just said she'd give it all up and go off travelling. 'You could come too.'

'You're forgetting,' he told her, 'I already did that, ten years ago.'

She was hard to live with, jumpy. Presumably it would change, she'd settle. 'She can't make any decisions,' he told Gayle, 'she doesn't know what she's doing.'

'So what?' said Gayle. 'Let her mess around if she wants. All her grown-up life she's had that pain, remember. She's never had a life without it.'

*

Will and Gayle went to Frank's on a Saturday morning. It was the first time since Donna's cure and almost two weeks had passed. The tree by the church was studded with early lilac and Gayle picked a blossom and stuck it in Kitty's topknot.

Frank took a long time to answer the door and they were on the verge of leaving when they heard a scraping noise and the sound of a bolt drawing back. The glass shuddered in the frame and Frank looked out. He was unshaven and there was a speck of something red on his chin, but he was wearing a shirt and tie. 'Well, this is a surprise,' he said, and he seemed to mean it. 'I'm touched.'

Will shook his hand. It was surprisingly rough, the firm grip of a younger man with something to prove. 'How're you doing?'

'Top of the world,' Frank said. 'Hallelujah!'

'Would you be offended if I did some washing-up for you?' Gayle asked.

'You can't,' he said morosely, 'the Ascot's given up the ghost.'

'Have you got someone coming to fix it?'

He made a face.

'We'll sort it out,' Will said because it seemed to be what Gayle expected. Gayle had done some shopping for Frank – Cheddar cheese, apples, bananas and wholemeal bread and eggs.

'You've spoilt me,' he said, 'feasts fit for Christ's own table.'

'Nonsense,' she said, 'you should look after yourself.'

Frank whistled as he put the kettle on. Will, helping Gayle unpack the shopping, realized Frank had neither looked at nor spoken to him.

Kitty stood in the kitchen doorway plaiting and unplaiting the multicoloured vinyl ribbons which hung in place of a door. 'Can we get a door like this?' she asked and they all laughed.

'You've recovered so well,' Gayle said to Frank, 'it's marvellous. I didn't think you'd be fit so soon.'

'Jesus is my remedy,' he said, thumping his chest – and Will thought he seemed taller and stronger looking than ever before, with his big feet and thick neck and silvery hair, and none of the creeping frailty you'd expect in a man of seventy. He seemed too big for his flat – his head looming too close to the cupboards, his feet touching the furniture now and then. He stood close to Will and did not really look at him. He didn't look like a man who needed anything done for him.

'We can't thank you enough for Donna,' Gayle said with an awkwardness which was untypical.

'No,' Will echoed lamely, 'we can't.'

Frank smiled and licked his lips, 'Don't thank me,' he said, 'thank Jesus Christ.'

*

Gayle knew exactly what was up with Frank. He was lonely. She knew it because he went out of his way to tell them he'd been out and only just got back, when in fact he had his slippers on and he had to unbolt the door.

The three rooms he lived in were piled high with junk and each time they went he insisted upon giving Kitty more things to take home: dirty fur and pilled wool and bits of lurex and greasy, bent and broken plastic. Pencil sharpeners, dolls whose legs hung out of their sockets, PVC purses, a broken tennis racket. 'You're three,' he told her with a sweep of his hands, 'choose three presents, one for every year of your age.'

'There's nothing for children here,' Kitty said in a bored voice.

'In that case, I'll choose for you,' he said and he started picking items off the shelves and out of cardboard boxes, stuffing them in a wrinkled carrier bag pulled from behind the old gas cooker.

They didn't feel they could refuse after what he'd done for Donna.

'How's your wife?' he asked Will quite out of the blue. 'Doing all right, is she?'

Gayle saw that Will was taken by surprise. There was an embarrassment between them and Frank, about the fact that Donna never came. It wouldn't be odd for Frank to ask Will about her, except that he never did. 'Fine,' he said, she's fine. No doubt she'll drop by one of these days.'

'She should do that,' Frank said with a burst of certainty, 'she should do it.'

'Well,' said Will, 'I'm sure she will.'

'Good,' said Frank, turning back to his bag, 'oh good.'

They had to take the junk. It would have been too much of a risk, to hurt his feelings. They did not even bother to take it inside when they got home – just dropped the lot straight in the dustbin, and the grimy carrier bag too.

*

Annie tossed a laundry bag in the air and caught it. You weren't supposed to throw things on the wards. Annie had already been spoken to in Sister's office for pushing a commode chair down the corridor too fast. 'Geoff says I ought to get something done about my face,' she said.

'What?' said Gayle.

'My face. He says it's silly to live with it – that I should do something.'

'Great. I thought he loved you.'

'He does. He just knows how much I hate it.'

'Well, you've lived with it this long,' Gayle said, wondering whether her own life would be altered all that much by having a great purple stain down the side of her face.

'So what?' said Annie, almost cross. 'That's no attitude.'

'Well, so what're you going to do?'

Annie pulled a load of drawsheets from the skip, stuffed them in the bag. They reeked of urine. 'I wondered if I could see your man, Frank?'

'Frank?'

'Would you ask him? About my face? See if he does birthmarks?'

Gayle laughed. 'He's not some cosmetic surgeon.' It dawned on her that she was reluctant to test Frank again, but couldn't quite say why. After all, Frank Chapman and his powers didn't belong to her. 'All right,' she said, 'I don't see why not.'

*

'I'll go and get us some croissants, shall I?' Donna said on Sunday morning.

Will looked at the clock, 'The shop's not even open yet.'

She pulled on her jeans. 'Well, I'll go and wait. It's a lovely morning. I'll walk. Get a paper.'

She was gone before he could continue the conversation. He knew she couldn't stay. The shop would not open for an hour. It was ten minutes away by foot, seven at the pace she went these days. It was as though she had to get out.

She wasn't being cool with him, far from it – she was all over him when they went to bed these days, sexually alert, demanding and responsive. He couldn't fault her. But suddenly she did not want to lie there next to him doing nothing – did not want to get caught on the spot long enough to have to speak or think or whatever it was she clearly thought he might make her do.

*

She did not go to the croissant shop. She got on a bus and went to Brixton, got out by Mothercare, walked back to Frank's place. The streets were empty, litter blew in the gutters, a phone box on the corner had been smashed up and leaflets flapped around its base.

There was a battered maroon Ford Cortina parked opposite Frank's flat and Donna leaned against it and watched his door. It was the door through which she'd gone that morning with her stick – the door which now swallowed Will and Gayle and Kitty most weekends because of her. The paint on the door was scratched and peeling and there were dirty panes of glass with some thick netting hung on the inside which she knew smelled of human skin and sour milk.

She waited, half-standing, half-sitting on the car, which was filthy and on which someone had scrawled, 'Fit fucker bites' in the dust. Like everything else, the words made no sense.

The Sunday morning air smelled peculiarly fresh – of petals and light and of spring. Donna sat, breathing, and she stared at the door so long it grew far away and fuzzy. She knew Frank wouldn't come out. It was like watching an animal's lair. You watched even though you knew there'd be no sighting. You watched to get your bearings and out of curiosity and to be ready for the next time.

*

Donna told Will she would come with them to see Frank. 'Just once,' she said, 'to thank him. But I'm not listening to any Jesus stuff. If you and Gayle choose to put up with all that rubbish, that's up to you.'

She couldn't see why Will still went. She did not believe him when he said he thought he should. Will never did anything for that reason. 'It's so out of character for you, to go visiting an old man suddenly. Such a change. I don't understand it.'

She was lying on the sofa eating a yoghurt. He looked at her. 'Why should it be a change? Anyway, everything's changed. Our lives have been altered beyond recognition by your cure.'

She hated it when he referred to her 'cure' – as if it were some public event, a turning point. She had forgotten what it had been like, to be unable to move. She had accepted her new state as a natural thing, a loose, comfortable thing which wrapped around her, which was rightfully hers.

'Yes,' she said, 'but this. You haven't got time to sit around with him.'

'I don't know. People can rise above their usual behaviour patterns.'

'He's creepy,' Donna told him, because she knew, 'he's a creep, but I'll come this time.'

'I'm getting to like him. It's surprising what you can get to like if you try.'

But it was a lie. She knew Will wasn't telling the truth. She knew he was just making a point – going out of his way to be generous, copying Gayle.

*

Frank kept his eyes fixed rigidly on her the whole time she was there, as she knew he would. It was a bright morning and they sat crammed in the tiny dark room – she in her denim jacket, squeezing the foil of a bunch of bluebells she'd pulled from the springy earth of the waste ground behind their flat. Kitty leaned up against one of her legs, picking her nose, staring at Frank.

'I didn't think it would work,' she told Frank, 'it was amazing, whatever it was that you did.' What he did. She thought of Tommy in the drawer. Her blood rolled in her head which was tight as a drum.

'Don't thank me,' Frank said, even though she'd taken care not to say the actual word thank you, 'I only laid on hands. Thank Jesus, Who died at Calvary for your sins.' He set his chin at an angle and his spit sprayed the air.

Donna shivered. 'Where do you want me to put these? Is there a vase?'

He was silent.

'A jug or something? What do you want me to do with them?' she said.

'Donna,' he said, 'Donna.'

Will looked at Gayle. 'Tell him how you've been,' Gayle urged, pulling at the skin around her nails.

'Donna,' Frank said again. She could not look at him, could not speak to him. She felt trapped, suffocated – her limbs moulding themselves to the dark constrictions of the room. She felt as though he were going to take something from her – something she'd do anything to keep. She looked at his big, voluptuous hands, the healing hands, the hands which had sneaked up and healed her and she promised herself she'd never go near them again.

'Well, I'm off.' The words shuddered from her lips and she jumped up – yes jumped, because now she could quite easily. Kitty had crept up and was holding onto her hand, but she peeled the little fingers off one by one. Remorseless.

'Wait for us,' Gayle said, 'we won't be long.' She was groping in her pocket and Donna knew she was fingering her cigarettes as if they were a charm.

'No.' Donna moved to the door and clicked up the catch before Will – especially Will – could say anything to stop her. 'I can't. I'll see you later.'

She didn't look at Frank.

She didn't care that she'd left them, she didn't care at all. She moved with relief onto Brixton High Street and past the market where coloured handkerchiefs flapped in the breeze and oranges and potatoes were piled high. A man sat in the middle of the pavement playing an accordion, with a corrugated cardboard sign by his legs, one of which was a stump, the trouser leg loosely folded over.

She crossed the road and went into the Body Shop and stared at the green wooden shelves and bought a cruelty-free lip balm. Then she sauntered home, up Acre Lane, in the sunshine.

She wondered what Frank made of it all: deprived of a vital opportunity to rant.

*

'Oh,' he says as innocently as he can, 'oh what a shame, she's left her stick.'

'She's doesn't use it any more,' the so-called boyfriend tells him, 'she brought it to give to you, but she must have forgotten. She wants you to have it.'

And he passes it over.

Frank lets the palm of his hand close over the silver knob. The clean coldness of Donna's stick.

'Hallelujah,' he says, 'how kind. It's a really good one.'

*

Before they left, Gayle said to him, 'I don't suppose you'd see a friend of mine, for healing?'

'Who?' he asked her. 'What's wrong?'

'Annie Corbaci. Someone at work. She's not sick. She has this birthmark all over her face.'

Frank shot her a look. 'Those birthmarks. They can be a sight.'

'Would you see her?'

'Send her along,' he said. As they said goodbye, he added, 'Tommy was born with six toes on each foot. Sign of the devil, you know.'

They left before he could get going.

*

Suddenly it was May and Donna took Will's penis in her hands and tried to mould it, stroke it, make it live for her. He laughed, lifted the cradle of his pelvis, touched her cheek and pulled away. 'Why do you never fuck me any more?' she said.

'I do.'

'You don't.'

'I don't know,' he replied and this time it was clear that he was telling the truth.

*

Will and Gayle agreed that they would always keep the visits short and leave before Frank got going on Jesus. After about half an hour, he would not be able to contain himself – would rise and reach for his tracts. His voice would deepen. His eyes would take on a fanatical glaze. He would get worked up.

'You see, young woman, Jesus died at Calvary for our sins,' he told Kitty, standing up and unfurling his thick clenched fists. 'You'll see, blood must be spilled.'

Kitty stood on the carpet in her socks – which were stained at the heel and toe with navy dye from her sandals (it had been raining when they arrived) and watched him with an open mouth.

'Time to go,' said Gayle.

'Blood—' said Frank.

'OK, Frank, that's enough. Please don't talk to her like that.' Gayle lifted Kitty on her lap and began to buckle her shoes, 'If you carry on, I won't be able to bring her any more – I mean it.'

He raised up both his hands. 'Persecute me then, you too. It won't make no difference, you'll see. They all do it in the end. You shuffle and shuffle as often as you like, and when you deal it all comes out the same.'

'No one's persecuting anyone,' Will said.

'It's all very well for you to talk,' said Frank, 'you're well in there, you are.'

'Meaning what?' Will felt a change in the room as though someone had lifted a curtain, let in a wind.

'Persecute me,' Frank said bitterly, 'we won't be seeing each other any more.'

'Shut up,' Gayle said, 'we're your friends, not your bloody

Church. Don't shoot yourself in the bloody foot, you silly man.'

'You owe me,' he said to her and he lifted one trembling finger in the air.

'Really?' She turned and looked at him and her eyes were wild and cross. 'Do I? I think we all owe each other. Where's your humanity, Frank?'

'You'll see,' he said, slow as anything, 'you will see.' He had drawn himself up to his full height.

'Come off it,' said Gayle, letting Kitty slip back off her lap and standing up.

'I've – been – eaten by a – boa – constrictor,' sang Kitty, placing both her hands over her ears.

*

'That was brave,' Will said to her on the way home, 'he didn't like that at all.'

'Not really,' she said, 'I'm not scared of him and he knows it. Sometimes I hate him, when he tries it on like that.'

'Mummy, who do you hate?' said Kitty.

'No one.'

'If you hate people, you go to Hell,' Kitty said.

'Who told you that?' Gayle looked round sharply.

'Hilary.'

'Well, she's wrong,' said Gayle, 'I'll have to talk to her. There's no such place as Hell. Is there, Will?'

'Absolutely not,' he said.

*

Gayle wasn't brave. If she'd been brave, she'd have told Simon to go away and stop hanging round the flat, messing up her only sofa, draping his jeans on her radiators, using up the last of the milk and not replacing it, taking her money to buy beer, dropping flakes of tobacco all over everything.

'Are you a Christian?' he asked her.

'No, I'm not. Why?'

'No reason,' he said. 'Look, I've brought you some flowers.' He held out tulips, wrapped in white paper.

'With what money?'

'What do you mean what money? With mine.'

'I didn't think you had any.'

He paused, then he laughed. 'What do you take me for?'

'Why do you want to know if I'm a Christian suddenly?'

'Just wondered. Wanted to know where you stood, that's all.'

'No, you didn't.'

'Yes, I did.'

*

Annie had been to visit Frank and he had laid his hands along the side of her face and nothing had happened. Nothing had happened that day or the next day or the following week or a week or so after that. 'That's that then,' she said, lighting a cigarette in the sluice room, 'so much for your fucking miracle healer.'

Will and Donna knew it hadn't worked and said nothing. Frank said nothing either. Simon said it meant Donna's cure might all have been a coincidence, a case of mind over matter. Gayle didn't know what it meant. She didn't know whether to be surprised or not. She didn't know what to think.

*

The beginning of summer should have been wonderful, with Donna better and work on the LexCom pitch coming on pretty well. Will did not know why it didn't feel that way.

He was on edge, could not relax. He suffered terrible insomnia. When he slept he felt whatever it was expanded and nurtured itself, feeding off his temporary oblivion. In the old days, he used to wake and have Donna beg him to rub the worst bits of her back. Sometimes she would swear to herself as she staggered around, or cry softly in the bathroom. Now he often woke to find her already out of the shower, singing, rubbing mousse in her hair, making coffee.

One morning, he had a meeting in Gower Street. He went by cab, gripping his briefcase, his tie flapping in the breeze of the pushed-down window. There was a faint sweet warmth in the air and when they got to Gower Street and he stepped out onto the blossom-stained pavements, he felt off-balance as if his eyes were shut.

The meeting was in a dark, chilly room – expensive chrome and air-conditioning. Coffee burning on a plate in the corner. The inevitable woman in high heels with a flip chart and marker pen.

Once he'd made a point or two about image and grainy realism, he found himself fazing out, thinking of Frank Chapman and his flat. He saw the subterranean world of his weekends – Kitty plaiting the coloured vinyl strips, Frank talking away, Gayle with her cardigan sleeves rolled up, drying plates. Gayle telling Frank what was what. The expression of concentration on Gayle's face as she buttered a piece of bread for Kitty. The picture of this place – where they spent a relatively gloomy hour each week seeing to Frank – somehow pulled his head like a magnet. Whatever else he did, he always focused back on Frank's flat.

Every time there was laughter in the meeting – which sporadically there was – he joined in. But it was fake and he wasn't there: he was sitting instead on Frank's white vinyl armchair, watching Kitty play with a pair of wooden candlesticks which had Jesus on the Cross draped on their stems. 'Why is he asleep standing up?' asked Kitty. 'Why does he have a nappy on?'

He noticed the lining of Flip Chart's skirt was torn. It was really noticeable every time she bent forward. As the meeting ended, there was a lot of hand-shaking, trouser-smoothing. I agreed with your point, someone remarked to him, you were right. He had no memory of an opinion. The woman laughed at something one of the men said, and her laugh was raucous, surprising, and he realized she was younger than he'd thought.

He managed to decline sharing a cab with anyone and began to walk back to Soho. But he was drawn instead into the leafy cool of a square, where he sank onto a bench and fixed his eyes on the dry, clipped grass, the concrete path, the litter lifted by the warm air. A central bed had been planted densely with flowers and their sickly scent wafted across now and then.

He placed his briefcase on his knees, rested his forehead in his hands and for no reason he could think of, began to cry.

*

At six o'clock, Betty said why didn't he come to the wine bar, just for a quick one?

Go on, a quick drink takes less than ten minutes, she said, holding up ten slender fingers. He laughed and said OK why not, and by quarter past was sitting in the soothing tobacco darkness with her, drinking red wine and hearing about a Keanu Reeves film.

'He built up muscle for it,' she said and then paused. 'Are you interested in this? You're not, are you?'

'I love it,' he said, 'nothing interests me more than Keanu Reeves' pectorals.' She laughed and asked if he and Donna went to the pictures much and he said not enough, because Donna's back always used to play up, but now she was better they intended to do it more. 'A good film always cheers me up,' she said. 'Before I met Mat, I always went on Sunday afternoons at Swiss Cottage.' She looked suddenly nostalgic.

Then she confided that John Beanie had hinted at a promotion for her – particularly if they moved offices as they were planning to. Will had known there was a chance of this, though he was surprised John had mentioned it to her as it had not been discussed in any depth at management level as yet. They wanted her to be account handler, she said, so long as she didn't get pregnant in the next year. She looked down when she said this and picked at her long fingernails.

'Don't you want to, though,' he asked her, 'start having kids?'

'I don't know,' she said. 'Sometimes yes, sometimes no. Mat does. I'm totally torn, if you want the truth.'

They were both silent. 'We haven't even set a date for the wedding yet,' she laughed, 'it could all fall through just like that.' This idea cheered them both.

'What would I do without you?' he said – and he actually meant whichever option she went for – and she laughed and said she was sure he'd manage perfectly well. He was about to argue with this but he didn't want to sound too sorry for himself, so he switched to flirting with her instead.

'If he ditches you, you can always have me,' he laughed.

'I'll bear that in mind,' she laughed back, and they decided to order a bottle.

He went home at nine o'clock on the Northern Line, drunk and unhappy enough not to mind at all when the train was held up for twenty minutes by signal failure at Kennington.

*

He hasn't managed to banish the little nurse's birthmark. Jesus has let him down. She held her face up to the light, showed him her disfigurement and he did his best, invoking the Holy Spirit, but he felt no change beneath his palms. 'It'll happen,' he said, but he knew it would not.

'Shall I pay you something?' she asked him, her whole face flushed in her eagerness. He bent towards her, touched her head.

'Say a prayer when you get home,' he said. And that was that.

Now he stands opposite the tube station on Brixton High Street, between Morley's and the Body Shop, and spreads the

Word and the Truth and talks about divine healing. He works at getting the idea of repentance into people's heads. He bellows the Good News into the wind, tells them it's never too late. That Jesus is a muscle man when it comes to bearing the load of their sin. Sometimes they take his pamphlets, sometimes they chuck them back at him. No skin off his nose if they'd rather roast in Satan's fires.

One day, a blackie with a horrifically deformed face like a cauliflower walks by. Hard to tell if male or female, the face is so swollen and turned in on itself. He can hardly bear to look. 'I don't know what happened to your face, miss,' he says, 'but Jesus can put it right for you just like that—' He snaps his fingers where he imagines her eyes must be.

She comes right up close, so he can smell the garlic breeze coming from between her lips, 'It's Mrs,' she says, 'and you can just fuck off back to where you came from and mind your own business, old man,' and she disappears into the Lambeth Building Society.

'The Lord offers His healing powers for nothing, madam,' he calls after her, 'more than you can say for the building society.' A good point, that.

*

Towards the end of May, their mother came up to town. She had lunch with Donna and then came over to see Gayle and Kitty.

'You look tired,' her mother said.

'I'm fine.' Gayle took her coat and her bags, led her into the kitchen.

'I can't get over Donna. It's unbelievable, isn't it?'

'What have you got for me?' Kitty was running a slight temperature and was glassy-eyed and difficult but would not have a sleep.

'Slow down, Kitty.' Gayle filled the kettle.

'Where's Simon? I was hoping to see him.'

'I don't know. Gone out.'

'Put your hand on my head, Grandma,' Kitty said. 'Pretty hot?'

'Poor love, she should be in bed.'

'You can't get a three-year-old to stay in bed.'

'I always kept you in bed at that age.' She delved in her bag and produced a sticker book.

'Snow White!' shouted Kitty.

'What do you say?' said Gayle, but Kitty was too absorbed to hear. Her mother went and got a hanger for her jacket, but Gayle knew she was secretly inspecting the flat. She put the tea and mugs on the table. 'Clean enough for you?' Gayle said when she came back in.

Her mother ignored her. 'How's the hospital?'

'Fine.'

'You never think of doing anything else?'

'Such as?'

'Something managerial, earn proper money.'

'I don't want to work in an office,' Gayle said, 'I'm satisfied with this.'

'Goodness,' her mother took out a phial of sweeteners and released one into her tea, 'I don't know what you all have against offices. If I were your age, with your brain and your energy and your opportunities. Kitty will be at school all day before you know it, and then what? You could travel, have a company car.'

Gayle laughed.

'You could go to business school with a brain like yours.' She paused, then, 'I wouldn't be surprised if Donna didn't do something now she's better,' she said.

'Something?'

'Well, she could train – get a grant.'

'Like Simon?'

'I'll believe that when I see it. No, I think Donna's serious. She works hard, that girl.' Finally she looked at Gayle. 'How often do you get your hair trimmed?'

Gayle shrugged.

'Well, it could do with it,' she said, 'it won't grow properly if you don't trim it. I get mine snipped about every four to six weeks, you know.'

'I bet you do,' Gayle said.

*

At seven forty that morning, Amy Franklin had burst into one of the large hospital bathrooms holding an open pair of scissors, blades flashing in the artificial light. She'd chased a nursing auxiliary around the bath, but finally been talked down by Sister. No one was hurt, but the auxiliary was treated for shock.

Sometimes, when Gayle stood by the swing doors of Thompson and looked down the corridor, the whole building seemed out of kilter, at odds with the rest of the world.

Seemed to sway disarmingly.

*

Her mother finished her tea. Went to the sink to rinse her mug. 'You don't have to do that,' Gayle said.

'Oh, I don't mind.' She looked around for a space on the draining board, gave up, brought it back to the table. Gayle watched. Kitty had fallen asleep on the floor, cheek resting on her sticker book.

'OK, I've a proposition to make,' her mother said at last, 'about the summer. I've been offered a house in Suffolk for the first two weeks of July, practically rent-free – just bills. I could only do a long weekend. I wondered how much holiday you had. Do you think Donna and Will would go too – maybe even Simon?' Gayle watched as her mother worked one finger over the sharp cluster of her engagement diamond. 'It would do you all a power of good, in my opinion, to get out of London.'

two

Will didn't meet Gayle until he'd known Donna for more than a year.

She was living in Southampton then, drifting, waitressing, making a point of never coming home. One weekend, Donna took him to visit.

The house was close to the market. Maroon paint on brick – discarded yam and green banana crushed under foot, torn newspaper floating in the gutters where stray dogs crouched, muscles straining, tails bent up.

She was in bed. The air was dusty, the curtains drawn. 'Hi.' She clicked on a bedside light. An older man in a pale, clean suit sat on the end of her bed. When they came in, he jumped up, exuding sprucey male perfume. 'Mike,' she extended a finger, 'he owns three yachts.' He nodded to them and she laughed.

There was an Average White Band poster on the wall, a few photos Blu-tacked up, a pile of novels and magazines by the bed, a bean bag and an ashtray full of stubs and brown apple cores which filled the air with their decaying sweetness.

Donna said, 'You look terrible.'

Gayle leaned up on an elbow, felt around for cigarettes on the bedside table. 'I'll survive.' She laughed again, tried to strike a match and spilled the box. Donna helped her to collect them up from among the bedclothes.

'I'm off, then,' Mike said and was gone.

*

'Do you remember when we first met?' Will asked Gayle on the way back from Frank's.

'No,' she said, 'remind me.'

'At your place in Southampton. You were pretty sick. I don't think we liked each other.'

She frowned, looked away while she thought about it and then shook her head. 'No,' she said, 'I don't remember.'

*

They stayed in Southampton for three days – hanging out in pubs and bars, eating takeaways, sitting around waiting for Gayle to wake up from her frequent sleeps. 'I'm not very good company, am I?' she smiled, rolling her tiny limp cigarettes which left a dusting of tobacco in the grimy folds of the bedclothes.

Mike never came back.

Finally, they hitched home. It was as if they'd never been there.

Donna told him later that Mike had given Gayle herpes – that it recurred now and then and made her very ill and there wasn't much that could be done. It was the first thing Gayle got from sleeping with men. The second was a baby.

*

He didn't see her after that for several years, until she came and stayed with them for a weekend in the summer when Kitty was a baby.

He came in to see a pushchair folded in the hall. She was sitting on the floor watching TV with the curtains half-drawn and the remote control in her hand. Shorts and bare brown legs and an ashtray and two empty cans of Diet Pepsi. A scattering of brightly coloured baby things all over the floor, a bottle warming in a Pyrex jug on the table. Kitty, in just a nappy and vest, fiddling with the video player.

Gayle looked at him and smiled.

'I hope she's not going to break that,' was all he could find to say to her.

*

In early June the weather grew clear and constant and almost hot.

Kitty came dancing out of the house and into his car wearing just a dress and sandals and no cardigan. 'Which would you rather,' she said, 'be eaten by a boa constrictor or fall off the top of the world?' Gayle followed her down the steps, pausing for a second to lock the door, and these days she looked somehow different. He couldn't say exactly how. She smiled more, for one thing.

As they drove back, with Kit asleep in the back of the car, she turned and said, 'I wonder if you'd do me a favour? Another one, I mean. I know that coming along to see Frank all the time is a favour.'

'No, it isn't,' he said.

'It's Harry. I told you we sort of resumed contact? Well, he wants to come and see Kitty. I just can't face it.'

'What can I do?'

'Be there.' She bit the end of her finger. 'But only if you could bear to. I would understand of course if you can't. I know it's a lot to ask.'

'Donna doesn't know anything about Harry, does she?' he said.

She gave him a quick look. 'She'd make too much of it. He's really not at all important. He was an accident of my youth. The truth is I'd like to deprive him absolutely of Kitty, but I'm not sure that would be right for her.'

'And what's Kitty like about it?'

'Oh, she doesn't know. Harry and I have agreed that he'll just visit as a friend.'

Harry and I have agreed.

'What's he like?' Will asked her.

She smiled slightly. 'I don't know. Not trustworthy. He depresses the hell out of me. He thinks we're still friends.'

'And are you?'

'He thinks we are.' She glanced back to check that Kitty was still asleep.

'OK.'

'You'll come?'

'If you want me to.'

She said he'd never know how grateful she was.

As he drove them home, it occurred to him that (except when they had the comfortable distraction of Kitty) they still couldn't talk to each other – that a new diffidence had set in. They could no longer look at each other when they spoke, they looked away instead at anything at all. They clung to Kitty's constant stream of questions. If Donna was there, they both addressed themselves to her.

Somewhere along the line they'd stopped disliking each other, but had then got stuck. It was as if they thought their new-found intimacy might be less unwelcome and dangerous if they made a point of including the whole world.

*

'To the seaside?' he echoes when Gayle breaks the news. 'That's nice. All of you?'

'All of us,' she says, 'even Simon.'

'Simon?'

'Our brother. He never leaves the city if he can help it.'

'And Donna?'

'Donna too. What will you do? Will you be OK?'

'Jesus will keep me company.'

'Well,' she says, 'we're not going till July. We'll send you a postcard.'

'Oh good,' he says.

*

A week later, Gayle was getting a bag out of the back of Will's car, when Kitty, doing butterfly jumps on the pavement, stepped out into the road. A removal van thundered by, missing her by an inch or so, sucking her into its wake as it moved the air.

Gayle stood under a tree which emptied its blossom steadily like snow and put her face in her hands and shook. Kitty, watching, began to cry.

Will took Kitty's hand but Gayle could not move.

'That could have been it,' she said quietly to Will and, without thinking, he put his fingertips on her shoulders and then pulled her close. Still shaking, she said, 'I thought that was it.'

He held her close a little while still after she'd stopped shaking and then let go.

*

'Well, she's had them,' Annie said, 'Geoff's wife. Two boys.'

'Oh. Is he pleased?'

'Delighted. Over the fucking moon. He wanted boys.'

'They always do.'

'I can't imagine he'll leave her now.'

'No?'

'Not now he's got his two boys.' Annie's face was definite, pink, flushed with excitement – pleasure, almost.

*

Everyone was excited about the house. 'It's almost on the sea,' Donna, who'd just spoken to their mother, said, 'and big. Kitty might have to go in a cot, but there's masses of room for everyone.'

Gayle said if it was so big, shouldn't they ask Frank, just for a day or two? He would love the break.

Donna went crazy. 'I can't believe you! This is a family holiday. OK, let's fill the place up. Let's just ask any old Tom, Dick and Harry then. I'll go and find some people off the street, shall I?'

'He's not any old Tom, Dick or Harry,' Gayle said.

'We found him lying on the ground,' said Donna.

'Luckily for you, we did,' said Gayle.

Donna said quietly, 'If you're going to use it against me for the rest of my life then I might as well not be better.'

'Oh, don't be so stupid,' Gayle told her, 'forget it. Frank's better off in London than at the fucking seaside with some fucking primadonna.'

'No pun intended,' added Will.

*

They did not speak about it for several days. Then Donna said to him suddenly, 'I understand that Gayle cares about Frank in some weird way, but surely he'll be OK for a couple of weeks?'

'I shouldn't worry,' Will said. 'Even if she asked him, he'd never come. What would he do in a house by the sea with all of us?'

*

At home, Gayle helped Kitty make a calendar of days till they went on holiday, put it up by her bed. Each night when she tucked Kitty in, they crossed another off with a blue crayon which hung on a piece of string.

Underneath, Kitty drew a picture of all her favourite people swimming in a squiggly blue crayon sea: Donna and Will, and Grandma and Mummy and Si – and Frank Chapman wearing multicoloured armbands and waving Donna's stick.

*

Gayle sat in Will's car outside Frank Chapman's flat and lit a cigarette. 'What's the matter?' he asked her. 'You look fed up.'

'Nothing,' she said, 'just everything. Donna's moods, and Frank and the fact that Harry's coming round.'

He sighed and held his keys, embarrassed.

'What?' she said.

He searched for words. He didn't know what to say. 'Nothing. I'm just surprised. I never knew you got upset like this.'

'What?'

'I always thought you kept everything at arm's length. The way you handle things. All this time,' he told her, 'I thought you were so tough.'

'I am tough.'

'No, you're not.'

'I can't help what you did or didn't think,' she said lightly, and a trace of her old anger momentarily reappeared.

*

A week before they went away – and after several calls to rearrange – Harry came round.

He was – he had to be – smaller than Will had imagined, fair haired and dressed in the half-heartedly aggressive style of leftover punk. He had a trace of Kitty's fed-up, expectant look, but none of her colouring which was undeniably all Gayle's. Attractive to women? Possibly, Will couldn't judge. He watched him brush Gayle's cheek with his lips and touch her arm. They stood in the kitchen where she diffidently introduced them.

'I feel I know Donna,' Harry told him and Will could hear the dry nervousness of his mouth, 'I used to hear so much about her.' He laughed and Will nodded and smiled and Gayle went off to fetch Kitty – leaving them standing together in the tang of her perfume.

'So, hey, doesn't she look wonderful?' Harry took a pack of cigarettes from his pocket and offered them to Will, who shook his head. 'Really good. Terrific.'

Will looked at the fridge. 'D'you want a drink?' He didn't particularly want to play host. Luckily, Gayle came straight back in.

'She won't come out. She's under my bed. I don't want to start a tantrum now. I don't know. We might all have to go in there.'

Harry was smiling.

'Do you want me to try?' said Will. Desperate to leave the room.

She was lying under Gayle's bed with a crowd of stuffed toys and a dirty old baby blanket.

'I've taken my knickers off,' she told him.

'Fine,' he dropped on his knees to the floor, 'now tell me why you won't come out.'

'Because I don't want to.'

He sighed. He didn't know what you did with kids. He didn't know what lies or promises might persuade her so instead he stood up and looked around and realized it was the first time he'd been in Gayle's room.

It was more an office than a bedroom – a room full of administrative stuff like chequebooks and box files and bills clipped together with bulldog clips. There was a cork board pinned with lists and receipts and coupons, and on the desk a thick black diary covered in a dusting of powder. Next to that, a pile of bright, folded kids' clothes. An ironing board and upturned iron. A hairbrush laced with her dark hair. A bottle of baby lotion knocked over on its side.

Carefully, he stood it up.

The drawer of the desk – which was also a dressing-table – was open, and he stepped closer to have a look. Postcards, bits of make-up, hair stuff. A tube of Savlon squeezed right in the middle. On the bed, a bra, a pair of leggings pulled off in a hurry, inside out, and a brown-paper carrier bag. He touched the neck of the bag, to see inside.

'What are you doing?'

He'd forgotten all about Kitty. 'Looking at your mum's things,' he said.

She slid out, her hair drifting upwards with static, her skirt halfway up her bottom which, as she'd promised, was bare.

'Come on, then.' He found her knickers and helped her put them on – her small hand on his shoulder as she stepped through the holes. 'We'd better go and meet Mummy's friend.'

They were sitting at the kitchen table opposite each other, a bottle of wine open between them. They both looked up very quickly, Gayle's cheeks were flushed.

'Well, how did you manage that?' Gayle looked at Will with genuine surprise.

'Hello, love,' Harry said to Kitty, just looking at her.

She held tight onto Will's hand. 'He's been looking at your things,' she told her mother proudly.

*

'So,' Gayle said afterwards, 'what did you think?'

'He was OK.'

'You didn't like him, did you?' she said. 'I could tell you didn't.'

'I didn't not like him. I didn't think anything.' He looked at Kitty, who was watching TV. 'He didn't have much to say to her,' he remarked quietly.

'Of course he didn't,' Gayle had been made lively by the wine, 'he's a bastard.'

Will smiled. 'If you say so.'

'Why're you smiling?' She poured the last of the second bottle of red wine into their glasses, kicked off her shoes. The sole was splitting off one of them and she picked it up again briefly and inspected it. 'I hate it when you smile like that.'

'I've never seen you so worked up about someone before,' he said truthfully.

'I'm not worked up,' she said, 'Christ, that would be an insult. I just know him – you don't.'

'I know,' he said.

'It's an insult. I'd hate you to think I was worked up over him,' she said again.

He looked at her. She looked back at him.

'It was really nice of you to come,' she said, 'I really appreciate it. It made a difference. Maybe I'll see you at the weekend.'

'Yes,' he said.

At the door, they stood apart.

'You're very patronizing when you just smile like that, you know,' she said, 'it must drive everyone mad.' But she smiled as she said it and suddenly all he wanted in the world was to pick her up off the floor and kiss both her cheeks like Harry had done – press himself hard into some soft, unsuspecting part of her.

*

That night Gayle dreamed that she was asleep and couldn't wake up, and when she did actually wake up she thought for a moment she was still asleep and falling down a black shaft.

*

'Come on,' Donna said, 'let's do it, let's fuck.'

She was getting used to her body again. Her limbs vibrated with his laughter as they played. Will laughed.

She took off his clothes and kissed him. 'I'm so glad we're going away,' she said, 'I can't wait to get out of London.' She sat astride him and held his penis. The window was open but the blinds were drawn. It was still quite early and they could hear the sounds of the street. 'I just love you,' she said, 'I really do. We could really have a baby now. I just feel I could be very easily made pregnant.'

'I think we should wait,' he said, stroking her.

'For what?' He was beginning to drive her mad with his waiting.

'For everything to settle down. After the holiday, after I've finished on this pitch. Autumn's a good time.'

'Autumn?' She felt that he was stiff and she put him inside her and as she bent herself to make him go all the way in, she put her head down and kissed him. 'I don't want things to settle down,' she said, 'you can wait, but I'm not waiting. I'm sick to death of waiting for things.'

He said nothing.

'I don't want things to settle,' she said.

'Sure,' he said.

'What are you thinking?' she asked him suddenly. She tightened her muscles a little and he shivered. His penis was inside her but they weren't making love.

He sighed. 'The truth?'

'The truth.'

'I suppose I'm thinking about work, about the LexCom account. That I shouldn't really be going away right now.' He laced his fingers behind his head and frowned.

'Fine.' She slid off him, left him sticking up there. She didn't know what it was. They loved each other, didn't they? But now that she was out of pain and able to do everything and anything, the force that had held them together had shrunk to nothing. Now she was cured, part of her was in direct opposition to a part of him.

*

It wasn't the truth. That wasn't what he was thinking about. He knew enough about himself to know it wasn't.

*

'I'm not sure you need come any more, to see Frank,' Gayle told him on the phone, 'it's not necessary.'

'What do you mean?'

'You're busy and I don't think it's fair on Donna either. It's not fair.'

'But I don't mind at all,' he said, 'you know I don't. I chose to do it. I count it as relaxation.'

'Well, maybe you should relax with Donna.'

'What do you mean?' he said. 'Donna's fine. I always came with you to see him, right from the start.'

'I know,' she said, 'I know you did. But still I feel I'm using you.'

'Don't be silly.'

'I think when we get back from Suffolk you should stop.'

'But I like Frank,' he insisted, 'you know I do. What's the matter? Why now?'

Silence. What did he expect her to say?

'Look,' she said, 'I'm right. Just think about it.'

*

She took Kitty shopping to the Arndale for holiday things – sunblock, a sensible sun hat with a brim, colouring books.

Kitty pleaded for a peaked hat with the Little Mermaid on, but finally settled for a plain white one with a pink gingham rim. Outside Mothercare, Gayle gave in and let her go on the pony which went up and down if you put 20p in the slot. Kitty never stopped laughing and shrieking the whole time it was moving. Near to them, a man selling membership for the AA winked. When the pony stopped, Kitty begged for more but Gayle kissed her and said no.

On the escalator, Kitty stood behind her, wearing the new sun hat.

'Keep your feet in the middle,' Gayle said, holding her hand, 'just keep still.'

'I am,' Kitty said.

The thing that happened next was impossible to explain. Gayle suddenly knew they had to get out, that someone was going to fall. It came in one blast, a wave. One moment she was standing there with Kitty and the next her heart was rocking. A kind of vertigo.

She thought: This must be what they call a panic attack; but at the same time she was thinking: We are going to die. Someone is going to die. The feeling was so strong that she began to sob. Tears fell down her neck and soaked her T-shirt, even though she had not been aware that she was crying.

Somehow, she got Kitty up into her arms and down the sinking steps. Somehow, though her whole body was trembling, she was careful and fast. She ran with Kitty in her arms, through the sliding doors and out onto the sunlit pavement by the Town Hall, where she knelt on the pavement. Kitty still had on her new hat. Gayle blinked in the light.

'I don't know what happened,' she said, half to Kitty, half to herself.

'You said I could have a dolly,' Kitty was reminding her and then a lorry veered off the High Street and smashed its way into the side of the building, right at the foot of the escalators. The pony which Kitty had ridden was rolled flat as dough.

It was reported on the regional news. The driver of the lorry was killed, and the AA man and two others, who'd been on the escalators, were taken to hospital and treated for shock. No one was clear as to what had happened, but it was presumed the driver had had a heart attack at the wheel.

*

'Everyone's dying,' Annie said, 'it's the time of year. Two more on Barton.'

'Who?'

'Annie Frost and that nice one, Phyllis Kale.'

'Ah.'

Annie turned a tap on hard, swilled a bedpan.

'How's Geoff?'

'Don't know. Haven't seen or heard from him all week.'

'I'm sorry.'

'Don't be. I'll survive. I always do.'

For a long time after her shift had ended, Gayle just sat by her locker, inert, waiting.

*

They walked in Battersea Park – Gayle, Donna, Simon, Will and Kitty. The sun was low and shadows stretched themselves like branches on the water. Ducks sank their feet in brown muck and silt and empty cartons.

Kitty raced off ahead as usual, veering off the path now and then onto the dry, flattened grass flicked with daisies.

'Kitty, wait!' Gayle called, walking with Simon. Donna and Will lagged slightly behind, separated by a foot or so of air.

It had been hot all day, bereft of wind, and the trees smelled sweet and stale. Small, jaded flocks of birds arrived confused, settled and flew off again into the fading light. Kitty tripped and fell over and Gayle rushed up to her.

'You're OK,' she said, brushing her down, 'what's hurting?'

'My heart,' Kitty said, 'my heart is hurting.'

'Join the club,' said Simon, dropping to his knees on the grass. And they all laughed.

They walked on, Kitty trailing a branch she'd picked up, Simon and Gayle lighting cigarettes, inhaling, blowing, cupping their elbows in their hands. Simon said something to Gayle and she laughed.

'We lead a charmed life, all of us,' Donna said, feeling suddenly, effortlessly., grateful. 'Don't we?'

But no one seemed to hear.

PART THREE

one

The house was less than half a mile from the sea and seemed to Donna to be full of light, nothing but light.

It was close enough for sand to have bloomed between the stripped boards of the floor, for salt to have blown about the door hinges and made them creak, for there to be pebbles and crabs' claws and dried sea lavender in the porch. Sand even gritted underfoot on the black lino of the bathroom floor, pooled at the foot of the lime-stained bowl of the old bath, hissed in the paper lining of drawers and underneath the beds. Shells and bird skulls and large, dull navy-blue stones were piled on the mantelpiece, next to polythene-covered handwritten instructions about TV and electricity and refuse collection.

In the lavatory, a wooden frame contained the words: NO PADS FLUSHED PLEASE. A plastic bottle of Harpic. A salt-bleached swimsuit forgotten on a rail.

The blankets in the airing cupboard smelled cold and damp, as did the curtains, which were rigorously patched. The furniture was dulled with dog hair, the rugs on the floor worn down to string in places. The bedrooms had tongue-and-groove walls painted baby blue – the stairs and landing were the same only in pink.

The kitchen had a big open fireplace. Simon threw

himself immediately down in a chair for a smoke and found half a pound of rancid butter under a cushion. In the hall another framed notice said, PLEASE LEAVE THIS PLACE EXACTLY AS YOU FIND IT THANKYOU. Under the notice, someone had left a load of coppers all piled up in their various sizes. Donna moved from room to room, carrying bags, moving pillows and blankets, adjusting the space to their needs. Simon said, 'I didn't think it would be this big.'

'It's huge,' Donna spread bedlinen on a garden chair to air, 'it's lovely.'

Kitty flew from room to room shouting and then tripped down the stairs and got a splinter in her knee. Gayle unpacked food and Donna opened and shut drawers and cupboards, observed that at least she'd brought a tin opener and a potato masher, in case they couldn't find one. Simon tried to switch on the water. 'It comes up from a well,' Donna said, 'sixty-four metres deep.'

'Who told you that?'

'Mum did.'

They both laughed at her.

*

All Donna wanted was for everyone to get on, to be happy. She gave Kitty a banana and went out to Will, who was standing in the garden with his back to them. There was a pear tree covered in thin yellow pears, its branches bending themselves around his head, as if he was meant to be there. 'Just look at that tree,' she said.

He said nothing, just stood with his hands in his pockets, looking at nothing.

'What's the matter with you?' she asked him – she felt bright, resilient, elastic. 'Why don't you talk to me?'

'I do,' he said. He was going to get away with it, she thought.

'I don't suppose anyone's brought tweezers,' Gayle called, 'I can't get this splinter out.' Outside, grass clear as water flattened in the sea wind.

'I want to go to the beach!' Kitty threw down the banana with one bite sucked out, trying to pull her shoes back on, trampling them without undoing the buckle. Then the phone rang.

'Already?' said Donna. 'Do we know where it is?'

*

'It might be the office.' Will dashed, glad to move away from Donna. He found an old-fashioned maroon plastic phone on the deep windowsill of the sitting room – a chilly, dusty room with flowered armchairs, sagging cushions – piles of *Country Life* and the parish magazine.

He was going to tease Betty about having to phone him so soon, but it wasn't her, it was Frank Chapman.

'Howdy,' he said in a slightly feeble voice, 'sorry to bother you and all that, only I've had a bit of an accident with a fork.'

*

On the beach at Kessingland, the tide was well out and behind the dunes, wind and time seemed blocked out.

Kitty's hair blew off her face, as Simon piggybacked her up and down, zigzagging away every time the water lapped his feet. Her shrieks carried toward them along with the restless churning of the sea.

'Well, I suppose he did well,' Gayle said, 'defending himself with just a fork.'

Donna stretched back on the white, cold sand, running her hands over her hip bones, which were level and relaxed. The feeling of limp, gliding health in her body was still a novelty to her. She put her hands down. The grass was so fine and dry it was almost black. No one was going to stop her flow, no one.

'Funny thing to choose, a fork,' Gayle said.

'Well, as opposed to what?' said Will.

'Anything.'

'I don't think choice came into it.'

'I still don't see how he got hurt by the fork, though,' Gayle said, 'if he was holding it.' She undid the laces of her trainers and did them up again, pulling each layer tight, tighter. They both watched her, then they all turned again to watch Kitty and Simon kicking the hem of the surf.

'Well, we can ask him,' Will said.

He sounded almost excited. He hates you, Will, she thought. And she also thought: Six hours, that's all we've had. Six hours and now he's back in our lives.

*

He arrived at five o'clock with two carrier bags and a bandaged wrist, and all of his usual misdirected gusto.

'Praise the Lord,' he said as he saw Will waiting on the platform at Beccles. He was finishing a pack of British Rail sandwiches and he folded the plastic container carefully in on itself before cramming it in the top of an already overflowing bin. 'Cheddar and onion,' he said, 'not that I could taste the onion.'

'Is this all you've got?' Will indicated the carrier bags.

'Light as dust,' Frank smiled. 'Didn't think you'd see me again so soon, did you?' he said softly as they got in the car.

Will thought he sounded almost triumphant – a kid getting his way. For some reason this aspect of Frank did not particularly bother him.

As they slowed and pulled up on the gravel, Gayle came out of the house wearing a long black T-shirt and bare feet, her arms wrapped shyly across her chest. She stepped up and kissed Frank on the cheek – a holiday thing she'd never have done in London. He said no thanks to a cup of tea, but accepted a Coca-Cola. Kitty was eating her tea. She watched, fascinated, as he pulled the tab on the can with his thumb.

'Most refreshing drink in the world,' he told her – told all of them – leaning back in his chair, 'praise the Lord.'

Then he told Kitty he'd something for her and produced from one of the carriers a pack of candy cigarettes.

'When you've eaten your pudding,' Gayle said, opening a tin of apricots. Kitty put each apricot half in her mouth and chewed it then spat it out. 'Oh, I give up,' said Gayle, removing the dish. Will saw that her feet were bare and each toenail was painted a dark plum colour. He found this hard to reconcile with the rest of her and the fact that it was hard to reconcile excited him.

Kitty got the packet open and ran around pretending to

puff. She licked the tips, which were coloured red. Then she crunched the white sticks with her back teeth. 'Tasty,' she said, and they all laughed.

'I hope you're not encouraging her to smoke,' Gayle said and she was still laughing.

'She knows the difference, doesn't she?' Frank said, leaning back and smiling. 'Doesn't she?' – flicking the edges of his fingers against the can.

'She's only three,' Donna said quickly.

'I'm not three, I'm three and a half,' said Kitty.

'Anyway,' said Gayle, and Will noticed that the sun had burned a patch of flesh under each eye and that her face seemed entirely different in the light from the sea, 'now that you're here, tell us what happened.'

Frank laughed and looked at Donna and Donna quickly looked away. Was she going to ignore him the whole time, then? She turned away and rinsed cutlery at the sink, drying it and putting it back in the drawer. At this point, Simon came in and sat down, keeping his eyes on Frank.

'Frank, this is Simon, Simon, Frank.'

'Oh,' Frank seemed not to hear Will or to see Simon, but pulled his great legs in so they crossed at the ankles, 'it was quite straightforward. He forced his way in when I was asleep – knew I'd just collected my pension. I grabbed the fork from my lunch. I'd just had Pot Noodles. If I'd been eating meat, he might have got a knife in his back – ha!'

He laughed, then laughed again, then sniffed and fished for his handkerchief. 'He caught my wrist with his pocket knife, however. Nicked a vein, but only a littl'un. Yes,' and he flourished his bandage, 'a neighbour went and called the police, praise Jesus.'

'But I don't understand,' Gayle sat down, 'who was he? Did you know him?'

'Oh no,' and he looked straight at them and poured the rest of the Coke from his can with a flourish, 'oh no, I didn't know him from Adam. Hello, Simon, nice to meet you. Good name, that, Simon, straight from the Bible.'

*

In his room, he kneels and shoves his face inside the thick pink candlewick of the bedspread and his nostrils are pricked by cheap detergent and the happiness of foreign beds.

'Tommy?' he whispers. 'Where are you? Can you hear me, your old dad?'

Tommy comes in sometimes from the town and just stands there in the doorway in his bell-bottoms and the T-shirt with the lurex lace all undone in the top. Disco clothes, he calls them. He wears a thin gold chain around his neck and those brown curls just bounce on his collar-bone. He chews gum – shifts it around in his mouth – a mouth surrounded by a smudge of beard. His lashes are dark as make-up.

'What is it?' Frank asks him, teapot poised, sensing – what? – something in the air. 'Why do you look like a girl? Are you a hippy?'

Tommy's boots have three-inch platforms. Like stilts. When he slams out and down the street to Jed's place, or Alex's or some bar, all he leaves is a faint incense whiff in the air, so Lola can come in and pull off her rain hood and straight away say, 'Tommy's been in, then?' and 'So where is he now?' and blame him, his own dad, for driving him away.

The Lord Jesus does not help much with family life. 'Life is no bowl of cherries,' Lola says till she's blue in the face, and 'If life gives you lemons, make lemonade!' – yet which is it to be, a disappointment or an abundance? Lola can go on and on until the cows come home, but in the end Tommy must be one thing or the other – a man or a woman, living or dead, bugger it!

*

'I don't want him here,' Donna said.

'I don't see why he is here,' said Simon.

'Calm yourselves,' Will said, 'I give him twenty-four hours. He won't stick it.'

'He has no one else,' Gayle said, 'he's our friend.'

'Yours, you mean,' Donna said, 'yours and Will's.'

'OK, ours,' Will admitted and Gayle flushed inwardly and did not know why. She touched her lips and tucked her hair behind her ears.

'Fucking up our holiday,' Donna said, 'it's beyond belief.'

'All right,' Will said, 'you get rid of him, then.' The whole discussion had been in a hoarse, hushed whisper whilst Frank was upstairs. The sky outside was dim, blue with thin, indecisive clouds.

Will walked out of the room and Gayle automatically relaxed.

*

Did he say bugger it? Sorry (forgive his French) – but life has short-changed him to such a fierce degree that someone is going to have to cough up. Spiritual things are not the answer – as Lola discovered – they don't help preserve your bones when you've gone in the ground. Brothers Wilson and Vernon never found a way to jilt the demons altogether – never found wives or lovers or daughters, never found ways of enlarging themselves without the aid of the Holy Ghost.

Why do the women cling to Will? If he could unravel the years, they would cling to him: lip to breast and knee to hip. A solid red line leading from him to them.

This trip is fitting in well with the plan. He unpacks his bags very carefully, not that they contain much. A Gibbs toothbrush, new in its box from the chemist. A hundred Good News tracts. A Cox's apple, the flesh turning brown where he sank his teeth in on the train. A pair of underpants, darned exactly where it mattered by Lola. The photo of Tommy. A box of matches – he doesn't know what for, since he's never smoked. Just seemed like a good thing to pack.

*

Donna went into the sitting room to look for her purse and glanced up to see Frank standing there. 'Sorry,' he said, 'sorry.'

She shrugged, made for the door, but he stopped her. 'You should forget I ever showed you that picture,' he said, and she froze and knew he was lying. 'I'm sorry,' he said again, 'you should forget it. The resemblance helped me work the magic.'

'Magic!' she said. 'Why are you here?'

He spread his palms. 'An old man in search of comfort.'

'Got yourself attacked again.'

He laughed. 'It suits you, being well. As it would have suited Tommy. What a waste it all is, waiting for Jesus to act on His whims.'

Donna shivered. Why did the mention of Tommy's name move her, cut her, hurt her? 'Forgive me,' Frank Chapman said, and she didn't know for what but she replied, 'I forgive you. Just please go soon.'

*

That night, they all sat among the wasps and the falling apples in the small overgrown walled garden and ate mackerel bought in Southwold that afternoon.

Gayle brought it out on a large white dish she'd found right at the back of the cupboard. The white china gave it a surgical look – flesh crammed with lemons, silver-blue ribbons of skin, dead eyes, new potatoes layered around like yellow-grey pebbles.

Frank entertained them with stories of his life – the boat he used to have on the Norfolk Broads just a matter of miles away, and of how he had dreamt of buying a schooner and taking off to the Caribbean, trading between the islands.

'It was my dream,' he said, 'only Lola wasn't having it. She liked to stop at home in one place. She'd lost another baby by then – jumped over a barrel in the fourth month. But I could've made a bob or two doing that, and the chance is gone so quick and then that's that.'

'Sounds a great life to me,' said Simon, rubbing the chill off his arms and yawning, 'it's a shame.'

By half-past nine, the light had faded to green and then

to black and a cooler wind blew in from the sea. At ten they lit an outdoor candle, which spluttered, wavered, then burned. They found another in a glass box like a lantern, and lit that too. By half-past eleven, all the corners of the house and garden were solid pools of darkness, and only the pallor of their arms and faces showed.

'A lovely evening,' someone said, and Gayle heard herself sigh.

*

Will watched them smoke, Simon and Gayle, lighting each other's cigarettes with the big box of Sainsbury's kitchen matches. Gayle played with the dead ones, doodling patterns on her wrists with the charred ends.

When Donna flicked on the light in the kitchen to make coffee, they all suddenly sat forward in their chairs and Will saw the hairs and goosebumps standing up on Gayle's arms. She leaned back and reached for her cardigan, which had caught on the back of the chair. He saw how Simon jerked forward to release it for her.

'What an evening.' She tipped her chin to look at the sky. 'It's almost warm still.'

'Yes,' said Will, but they didn't look at each other.

Donna came out with the coffee. She seemed to have relaxed, opened out again. 'Look at the stars,' she said, 'you never see stars in London. This sky is just so black.'

'Pitch black,' said Simon. But Will looked up and saw nothing but light – endless, random bouquets of light.

'Well,' said Frank, 'I'm an old man who needs his sleep, if none of you mind. That was very enjoyable. God bless, Amen.'

Simon coughed and pulled his chair aside for Frank to pass. 'Sleep well. Hope you're comfortable up there.' Gayle turned her head as he passed.

'So how long's he staying?' Donna asked, when the stairs had stopped creaking and the light in his room glowed through the thin curtains.

'Oh, not long,' said Gayle, as if she knew.

*

After half an hour, Simon went up.

Donna said, 'Shall I check Kitty?'

'Oh, would you?' Gayle looked at her watch.

When Will was all alone with Gayle, she glanced at him and something dogged and unfinished in her glance made him smile. 'What?' she said.

'Nothing.' He dared himself to continue to look at her and carefully laid his hands on his knees. She met his gaze at first but then looked down at the table and laughed. The light all around them seemed green. The laugh blew the naked candle out. He could barely see her it was so dark.

*

When Tommy is fourteen, Frank takes him out of school to work in the office. It's a family business, and Tommy's the son and heir. That's a joke; Tommy doesn't think he's anyone's son. Doesn't think he can learn from anyone.

All the same, Frank teaches him what's what. Has him carting boxes about, answering the phone, taking bookings, making tea. He's been considering taking on a typist but now he decides the business can do without. Mr High and

Mighty can learn. An apprenticeship he calls it. It was good enough for the Son of God.

The wooden structure which they call the office is pretty small – a prefab, close to the river and the boats and the vapour of evaporating tar which clings around their mouths and noses on hot days. The pleasure boats make a mint and the summers are nonstop busy. Lola still caters, the office side is just him and Tommy.

Midmorning, he always gets Tommy to make a cup of tea. Before they drink it, he makes him thank Jesus, aloud. Watching Tommy shudder as he speaks the words exhilarates Frank, he cannot say why. Same as when he shouts at Lola. An almost physical thrill – the flesh warbling its power.

Tommy has a girlfriend, of course. He comes home with small eyes and smelling of hair. One day Frank catches him off the bus from town, a small, squarish bottle sticking out of a brown bag. 'I hope that's not alcohol.'

'Leave me alone.' Tommy tries to stare him out, twists the paper bag close around the neck of the bottle and takes a step away from him.

'What is it?'

'None of your fucking business.' Frank wrestles the bag from him and looks in. Perfume. The label says Smitty.

Frank laughs. 'Smitty?'

Tommy shrugs. His eyes are hooded for lack of sleep. Circles of hair on his face. Frank would like to strike him, he really would. 'You know I'd rather see you ten feet under,' he says, 'than have you get a young woman into trouble.'

Young woman – he loves the sullen roundness of those words. Tommy says nothing. His breath goes in and out – pale skinny chest heaving up and down under his tight, cheap shirt.

'Jesus sees everything,' Frank comments as he walks away. Away, because just the sight of Tommy makes his heart hurt and his eyes water these days.

*

It was only nine but Gayle and Kitty had been up for hours. A line of picture dominoes covered the table. Breakfast dishes were piled up by the sink.

'There's no hot water.' Donna let the big tap run and something juddered as she put her fingers under.

'For fuck's sake,' Will commented, 'this is a holiday.'

Kitty wanted to go to the beach. She was pulling at Gayle's shirt, exposing her bra strap. Gayle removed her fingers and pulled away. 'We ought to take her,' she said, 'she's been patient. She'll go crazy if we just hang around.'

'I'll come,' Will said, and Gayle quickly looked away.

'What's that man doing?' Donna asked. 'Is he still asleep?'

'He'll know where we've gone,' said Simon.

'It's not very friendly,' Gayle said, 'waking up on your first day to an empty house.'

'He'll handle it,' Will said.

'No,' she said, because she knew she was going to have to fight him, 'I'll stay. You all take Kitty.' She felt relieved. The sun bent its rays through the kitchen window and temporarily dazzled her. She put her hand across her eyes.

'That seems a shame,' Will said.

'Can't you stay, Si?' Donna said. 'You don't want to come.'

'I do. I'm coming.' Simon kicked his boots out from under a chair.

'Look,' Gayle said, 'I'm happy to stay, it's a break for me if you'll take Kitty. I'll read the paper. I'll enjoy the peace. Really.'

*

It's not that he hates Tommy – no, never that – it's just that he never expected that having a son would be so frightening. People lie. They say that children are a blessing – that you're blessed for ever once you have children – but that's a lie put about to get you off and doing it, hastening your own end.

Lola counted Tommy as a blessing and when she couldn't count on that blessing any longer, then she was defeated, she gave up. You can count on Jesus for ever and ever, Amen.

Every day, Tommy defies him in some way. Just as Donna snatched good health from his healing hands and dodged the rest, so Tommy laughs at him behind his back, behind a tight, straight hand – sneaking around, hiding behind death.

His friends start coming to the house. More and more when they realize they can eat Lola's food and put their feet on the furniture. They're no respecters of anything. They batter him with questions, like why doesn't he have a television. 'What would I watch if I did?'

They scratch their faces. '*Dad's Army. Colditz. Top of the Pops.*'

'Demons inhabit television sets,' he informs them and they lean back and snigger and steal glances at Tommy – poor Tommy, having a dad with a message to preach. Later, they roll tiny cigarettes, hunched in concentration over their tobacco tins, play moany records about peace and rainbows. They don't know what love is. He could tell 'em, if they'd listen. Instead, they grow their nails long as girls' to pluck the strings of their guitars – hair shoulder length and clean and glossy as girls' hair. Eventually Tommy says, 'Let's get out of here.' And, slam, slam, they're all gone.

It's after one evening like this that Tommy passes out in his room and Lola can't rouse him and the doctor is called. Loosening his shirt, they find a bruise the size of a pineapple across his chest.

*

Now he lies dressed and flat on his bed, the back of his head cradled on his meshed palms, listening to their voices come and go through the thin floorboards.

Eventually, he swings himself in one movement off the bed and moves on hands and knees to the low window. He watches them crunch over the gravel, light voices – the child swinging a pink bucket, head up, asking questions, Will walking with his nose down, behind.

He watches them disappear round the curve of the road towards the beach, leaving the house a still, frail shell containing only the echo of his wishful thinking.

*

The road was sandy, the verges lined with elder bushes and cow-parsley and frilled towers of mauve and pink weeds.

'Look,' Kitty pointed to a chubby yellow flower, 'what's this?'

'Ask Donna,' Simon said.

'Donna, what's this?'

Donna frowned. 'Egg and bacon.'

'Egg and bacon?' Kitty laughed loudly in an exaggerated and affected way she'd recently learnt. Simon chased her. The sea appeared again – a wide arc of colour, boisterous and light. The wind blew. Will felt Donna look at him.

'What is it?' she said as they reached the top of the steep white steps down. He put his hand on the railing.

'What's what?'

'You don't look very happy.'

'Oh, Christ,' he said, 'please don't start.'

She was quiet for a moment. He looked out at the sea. He knew he was being very uncaring, very hard. It suddenly seemed unimportant, whatever there was between them. She had been racing around for so long – using this new energy of hers – and he felt that though he cared for her, he could no longer act. And because he couldn't act, he could save neither of them. That was it, so his caring for her was worthless. She looked pained and he almost enjoyed her expression, almost wanted it.

Suddenly she said, 'Look at me.' He looked. 'It's a beautiful day,' she said, wrapping her arms around herself, 'and we're on holiday and I'm better, and look at me, I just want to cry.'

'Why?' He put the question with a calm, intellectual interest, unkindly. He looked as if to a script. He had lost the ability to respond emotionally to anything.

'I don't know why.'

They were down on the shingle now. The breakers huffed and sighed. Kitty had seen a dog and was shrieking.

'Well, I don't know either,' he said, 'it's up to you. You try and think of why.'

*

When they learn what is wrong with Tommy, Lola stands and howls.

She stands all night at the window in her nightie – sad and fat – moaning and hollering, staring at the dim, unmoving disc of the moon.

She lapses now and then into Hungarian – something he has not heard her do for years – and eventually she kneels down right where she is in front of the wardrobe and prays.

The curtains are wide open. The sky is flushed with constellations. He thinks he can make out the sprinkle of the Milky Way from where he lies, rigid with fury, in his pyjamas.

'You used to be pretty,' he says to her suddenly, as he makes out her bottom through the cloth of the nightgown.

She doesn't look at him. 'I hope you're not praying to that false Roman Catholic God of yours,' he says, 'because I doubt he knows bugger all about leukaemia.'

*

When Frank crosses the landing to use the toilet, the floorboards creak. Going slowly makes it worse so in the end he just dashes.

Well here I am, he thinks as he drops his trousers and sits on the wooden seat. The walls are pink. He has made it into someone else's life at last. He feels a rush of excitement; well, it's been such a long time.

He looks into the wastebasket in front of him. There's a used tissue and a piece of cotton wool and the cardboard wrapping from a child's toothbrush with a dinosaur printed on it. Frank takes it out and looks. The dinosaur has a speech bubble. Part of it has been torn off, the only bit left says 'easy reach'. He throws it back and then he notices a thin white cardboard tube with another one inside. The edge is rimmed with a black line of dried blood. He doesn't pick it up, just has a good look.

When he's used the toilet and is about to flush, he sees a block of something hanging there in the bowl – something turquoise and fresh and sweet. He remembers that Lola used to put one in the toilet at the café. A crystal, salt and flower smell.

*

The tide was in and the morning sea was scorched with light – a perfect, huge reflection of the sky.

The shingled band where Simon and Kitty had piggy-backed yesterday was now a deep swell of water. This drove Kitty wild and she raced up and down barefoot, tossing stones in. Simon, it had to be said, was patient, flinging them again and again for her so they bounced, even where the water was choppy. Further along the beach, a dog was barking at the waves. Simon sat where the shingle formed a ridge and lit a cigarette, cupping the flame against the wind.

Donna's hair blew against her cheek. She turned her head

away, shaded her eyes with her hands. He saw tears on her cheeks and tried to put a hand on her arm. 'No, get off,' she said, moving away.

'I want to swim,' said Kitty, running up.

'You must be joking,' Will said. One or two idiots bobbed out there already. It was hard to think of anything worse.

*

Tell us, they beseeched him, in the little Gospel Hall in Surrey, what must we do? Christ becomes so very real when a loved one goes.

When the disciple he picked up in Kennington arrives on his doorstep, he tries to explain the manifold benefits of purging and prayer. He gets a Pyrex dish for the bile, a towel, air-freshener. He raises his arms, feels the sticky cling of his armpits. 'I always sweat when Jesus is close by,' he laughs.

'Don't you come near me,' the disciple says.

'It's quite all right.'

'Don't touch me.'

'Calmly now,' and he moves in.

In Surrey, they held the boy forcibly over the bowl – four or five strong men it took, to control the demons, let them pass out.

Afterwards there was a stench of vomit and of urine where he'd lost control of himself – screaming like a splayed cat, head flung back. The deliverance was a climax. They wiped his mouth gently with a napkin, prayed over him: O dear Lord, thank you Jesus, thank you Holy Spirit, thank you Holy Angels for our protection.

That was Surrey. But the new disciple just panics and goes for him, grabbing the nearest thing, which happens to be a fork.

*

Gayle sat alone in the kitchen – tried to read the newspaper. She stood, then sat again, then did not move for a moment or two. She forced herself to keep still. She heard Frank creak along to the bathroom upstairs and wondered whether to shout up and offer him a cup of tea. She decided she would wait until he came down.

Finally she stood and put a kettle on to boil so she could wash up even if the water wasn't yet hot enough. On the windowsill a crane-fly was dragging its legs, fussing against the glass. The window was specked with dirt. She tried to open it to let the insect out, but the catch had long ago been painted over and stuck shut and she had to give up. She went to the back door to see if there was a fishing net or something she could lift the insect out with.

She saw that the candles from last night were still on the garden table, melting in the sun. She fetched them in.

When she came back in, tears were running down her face, soaking the neck of her T-shirt. She did not know why – could not imagine what had gone so wrong. Everything which had been substantial beneath her had dissolved and she was falling. She put the candles down next to the sink and saw that her hands were trembling, unsure of where to go next.

Light was sucked from the room, flung into the garden, leaving her gasping, in darkness. All life's expectation gone, everything under water.

She began to speak to herself – to soften the blow. There was absolutely nothing, no one, around to prevent her speaking. She had no idea what she was saying.

*

Will looked at his watch. There was nothing he could say to Donna, nothing that would do the job.

Kitty, poking under a rock, had found something crawling and Simon was helping her examine it and Donna was saying various careful and excited things. Even as he moved closer to tell her, he was already turning.

In that instant he decided not to explain. He walked with his eyes fixed on the distance. He knew she saw him go, but she didn't call after him.

*

Tommy knows he's dying. He must know it because Lola won't stop crying all around him – in every room and all around his bed. The noise of her crying is eventually ingested by the house, as if it might lodge in the walls, permeate the floorboards. As if the air they breathe is infested with her tears.

She brings him boiled cabbage and chicken broth and toad-in-the-hole mashed with a fork, holds the spoon piled near his lips, but he won't eat. She thinks he needs meat – that if he could just eat flesh, his own would be saved. On the wall of his room there's a Slade poster. Instruments brandished like war tools.

After three weeks, Dr Gillot says, 'This is it. Now his strength will go, that's what will happen now.' And he stares at an open bottle of milk on the table.

'Hallelujah!' Frank says. 'We'll see what Jesus has to say about that.' On his knees in his dark, humming office he prays hard for his only son.

Easter. Palm Sunday. Lola sits by the narrow bed and strokes the depleted face. 'Poor baby,' she says now and then, to the wall, to the sheets. Frank comes in and Tommy turns away. 'Don't turn away from me,' he says, 'I'm your father.'

'Frank,' Lola begins.

'I don't want you,' Tommy says. Two bruisy shadows have come to roost under his eyes. There are unidentifiable spots on one of his hands.

Lola begins to cry.

When his mates come round he almost sits up, but he no longer tries to smoke. They murmur away together. When the girlfriend comes round – hair tied back with an elastic band and carrying a box of After Eights – they weep and cling on to each other and Frank overhears him say he loves her. She's called Elaine. Frank's never seen her before, but Lola has. Says she's from the youth club. What youth club? He didn't know Tommy went to any youth club.

Lola sits in the kitchen and stares at her two fists as though she never knew she had them.

The doctor has given her a bottle of something and it sits out of the way on the shelf in the hall, but Tommy has told her again and again that he isn't in any pain.

Then one night he screams for the bottle.

*

He is on his way downstairs – slowly, slowly, gripping the banister in the dark, ticking stairwell – at the bottom a pool of light. He stops because someone is crying. Then he hears quick footsteps on the gravel – almost a run. He pulls back, dipping noiselessly into the blinding sunshine of his room.

The kitchen door bangs.

*

He reached the house before he'd worked out what he was going to say – or maybe he wasn't going to speak at all. Maybe he was a child again, petrified, upset, without words.

She stood up as he came in and he saw she was crying and that stopped him for a moment. Maybe she understood his face or maybe she didn't, but he never found out because before they could go on in either direction or any direction, or even move at all, the phone rang.

She ran to answer it and he followed and as he moved into the doorframe, she listened to what she was being told and her crying stopped.

*

'What is it?' Will asked her.

She looked at him, standing there. She had finished listening and had said one or two words – a word here and there, a yes, a thank you, an Oh God.

'Annie's dead,' she told him, 'Annie who works with me. She's been killed.' She said it without any terror or drama or jumpiness, as if she'd already practised saying it to herself and she knew the words already and had great confidence in her ability to speak them out loud. 'Annie,' she said again, because she felt she needed to clarify, 'she was knocked off her moped. You know, Annie. Who was going out with the video manager.'

*

He said, 'You come and sit down and I'll get you something.'

'I don't need anything.'

'Come and sit down anyway.'

She sat, but not on the chair he pulled up.

He had been running. He had run up from the beach – left Donna and Simon and Kitty looking at things which lived under rocks and had been running to tell her something – get or give her something. Now there was nothing he could give her that would make a difference. 'Whisky? Brandy? You should have some alcohol.' She shook her head. He felt terrible for her. And for himself. This news meant he couldn't do anything for her.

*

The week after Easter, Lola says to him that they must make arrangements with the pastor.

She says the word burial – speaks the words as if each one hurts. She's bitten her lips till they are aflame with congealed blood and her nails down to the quick. Everywhere, she exposes her flesh, opens herself, creates new sores.

'I want a proper burial,' she nags. But he's not having any of it. He takes her by the shoulders and looks into her eyes.

'Burial?' he explodes. 'What d'you mean? He's not going

in any hole in the ground, our Tommy, no, sir! I've had a word with Jesus and He's given me a sign. We're going to raise him up from the dead, bring him back. He'll be curled up warm and breathing in his own bed before April's out – thank you Jesus, Amen!

Lola leaves the room – tries to slam the door, but there's a shopping bag in the way.

*

Donna put her arms around Gayle.

'How old was she?' Simon asked.

'Twenty-five, twenty-six.'

'Did she wear a crash helmet?'

'Oh, for Heaven's sake, Si.'

Annie had died on her moped. They thought her wheel had struck a stone. She had lived for fifteen minutes after that.

Gayle sat, open mouthed, dry eyed. She looked at Will and he looked at her. There was only Will in the room, she saw no one else. Her mouth was open like a wound. She felt the tears should properly come from there.

*

That night, Will dreamed of someone sucking his cock – damp strands of hair falling over his groin, a mouth both familiar and not familiar, the certainty that he would soon grip his thighs and turn himself inside out.

Who are you, he begged, between the long, taut strokes of his pleasure, tell me who you are? But the lips stayed rolling up and down on his cock and the shadowy head would not turn and it remained a nameless, faceless ecstasy.

*

Donna dreamed in fits and starts – flying over the sea, seeing how the clouds darkened large patches of water to navy blue and then how quickly it changed and the water was wrinkled and sparkling with light again.

It was a fantastic, indescribable sensation and when she woke she was still smiling with the memory of it.

*

Gayle dreamed bits of dreams all joined together and owls calling and one moment it was night and the next moment day, and Annie was sitting on the sofa reading her horoscope in a magazine. 'Annie,' she said.

Annie smiled. 'Hey, listen to this,' and began to read but the words were not properly formed and they seemed to spring from everywhere but her mouth.

*

Frank does not dream.

He lies on the bed and stares into the dark with open eyes until he can make out the wardrobe and the basin and the chest of drawers with the smooth oblong of glass on top. He stares at the window as it changes colour, absorbing something which barely resembles light.

He had a brother, Arthur Lawrence Chapman. They liked to play by the river. The water was dark and slippery, sticky with mud. He didn't know how to love Arthur, his own brother, and that's how the accident happened. Jesus, the Ultimate Manager, set the scene – punished him for his lack of love. When a boy isn't loved, he falls, you see – and though the fall is pure slow motion and you are watching, there's nothing you can do.

It's not your fault when the waters zip tight over his head – then back up for a moment, cuff, collar, nose, fingertips – then down again. Birds glancing down on that riverbank from above would have seen a small boy sinking, screams ripping the air.

Arthur Chapman aged three and a half.

Beetles rummaging on the slippery bark of that willow would have witnessed a chubby, grubby hand easing an even chubbier one off, scraping away under the little fingertips, pinching, digging, before employing a final push. Frank Chapman aged nine.

A single scream slicing the air.

You're glad he's gone, glad you can never forgive yourself, glad Jesus showed you how to take it like a man. For the rest of your life, you are what is known as glad, but glad's a funny word for it.

The current was strong. Arthur's drowned body fetched up at the bottom of the weir a mile on, where his jacket caught on a branch and held him, face down, under that unforgiving April sky.

two

Their mother arrived the next morning. 'This house smells of gas,' she said.

Donna sniffed. It was typical of her to smell something as soon as she arrived. 'I don't think so.'

'It does.'

'Well, no one else has noticed it.'

'We should get it checked, all the same.'

'Hi.' Gayle walked in.

'Sweetheart,' their mother said, 'I'm so sorry about your friend.'

'It's OK,' said Gayle.

'It's terrible. Are you all right?'

'I'm fine,' Gayle replied.

'Good job you're away, probably.'

*

They had tea on the lawn. Will kissed Karin, and Gayle introduced and explained Frank. 'I don't know how you did it,' Karin said to him, 'but you changed my daughter's life.'

'In Christ's name,' Frank said and gave a little half-bow.

'Are you a homoeopath or what?'

'A healer,' Gayle said quickly.

'Well, whatever. We can't thank you enough. Look at

her,' she hugged Donna, 'every time I see you, I'm amazed all over again.'

'Hallelujah,' Frank said, but surprisingly subdued.

The weather had turned very hot, with no breath of wind inland. Someone had the radio on quite loud in a nearby house and male voices interlaced with classical music lapped into earshot now and then. Frank was very restrained and ordinary, polite and quiet. He asked Karin if she lived near the Sussex Downs.

'Not far away,' she smiled at him, uncertain.

'Have you ever been to Brockwell Park?' he asked.

'Is that where they have the concerts?'

'No, Mum, that's Kenwood,' Donna said.

Kitty stood naked in a plastic bowl of water, watching a ladybird crawl over the end of her finger. Everyone turned to watch her.

'Kitty,' Gayle said, 'hat.'

The ladybird flew off, a black frizz of wings.

'I've got too much on, I have,' Karin said, pulling at her viscose blouse.

Will and Gayle sat close to each other. Each time she moved, he imagined he felt a compression of the air between them – her effect, the red-hot thread of her energy.

*

Gayle looked at him and thought: What have I done? What have I done? What have I?

*

'I love you,' Kitty said to Will, wrapping her arms around his neck, 'you're my best one. I love you and love you.'

She kissed him, butterfly touches moistened with three-year-old spit, smacking against his unshaven jaw.

He put his arm around her, her skin so smooth your hand slipped right through it. He couldn't look at Gayle.

*

Frank walked with them to the beach. It was almost six and very hot. Families were spread out on their towels, showing no signs of packing up. A Mr Whippy van had a knot of people around it.

'Hallelujah!' Frank said now and then. 'Praise the Lord!'

Donna noticed that his pants were pulled up too high, overlapped the tops of his trousers. There were stains of something on his shirt. He smelled musty, of public transport and post office queues. His dull inner-city clothes looked odd on the sand, like a body washed up – inert and unlikely and sad. The hot breeze blew his hair so it stood on end – whiter than white.

'Well, thank God for a little air,' her mother said.

Kitty found a spider crab, then lost it, then found it again. They all sat down and let her bring them tea parties in her bucket – sand and water sploshing, choices to be made.

'Ha! Breeze sure makes you peckish,' Frank said to Simon. As he spoke, a spray of saliva caught the light and sparkled. Simon smiled and looked away.

They'd left Gayle and Will to prepare supper.

*

Gayle and Will were lying on the kitchen floor in each other's arms – still and clothed and mouth on mouth. Not moving or speaking.

He held her against him. Gayle, against him. He could feel her shoulder blades and the sudden flesh bloom of her upper arms. If he looked – if he dared – he could make out the intricate weave of broken veins on the side of her nose, the dark definition of her lashes, the sun-bleached sweep of hairs on her jaw, the faint, chocolaty dust of her eye make-up. But just now, her eyes were closed. Right now, it was impossible for either of them to look.

Ten minutes ago he'd looked, they both had. She had put vegetables on the table, soil clinging to their roots, felt around in the half-open drawer for a knife.

'None of these are sharp,' she'd said, and he'd come to look, and then in a swift, reckless movement found himself closing against her, holding her body against the sink.

'Hey,' was all she said, but it was a sigh not an exclamation. He heard her gasp as he cupped her jaw in his hands so he could properly taste her mouth. Her lips were cool, unsurprised. Gently, he pushed the drawer shut, but it wouldn't go all the way and it stuck. Her arms came around him and he felt them meet on his back. Together they tipped down to the floor. The world tipped, in sympathy.

He was nearly in tears, moved and frightened by what he had done. Dared to do. But she did not push him away.

Now he was on top and her hands were around his neck and her teeth were chattering. He had an erection and he shifted his thighs to conceal it. Somewhere within the wood and brick and fabric of the house a clock struck the half-hour. She stiffened in his arms.

'Relax,' he whispered, instantly regretting that he sounded as if he'd planned it. Which he hadn't.

He rolled off her and pulled her to him and moved his hand down the back of her T-shirt till he reached the small of her back. He wanted so very much to move it lower but he couldn't. His hand was shaking.

She gave a little laugh.

'Don't laugh,' he said, though he knew the laughter meant nothing, wasn't real.

*

After ten minutes or maybe half an hour, she rolled herself on top of him and kissed him. Her lips were light and cautious, tentative, then less so. He felt her nose nudging his, her tongue lifting his lips. Wet. The weight of her hips across his.

The sensations were amazingly intense, as if he were an adolescent discovering it all for the first time again. At one point it became unbearable, and his body seemed to panic. He closed his eyes. When she lifted her face, he breathed again.

Still neither of them spoke. This can't be happening, he told himself. He remembered she was Donna's sister. Kitty's mother. He smiled. 'What?' She pulled her head back to look at him.

'Nothing,' he said, 'just you.'

Then they kissed properly, not gently but in an equal way, enjoying the new certainty of each other's mouths. Again, they did not try to speak. The kitchen floor was filthy – there were dog hairs in the matting and dry bits of pasta and most probably fleas – but he knew if they moved it might change, they might lose it.

After a while, though, she got up anyway.

She said she'd be back in a minute. He moved to sit shakily at the kitchen table, stared at the space where they'd been. Then he heard her going upstairs. He felt so nervous and aroused. His heart was racing. She stayed up there, but he didn't go up after her. He didn't know why.

Maybe it wasn't like that. Maybe he just didn't feel predatory about this.

*

They'd done nothing about supper, of course. The peas were unshelled, the potatoes unpeeled. Lunch plates still piled in the sink. They had to make something up.

'Gayle passed out,' he announced as they all banged open the back door, walked over the exact fragment of floor where they'd just held each other, 'I made her lie down. She's on the sofa.'

'Oh dear,' said Karin.

'She just fainted?' Donna said, pulling off Kitty's hat, revealing Kitty's hair stuck to her head with sweat. 'Just like that?'

'Just like that,' he shrugged, unsmiling, 'the lengths a person will go to, to get out of peeling potatoes.' Simon looked at him hard, before going into the downstairs lavatory and sliding the door shut.

'What has Mummy done? What?' Kitty shouted, bouncing and weaving between their legs. She'd pulled off her shorts and was somehow naked again.

'It's all right,' Karin said, 'she'll be fine. You stay with me, let Mummy rest a minute.'

Karin got going on supper. The lavatory flushed and Simon sloped back in. 'Where's your friend Frank?' Karin asked him.

'He's not my friend.' Simon got a beer from the fridge and poured his mother a Martini. Cubes of ice were shaken out, fell on the table.

'These knives are all blunt,' Karin complained, 'you'd think there'd be one sharp one.' Kitty knelt up on a stool and begged raw peas.

'Is she OK?' Simon said to Donna who'd come back in. She nodded. She looked very pale herself.

'It'll be grief,' Karin said suddenly, 'grief does you in.'

*

Donna poured herself a drink and listened to them all. She listened to the ice in her glass expand and crack and distort. She saw Frank standing in the garden looking at the red-brick back wall which was mossy and had some kind of vegetable growing up it. She saw Will tip his chair back against the wall, watching Kitty. She saw Simon watching Will.

And she knew then she'd been tricked, not just by Frank Chapman, but by them all. She knew she'd allowed herself to be stripped of her original pain – pared down, minimized, bought off – only to be introduced to a brand-new one.

*

Gayle lay under a blanket on the cool, sagging sofa listening to her heart go bang. Frank put his head around the door, frowned at the room, then found her. 'You should have come to the beach,' he said.

'Should I?'

'You know you should.'

He looked straight at her and she laughed, because she wasn't going to give him an inch. None of them were going to now.

*

Donna walks into the garden and Frank follows. 'I killed my own brother,' he says.

'What?' Turning her pretty boy's head – long black lashes, tight brave lips.

'I had a little brother and I killed him.'

'Oh?' Butter wouldn't melt. They are down at the bottom of the garden, where the heat has petrified the rosebuds on their stems. Wasps bump against them – flick, flick. 'What do you mean?'

'What I say. I made him die. Do you mind me telling you? Do you?'

Lola never loved him – not once in their marriage. Why did she wait and tell him – finally, unkindly – when they were old people and it was too late? He'd been used up.

Donna shrugs. Moves her lips around the circle of her glass. She's thinking and her eyes are glassy with disbelief. Sometimes when she moves, she is so free and so like Tommy he wants to stop her in midair, mark the shape of her flight. 'No,' she says, 'I don't mind.'

'You don't believe me.'

'I believe you. I've heard you.'

But he knew she wouldn't believe him and he doesn't want to be let off – he wants more. He wants blood, his own and others'. He wants to spill his own blood for her – either that, or hers for him. 'You want to watch your boyfriend and your sister,' he tells her, 'the two of them together – you want to watch out for them.'

Her eyes do not move. She continues to look at the browning grass with the molehills on it. 'Do I?' she says.

He would like to have more effect. He would like to confess some more, but it's as if he is forgotten.

*

Upstairs, stripping Kitty for the bath, Gayle muttered in passing to Will, '*Rien devant l'enfant*.'

The taps gushed loudly so they could not be heard. He noticed how lovely her hands were – the nails white and straight, the fingers naked of jewellery – as she quickly turned off the taps. She swished some blue bubbly stuff into the water.

'What do you take me for?' he asked her, hurt. She straightened and her face was level with his.

Kitty sat on the loo, one hand braced on each side of the seat, watching them, dazed with sun and fatigue.

He realized he loved Gayle so much he'd worn her down to nothing in his sight – that if he didn't move away she'd disappear. And he didn't want to be that close, not if it meant she wasn't there any more.

*

Later, Frank sits in a room gobbled up by shadows, whilst Simon rakes the ashes to make a fire. The mother comes in, all enthusiasm and small remarks, and asks him about himself – sits on another chair, smooths her skirt, inclines her head at him. 'Are you from London, originally?' she asks him.

He says no and tells her about Silver Street and the *Jean Sweet* and the tidal river. She asks if he has any children and he says yes, just the one.

He likes being questioned – enjoys the interest. Could have done with more of it in his life. He straightens his back and spreads his fingers over the nice cool cushions.

*

Gayle went up to kiss Kitty goodnight.

She sat on the bed and looked in the mirror. She picked up her hair, wound it in her hand, held it against the top of her head, then dropped it again. She looked hard at herself. The reflection was hostile, animal. Whenever she thought of Will, it was not on top of her on the kitchen floor, but in his car, on the way to Frank's – or actually in the flat, against that backdrop of junk and dust and peculiar tension.

Everything that had happened had happened because of Frank. Even Annie seemed to be traceable back, by a thin line.

Kitty was watching from her cot.

'Get me out.' She stretched out bare arms.

'No,' Gayle said, 'it's bedtime. Go to sleep.'

'I don't like it in this cot.'

'Come on, Kitty, lie down.'

'I'm not a baby.'

'Kitty—'

'What are you doing?'

'I don't know. Go to sleep.'

She pushed Kitty down in the cot, snugged the blanket over her, ran a hand over her cold shiny hair. The crown of Kitty's head was a perfect combination of hard and soft and round and still. Everything Gayle normally knew and thought had disappeared. So many barriers had been removed. She couldn't remember how it had begun, or if it had begun with Frank.

*

That evening at supper, Frank seemed uncertain, on edge. He had had a bath but had not changed his clothes, though his hair was wet and combed to the side and he smelled faintly of soap. Will saw that Karin did not know what to make of him, how to behave. She sat away from him, but listened to everything he said with a fixed smile on her face. She clearly thought it was because of Donna that he was staying there with them, and that they owed him something and that they must therefore comply.

At one point, she asked him again about his son and Frank told her he had died of leukaemia at the age of fourteen.

'Oh,' her hand flew to her mouth, 'oh dear, I'm so sorry.'

'Don't be,' he said, 'he's up there hobnobbing with Jesus Christ now. I rejoiced for him as he drew his last breath.'

'Well, it's good,' Karin searched for the words, 'that you have your faith.'

'Didn't you ever try to heal him?' Simon said suddenly.

'I did,' said Frank, 'but Jesus had other plans.'

There was a pause, then Karin said, 'I had an experience once. After my husband died. He had this digital clock by the bed. A radio alarm clock. After he died I was very angry, for a number of reasons. I came into the bedroom one morning at about nine and I said, "OK, if you're there, show me!"'

Simon laughed, but everyone else was silent. Frank put down his knife and fork and rested his hands in his lap. 'I was very angry,' Karin went on, 'as I say, it was nine o'clock. The moment I spoke, the numbers flicked fast-forward to eleven ten, and the radio came on.'

'Really?' said Donna.

'Jimmy Young,' she said. This time, Will laughed.

'But that's nothing to do with faith,' Gayle said.

'OK,' she told them all, 'you're so clever. How do you explain it?'

'An electrical fault,' said Simon.

'Why should it be him doing it?' Donna asked.

'Well, it was his clock, wasn't it? He just went for the nearest thing.'

Frank said, 'You want to watch it, messing about with spirits. You'll please the Devil no end and there'll be no chance of Life Everlasting.' His voice soared to a shout and he jumped to his feet, knocking his chair back against the wall. 'Hallelujah! Deliver this room from demons!'

'Hey,' said Simon.

Karin looked shocked. 'Can we talk about something else?' Donna said. She looked tired and edgy and fed up.

'It wasn't an electrical fault,' Karin insisted, without

looking at Frank, 'the clock still works fine to this day.' She poured some more wine.

'Please,' Donna said again.

Will turned and looked at Gayle and when she looked back, he smiled. He carried on looking at her until she looked away again. Donna began clearing the plates and Will got up to help.

Frank seemed to have switched off. He stared out of the window which was now thick dark black against the kitchen light. Donna brought out the strawberries, but no one was very hungry any more. They decided it was too cold for coffee in the garden. A dark, fishy wind was blowing up from the sea.

One by one, they drifted up to bed.

*

Kitty was sitting up in the cot crying when Gayle went in. She felt her forehead, which seemed hot.

'Rabbit's naughty,' Kitty said, shaking the knitted animal who'd gone all flat and shapeless, 'he's going to have to change, you know.' Her voice was thin and bolshie and delirious.

'Shh,' Gayle said, stroking her damp hair.

'He keeps telling me things that aren't true,' Kitty mumbled.

'I'm going to get you some Calpol,' Gayle said.

She went to the bathroom to get it, but by the time she'd got back Kitty was asleep again, the rabbit squashed up under her chin. Her mouth was open, her cheeks red. There was a film of sweat around her nose. Gayle tucked the rabbit back into the crook of her arm and touched her again. She still seemed hot. She pulled up her pyjama top and uncovered her – sat for a long time just watching her breathe.

*

When Tommy's lain there dead for fifteen minutes or so, he says right then, let's get to it.

He phones them all: Tom Willis, Brother Leitch, Brother Barnham, Jeremy Blather, Sid Darcy and his nosy wife Miriam. They've been on standby ever since that afternoon when Tommy's breathing changed and Lola tried to telephone the nurse. In the end Tommy died quick as a flash – slipping out easily between one minute and the next. They'd had no time to get help. But he's prepared in advance, Boy Scout that he is.

Lola's hair has come all undone and she tramps around in her stockinged feet coughing down the tears and saying baby, baby, come back to me. She doesn't see how Tommy can be dead if his skin's still warm. His eyes are still open, still wet with his last-minute, panicky tears. There's a biro mark on his thumb, from writing a note to Elaine.

'Close them,' she growls at Frank, 'close his eyes.'

'Shut up,' he says, 'any minute now he'll be awake. He'll want them open.'

'I'll get her out,' he tells Sid and Miriam as they creep in and stare respectfully at the wide-eyed dead boy on the bed, 'we have to be quick.'

'Oh dear.' Miriam takes off her outdoor boots and puts on elasticated nylon slippers without once taking her eyes off Tommy. 'Oh my dear, oh dear.'

'Hallelujah!' shouts Sid, raising both arms to the Lord and then Brother Leitch comes in saying he hopes he isn't late only his wife had to go to a separate healing meeting and he can't get hold of her. Soon they all crowd the tiny room – their macs and jackets piled any old how on the armchair, arms bared, hands held in prayer.

'What're they all doing here?' Lola cries. 'Get them out!'

'Lola,' he takes her shoulders and turns her through ninety degrees, 'go in the kitchen and make a cup of tea for Tommy – yes, for your own dear, living son – we're going to wake him up now. Hallelujah!'

*

He lay in bed awake next to Donna whilst the house slept. Her bottom was hunched up, uncovered, and her mouth was open. She had the palm of her hand up against it as if in surprise – as if there was something she'd been told and she couldn't quite bring herself to believe it.

In the garden or maybe beyond, he could hear some animal making a sharp, complaining noise – maybe a fox or cat. He didn't know what time it was, but could tell by the thick and certain quality of the dark that it was nowhere near dawn.

He couldn't sleep – not in the same house as her. He couldn't stop thinking. It was as if he had no substance without her. He wanted only to be engaged in an activity which affected her, or which at least would have some consequence which involved her. He wanted to spend time making their relationship progress, or else if he could not, to spend time talking about it. Part of him actually wanted to wake Donna up and find a valid excuse to talk about Gayle.

Part of him actually wanted everyone to know what was going on.

About an hour later, he heard someone go downstairs, heard the throb of a tap in the kitchen, the click of the cupboard. He pulled his shorts on and went softly down too.

She was standing there in her long T-shirt, waiting for the kettle to boil.

'Oh,' she whispered.

'It's you,' he said. He felt so nervous and embarrassed – his chest all bare – he wished he'd put something on.

'Yes, it's me.'

'I knew it was.'

'Yes.'

'Can't you sleep?'

'Kitty woke me.'

'I didn't hear her.' He felt immediately negligent. 'Is she OK?'

She shrugged. 'A temperature. I don't think it's anything.' He looked at her standing there next to the cloud of steam. She switched off the kettle.

'What're we going to do?' he said.

'Do?' she repeated.

They still stood at opposite ends of the room. She didn't look tired or uncertain. He wondered why it had taken him so long to understand how beautiful she was – her eyes, her wide, calm mouth, the arch of her eyebrows, her tangle of hair. All those years of not looking.

It crossed his mind that she must be naked under the T-shirt. He walked over to her. He put his arms around her, mostly to steady himself. Her hair was a cloud of black, he couldn't get used to it. He wanted to lift her T-shirt and touch her under it, but he didn't. Instead, he stroked her back, rubbed it in circles like a baby's.

He wanted to say, I want to sleep with you, but knew it would sound petulant, like a teenager pushing his luck. He said instead, 'I want you.'

She made a little noise, but didn't move closer.

He wanted to say: I want you instead of Donna, I want to swap, I made a mistake, I admit it now and I will do anything to be allowed to change. He said, 'I want you,' again.

She didn't say anything, but she didn't move away. As they kissed, he felt so unrecognizably nervous and horny and out of control.

Then there was a bumping on the stairs and they jumped apart. The door swung open and it was Kitty holding a pair of socks. Her cheeks were red and feverish, her eyes glazed.

'I don't want my socks on,' she said, swaying and scowling into the light.

*

They're at it all night, praying at the freshly dead boy's bed. The nurse never turns up, so they are left in peace, so to speak.

At one point he lifts the sheets and pulls up Tommy's pyjama top, exposes his bare skinny chest with its few dark hairs, so they'll be able to see when it kicks into action like a little pump, when he starts to breathe again.

'Leave him alone,' Lola says in no more than a whisper

from the kitchen doorway, 'close his eyes. He's a child.' She has backed off into a glazed, zombie state – and good riddance. The kettle has long ago boiled and cooled on the hob.

'Go away,' he says, 'you're ruining it. Your own son. Do you want him to remain dead for ever?'

He's harsh because it's the truth. But he also wants to punish her because he knows she is weak and she has ruined his life and he's kicking himself for ever having married her.

It turns out to be a long night. Now and then it gets going and then grinds to a halt again – thick and black – as if someone has just come along and whipped the stars and moon out of the sky, laid them in a box and jammed the lid on.

*

Kitty was better the next day, though on the verge of a cold. They all went into Southwold, bought fish and vegetables and bread and some clotted cream to have for tea, and Donna went to the chemist. Karin bought a film for her camera.

They sat on a bench on a grassy hill outside the Sailors' Reading Room, where the warm wind made their eyes water, and Frank held Kitty up to look through the binoculars. Kitty couldn't see and tried to close one eye.

'No,' Will helped steady her head, 'both eyes, twit!' Kitty shrieked with laughter. Gayle could not trust herself to look at Will, but she knew when he was watching her. Karin took a photo of them all gazing at the wide, sparkling panorama of the sea. Gayle counted the ships and boats with Kitty. Gulls floated in wide circles and screamed in the space above their heads. Somewhere inside her body, Gayle was flying and screaming, too.

They walked along the front, past the pier and the amusement arcades, to the boating lake.

'Look,' Gayle said, 'the water's full of tiny brown fish. Can you see them all wriggling?' and Kitty shrieked and coughed and jumped from foot to foot in delight.

Gayle and Simon took her in a pedal boat. The others watched from the side. The boats were plastic, with flat bottoms, in different colours and theirs was green. Weed and water floated on the bottom where you put your feet. A lot of kids were yelling and laughing. Frank sat away from them, on a bench in the sun, head thrown back, a smile on his face.

*

The bruise-black window drains to yellow and Tommy still lies so very stubbornly dead. In the slippery morning light he wears an expression on his face that spells it out for them – that says he is intending to remain dead. More fool him, then.

'Amen,' says Brother Barnham and sits down, head in hands.

'Give up?' Miriam has already got her coat on and is stuffing her thick, short feet into her outdoor shoes. Her face is pouched and fleshy with fatigue.

'Well, I don't like to say it, but it's not going to happen, is it?' says Sid. Who has had enough of hanging around a dead body.

Frank pulls the pyjama down over Tommy's chest. The

skin is a little cooler now. Through the doorway, he can see Lola rigid at the kitchen table. She has not moved in more than an hour.

'No need to rush off,' he says, because he can feel them jumping like rats from a ship and he does not want to be left alone with what is left of his family. 'Lola,' he calls, 'we'd like tea now, please.'

'If you've finished,' she says, without turning round, 'I'm calling the nurse and the undertaker and the pastor right now.'

Wearily, Brother Sid pulls the sheet over Tommy's face. Makes a corpse of him.

'No,' says Frank, because it is not Sid's decision. 'Not yet. Plenty of time for that,' and he whips the sheet back off again.

And – can you believe it? – he could swear Tommy's expression just changed.

*

'How long is that man going to stay?' Gayle's mother asked her as she knew she would.

'I don't know.'

'I know we are grateful to him about Donna and all that, but couldn't she just pay him something and be done with it?'

Gayle laughed. 'It's not quite like that.'

'Why not? Doesn't he operate like a professional?'

'Mum, you've seen, he's a religious man. He did it for Jesus and all that. Anyway, we have a relationship with him.'

Her mother said nothing, then, 'None of us are church goers.'

'He's hardly your normal C. of E. He's a born-again.'

'I hate all that evangelical nonsense. Gives me the creeps.'

*

They walked back along the sea front and bought Mr Whippy ice creams from a man with a port-wine stain over his face. Kitty bit the bottom off her cone and it dribbled all down the inside of her elbow. Karin wiped her with some Kleenex she had in her bag.

Will knew Gayle was making an effort not to walk near him. She was next to Donna, who walked with her head up and said little. The sea breeze was warm, lifting their clothes from their bodies, licking at their limbs. Kitty's hair kept getting in her ice cream. 'Why did that man have a dirty face?' Kitty asked.

'It's not dirt,' said Gayle, 'it's a birthmark. It's how he was born.'

'Does he like it?'

'I doubt it.'

Will knew she was thinking of Annie.

'Your friend wasn't looking to be healed,' Frank said suddenly.

'What?'

'The nurse, the little nurse who died. Marked out.'

'Annie? What do you mean, marked out?'

'Marked out for Jesus. Could have told you she was a goner.'

Gayle stopped in her tracks. 'Why didn't you, then, Frank? Why didn't you?'

'Ignore him,' Will said, and he took Gayle's elbow and pushed her forward, made her walk with him ahead of the rest. He didn't care what anyone thought.

'I knew a chap once,' Frank shouted from behind, 'with two artificial legs. Used to propel himself on crutches onto the pier at Cleethorpes in all weathers, sit down, unstrap 'em, leave his crutches along with his legs on the side, and hurl himself off into the water. I asked him why he had no fear and he replied, "Jesus gives full and free salvation – I look to Him." A torso with arms he was, if you think about it.'

'He's ranting,' Will told her. Gayle was crying, searching in her pockets for a tissue. He put an arm around her.

'Jesus put a song in his heart, pepped up his muscles,' Frank trilled, 'and he was an ex-Olympic swimmer.'

'There you are, then,' Simon said.

Frank told them how he used to give out tracts at Cleethorpes by the pier. How if people were asleep on their beach towels, he'd just wedge the tracts beneath their inert limbs.

'Must've blown away as soon as they got up,' Simon said.

'It was better when I had the sandwich board to wear,' Frank said, '"I'm a Fool for Jesus", it said, in black letters on the front. On the back: "Whose Fool Are You?"'

Kitty ran up to Will. 'Lift me up,' she said. He put her on his shoulders and she sang, 'Fool, fool, fool. . .' She smelled of little girl's knickers, of warm thighs and of pee.

He took his hand off Gayle's shoulder.

'Thank you Jesus!' Frank called out to the flat brown sea.

*

Gayle had had enough of Frank Chapman.

She dropped back behind Will and Kitty. It was all right to look at Will when he had Kitty. No one could tell. When she looked at him, the solid world went shaky. She could not believe what she had done. She remembered how it was on the floor with him – went over it again and again. When she thought about it, the back of her head felt soft, tight.

She had had enough of Frank Chapman. Any purpose he might have had was at an end.

Kitty clasped her hands under Will's chin, and he eased them back very gently so he wouldn't be choked. She noticed how he steadied her little thighs around his neck and how he carried her with a fierce, self-conscious pride, as if she were something carefully chosen, exotic and precious.

*

'What is it?' Simon asked Donna.

'I feel sick.'

'What? Sick like you're going to be sick?'

'I don't know. Just sick.'

*

At the car park, half of them piled into their mother's car, half into Will's.

Kitty had to go with Will because of the car seat, so

Gayle and Frank got in too. He sat in front, his elbow resting on the wound-down window. The car was scorching hot – so hot that Gayle had to wedge a towel under the metal fastenings of the harness so it didn't burn Kitty. There was an overpowering smell of ripe banana, because Kitty'd dropped a skin on the floor. Gayle got out of the car and took it to the concrete bin. She could feel Will watching her as she walked over the hot gravel. She could not bring herself to look at him.

Frank was very quiet in the car, subdued and forlorn. Gayle knew he wanted her to ask what was the matter, but she wouldn't. She felt she could no longer be responsible for his moods and his welfare. She had one child already and she could not cope with another.

As they drove up onto the Kessingland road, the sun slid behind a cloud and a band of purple touched the sea. The horizon was a fuzzy, inky line.

'Rain?' Frank said.

'I wouldn't mind,' she replied. The truth was, she no longer cared what happened to the weather or anything else. All her life she had tried to take control and what had happened?

Frank coughed. 'I'll go back tomorrow,' he said.

'Oh. Are you sure?' Gayle was amazed at the relief she felt.

She saw that Kitty was asleep, head tipped, mouth open.

'If you're sure,' she said.

'Yes,' he said, 'I think it's best.'

*

They were the first to pull in on the gravel drive. They'd lost Karin and the others somewhere past the turning for Kessingland.

As she opened the door and stood up, Gayle rested her hand for a moment on the car roof and Will covered it lightly with his, but he wasn't quick enough because Frank popped his head up then and saw them. They both pulled away stupidly. Frank just looked.

He said nothing but made a show of turning his back. Then he walked off towards the front door and whistled loudly whilst they got Kitty out. Overhead the sky was indigo, the air thick and sticky. Kitty cried, grumbling as she woke up. The car seat had made a livid dent in the side of her forehead.

Frank was still laughing and whistling as they unlocked the front door.

*

When Lola is out like a light on her bed and Sid and the others are gone, he comes down finally and makes himself a cuppa. Stares at the cooker. Recognizes hunger. Solves the problem by eating sardines straight from the tin, standing at the sink, spattering brine down his unchanged shirt. Prayer has the quality of fresh air – gives you the appetite of a wolf.

Soon he knows he must go back in there.

He slurps his tea heroically even though it's hot. Almost enjoys the burning on his lips. The yelp of pain. There's nothing he can't do, nothing.

Then he enters – he has to enter – and walks around the

room. He knows Tommy's there, he doesn't have to look. There is only the absence of pop music. He whistles the first song which comes to mind, which is 'My Bonny Lies Over the Ocean'. Tommy would've curled his lip. He deliberately does not look at the bed.

'You can't die,' he says then, 'Jesus says you're not to die.' And he snatches a look hoping to catch some sign of life. Tommy lies there like he's just overslept. All that's missing is a whiff of Lola frying bacon, calling him down.

But when he finally goes over and grasps Tommy's wrist and works his hand under the shoulder and lifts the chin and chest, there's no give at all and he can tell that if he persists the bones will shift in their sockets and crack. He tries to lay the body back down straight, but it won't quite go and some yellow stuff slides out of Tommy's nose and onto his hand.

Suddenly needing to go, he rushes across the yard and flings down his trousers and lets himself explode in the pan. In the chilly WC, he finally sobs his heart out like a six-year-old. He sees the yellow stuff is still on the back of his hand and he wipes it on some paper.

Then he lays his chin upon his knees and he must briefly pass out, for when he opens his eyes again the Lord Jesus Christ is standing there before him in the yard.

*

'It's parasitical, you know, what Gayle does,' Simon told Will as they slumped in the black shadows of the sitting room after supper.

'What?' Nearly everyone had gone to bed. In the kitchen, Donna was moving around, making camomile tea.

'What she does – the way she picks people up. Why d'you think she does it? It's far from altruistic. She needs it as much as they do. I know her.'

'Yeah?' Will tried not to show anything on his face.

'Yes,' Simon said, 'it's a kick, a thrill. Her problem. It's funny,' he stretched out his feet in socks, 'Donna thinks Gayle's the successful one, you know – the one who's sussed.'

'And she's not?'

Simon laughed. 'She's a mess. It's creepy, the extent to which she's a mess.'

Will laughed uncertainly. 'What do you mean, anyway?' he said and he couldn't help feeling he was falling into Simon's trap, whatever that was. 'She didn't pick Frank up. He went on and on to her about helping Donna.'

'And didn't she love it?' Simon said. 'She fucking loved it. I tell you, she gets off on it.'

'Whose side are you on?' Will stood up.

'Whose side are you?'

'I had no idea there was a war,' said Will.

'Well, you live and learn,' Simon said, staring at him, 'I'm sorry to disappoint you.'

'You're not disappointing me at all.' Will realized he'd already talked too much about Gayle. Maybe that was it – the trap. 'You sound almost jealous,' Will said at last. But Simon just continued to look at him steadily, triumphant.

*

The rain begins at four that morning, and it's very hot and sticky just before. Frank stands at the window watching the storm's progress, knowing it is a declaration of Jesus' love.

Far down the coast towards Lowestoft, a weak flash of lightning, then thunder. The beach lit for a moment – flat and hot. Another thunder-flash. Then long needles of rain, first singly, then in pairs, then great crowds of them – interrupting the surface of the sea and moving with force onto every face of that landscape and that house.

*

Frank left the following day. Gayle and Will drove him to the station. They were the only ones who would escort him anywhere. The sky was grey and overcast and heavy with more rain, though the heat was already drying the cracked earth.

'Weather's broken, then,' he said, 'hallelujah!' He picked up the same carrier bag he'd come with. 'See you in the Smoke.'

'Sure,' they said.

There was something going on in Beccles – a pageant or procession or something – which had slowed the traffic down. A policeman stopped them as a float went past. Crowds of children in fancy dress clothes stood in flip-flops and soaked plimsolls on the wet verge. 'You two make a lovely couple,' Frank remarked suddenly as they drew in under the Railway sign.

Gayle froze, pretending not to hear. He sniggered and she could almost feel his breath on her neck. We won't have to visit him any more in London, she thought. She realized it had been a means of seeing Will, though she hadn't known it at the time.

'Well, safe journey.' Will was cool, distant. He got out and shook Frank's hand, but kept his eyes down.

'Be good,' Frank said, 'and if you can't be good, be careful!' Gayle shuddered.

They left him near the tiny newspaper kiosk, smiling and looking around as if he expected any moment to see someone he knew. 'Invite me to the wedding!' he shouted then, with a sly, hostile energy.

They walked quickly to the car. 'I can't believe him,' Gayle whispered. Will's face was expressionless.

'Just forget it,' he said, 'he's pathetic. Forget him.'

'He's turned nasty,' she said, 'he thinks he's threatening us.'

Will took her hand and she felt her breath tighten and slow down. 'You,' he said.

'I wonder if we should have given him some money?' she said, because she was in a state about her hand being held, afraid to look at Will. 'Do you think he even has money for a ticket?'

'Stop it,' and he stroked her fingers slowly with his other hand.

*

They drove quickly out into the middle of the country – he gripped her hand between gear changes – and found a sandy clearing by the side of a field.

Not a soul around, nothing but the distant moan of a combine. The air was thick with humidity and the ground was damp. They'd no idea where they were, but it was inland and nowhere near Kessingland. A sign said: Holton, 1; Blythford, 2.

They made love fully clothed and in a panic of desire on three plastic carrier bags and a worn towel from the car boot. The moisture soaked through at the edges of the towel, and they got dirt in their nails from the ground. They used a condom which Will pulled from his pocket at the last moment without looking at her. She said nothing. She waited as he ripped it open, pulled it on.

She could not look into his face, because she would have seen what she was doing. Instead, she guided him into her fast and breathed in the wet potato smell of the field, closed her eyes to the rolling grey clouds.

They only dared take about ten minutes, after which they wiped themselves with baby wipes she kept in her bag for Kitty and drove back fast, swinging dangerously around the corners of the dark, stained country roads.

He held her knee as if it might fly off. She felt raw, wet, open, as if she might be covered in blood. Her fingers smelled powdery, of condom rubber.

'You didn't come,' he said, after a mile or so.

'I was too excited,' she replied, 'I like you too much.'

*

He opens his eyes and there's Jesus standing a few feet away in the yard – five or maybe seven feet, just the distance from here to there – across the blue brick paving. The Lord Jesus Christ. Hard to believe, but true. He Who died for our sins and by Whose Blood we can be saved!

It is seven or eight o'clock in the morning – the morning after the night they tried to raise Tommy up – and he hasn't slept for a couple of days or maybe longer. Somewhere a dog is barking its slow, painful bark. Down the road, he can hear the rumble of the milk float.

Frank's trousers are around his knees and Tommy has

passed on and there is Himself standing all lamb 'n' lettuce between the coalshed and the dustbins.

Frank blinks. He wonders if he's going to throw up. Never normally one to be lost for words, he finds to his dismay that he cannot speak.

*

Karin left the next day. It was bright again. The trees were wet and a bird was calling down the damp lawn.

'Listen,' said Kitty, 'it's the Silly Bird.'

'Why silly?' asked Will, pulling her against his legs.

'Because it's silly to call when there's no one there.'

'Kitty,' said Gayle, 'you've made a joke!'

After they'd gone, Kitty wandered in and out of the garden talking to the Silly Bird, plucking the fat juicy stalks of dandelions and lining them up on the kitchen table which was still sprinkled with Honey Nut Loops and brown breadcrumbs.

*

Amazing that the Son of God's so strapping, but here He is – big as the local bobby, hair long as a hippie's, only clean – and He's bearded, of course. He wears pure white robes and His feet are soft and white as a woman's despite the dust and grit of the yard, which does not get swept as much as it should.

On His palms there are the marks, blackish and laced with blood as if someone has just recently jabbed a screwdriver in and turned it. And spots of dark blood at His temples – smeared and scratchy like scabs which have been fiddled with. No crown of thorns, but here He is, the

Light of the World, standing there by Frank Chapman's dustbins.

He holds out his hands and smiles at Frank on the WC. There's a stink of refuse. A corpse in the house. And the stench from his own bowels is rotten, unbelievable. How much does Jesus smell, how much can He take, what does He know?

Frank wants to stand and wipe himself, but how can he? How can he take his eyes off the Lord? Sweat rolls down his back. The morning sun goes in and Jesus moves back against the little creosote fence and puts one hand down to grip the fence and raises the other slowly at Frank and makes a fist and shakes it. Frank sees that His eyes are huge: the irises yellow, the pupils gritty.

'I love you,' he says and his knees zoom up to his chin and – thuck – he's out cold again.

*

Will went up to the bedroom to clean his teeth and found Donna in there, sitting on the bed. When he came in, she pretended she'd been reading. He didn't want to start some conversation, so he said nothing.

'Hi,' she said at last.

'Hi.' He squeezed the toothpaste tube.

She sat there waiting for him to speak.

'What's the matter?' he said.

'I feel sick.'

'Sick?'

'Yes, sick,' she snapped, 'aren't I allowed to feel sick any more?'

He spat in the bowl. 'I don't know. I don't know what

you do and don't allow yourself to feel these days.' He didn't slam the door, but pulled it to quietly, secretly glad that she'd been the first to show aggression.

*

Later, the phone rang and Will went to pick it up but it cut off and there was no one there.

*

He overheard Gayle and Simon arguing in the sitting room. The door was shut but the odd word came to him. They were talking about Simon's new job – he was to be a dispatch rider as soon as he got back to London. The Unique Bike Company. Then he was going to see about a grant for his degree.

'Long hours, £450 a week,' he heard Simon say. There was silence then some mumbling, then: '. . . you didn't. You don't stick at things.' He caught Gayle's voice, but did not hear the rest.

Simon made an angry sound, then he heard Gayle say, 'You make me laugh,' and then Simon said something else which he didn't catch.

'. . . staying at the flat,' she said. She sounded patient, tired.

'. . . find somewhere,' he almost shouted.

Then the voices were very quiet and there was something he did not catch and then, 'I know what you want,' he heard Simon say.

There was silence then, after which he heard Simon walk out and kick the door shut with his foot.

*

Will went in and sat on the sofa and looked at her. She was standing by the window seat, her arms bunched in, curled around her chest. She'd pulled her hair back with a clip and was biting the skin on her lips and staring out at nothing.

'You're not his mother,' he said.

'Did you hear all that?' she asked him, turning round.

'No, not much.'

They were very likely in earshot of Donna and they knew it, so the conversation went on like this:

'Is he going to be living with you in London?'

'I don't know. Yes. For a while maybe.'

'You're mad. I don't know why you let him. What about the rest of your life?'

She refused to look at him. 'I want him to stick at this job.'

'Yes, but you're not responsible for him – what about you?'

'What about me? What do you mean? What rest of my life? Anyway, Kitty likes having Simon around.' She stared stubbornly out of the window where the Silly Bird was calling down the lawn.

'Oh, I see,' Will said, 'we're talking replacement father figures. Well, you must be able to do better than Simon.'

'You don't know what you're talking about,' she said.

They were both silent.

'What're you going to do, Gayle?' He wondered if he'd ever used her name before. It felt so new. He wanted to pluck her out of the air, sink his teeth in, eat her up.

'What do you mean?'

'You know what I mean.'

'I've no idea,' she said in an angry, plodding tone and still without looking at him, 'what are you going to do? What do you suggest?'

*

Donna lay on their stripped-down mattress with a dry throat. Her mouth tasted of metal and her breasts felt like a stranger's breasts. Everything she had ever wanted had come true – she was shaking, it had all come so true.

*

They hoovered and aired the beds and cleaned the bath. Gayle delegated jobs. Kitty raced around shouting as she had done when they'd arrived. 'Go in the garden,' Gayle said, 'we can get this done much quicker if you do.'

'Go and talk to silly bird,' said Simon.

'Not silly bird,' said Kitty, 'the Silly Bird.'

'Whatever. Go and talk to it,' and Gayle pushed her out of the back door.

Every time Will passed Gayle in the house, he felt a rush of smooth air. As if he could physically experience every single thing that stood between them.

When everything was done and the remnants of food were on the table in carrier bags and a black bag of rubbish was sealed and put in the dustbin and the car was virtually loaded, they sat for a few last minutes on the lawn, the four of them and Kitty.

'Well,' Simon said, 'here we all are again.'

Apples sliced up by the rain lay at their feet, smelled rotten. Simon lit a cigarette, because he wasn't allowed to smoke in the car.

'I think it was a mistake, having Frank here,' Donna said suddenly. She'd hardly spoken all morning.

'I don't know what Mum made of him,' Simon said. 'I thought it was quite funny, him and Mum at the table together.'

Gayle bent and lit her cigarette off Simon's. 'She wasn't keen,' she said, 'but then I wouldn't expect her to be.'

'Well, she did OK,' said Will.

'He's a taker,' Donna said, 'he doesn't give. I'm surprised you can't all see it. He's a taker.'

Simon blew smoke out. The sun bloomed and it was hot again. It was going to be another beautiful day. There were circles of sweat under the arms of his maroon shirt. He laughed at them from his cocoon of dark fabric. 'Well, Christ, aren't we all?' he said.

PART FOUR

one

London was clammy, the streets bereft of cars. As soon as Will was back at work, he phoned Gayle from the office. It was a quarter to eight. He imagined she'd be getting Kitty's breakfast. 'What?' she said, but her voice was warm.

'I want to see you.'

'Where are you?'

He heard Kitty in the background. 'Work.'

She hesitated. 'It's been less than twenty-four hours. We'll be round at the weekend.'

'Properly. I want to see you properly.'

She said nothing.

'Gayle—'

'Well, I'll think about it,' she said and put the phone down without saying goodbye.

*

He asked himself what he was doing – whether he was having an affair or simply leaving Donna. Whether he should leave Donna anyway, whether or not he had an affair. He didn't know the answers to any of these questions, and for the moment, he considered it enough that he asked.

More out of habit than anything else, he flirted with Betty. She told him she was still going out with the PE teacher but that they'd called off the engagement. A mutual decision. Neither of them felt ready to settle down. She had just moved flats to Notting Hill Gate and told him there'd be a party and she hoped he'd come. He said he'd love to, but would the PE teacher be there? She said no, she was afraid it would just be a gaggle of girls. He said he wouldn't complain.

The presentation to LexCom began at last in two and a half weeks and he now had to devote himself to work. Dan Mintoe was away in the South of France but phoned in every day, sometimes twice, and said he wanted to see something as soon as he got back. Will stayed at the office until ten and eleven each night, getting through a bottle of wine on his own as he worked, sometimes breaking off to read magazines and stare at nothing.

He thought about Gayle all the time.

'Busy?' the cleaner asked him. She was about seventeen and wore tight jeans done up with a silver belt and had a pretty face if you ignored the acne.

'Frantic.' He pushed his chair out of the way so she could hoover under his desk.

London remained very hot, most people still away, the streets dusty and purposeless. The Tube sucked and spewed people and the homeless sat begging on the pavement outside, messages written on corrugated cardboard, their feet tied up in rags. In the evenings, barbecue smells escaped from gardens and people in shorts called to each other as they stood hosing their yards. After Suffolk, the air smelled dark blue and brown and of evaporating carbon.

Donna said, 'I used to be frightened of all sorts of things and I'm not any more – isn't that funny?'

'Like what?' She sounded as though she were leading up to something.

'I don't know, lots of things. Now everything has fallen into place. Do you feel that too?'

She was looking at him and she was smiling, but the smile wasn't right and her eyes were speechless and hard. He didn't know what to say – what to avoid saying.

'I don't know.'

'Do we love each other?' she asked him.

'What a question. Of course.'

'But do we, really?'

'Why?'

'Why doesn't Gayle come round any more?'

'I don't know. Why?'

She didn't say why. These days she spent all her time questioning him, never enlightening him. He didn't know whether to believe half the things she said. 'I love you,' she told him one night as he fell into her bed half-drunk and oblivious with fatigue.

He tried to remember when he had last wanted her, had last been impressed by her and desired her. He couldn't think. But then if he tried to think back to the early days of their love, he could no longer imagine them either. He wondered whether his love had simply transferred from Donna to Gayle or whether there had been a period in between when it had just fallen off and dried up.

He knew it wasn't possible to love two women at once. Anyone who maintained otherwise was fooling himself unforgivably.

He fucked Donna anyway, hard and greedily in the dark, pressing his mouth into her hair, breathing her in and letting his saliva fall into the cracks and slopes of her flesh.

She held him tight. She seemed happy. She whispered things he couldn't bear to hear.

*

Donna didn't know whether she wanted to grow bigger or just disappear. People disappeared every day – people just like her. Well, just like her except for the fact that she had been the subject of a miracle. That fact would always make her extraordinary – would always make her both less and more likely to do certain things. But otherwise, they were like her – dark-haired girls last seen outside post offices, at bus stations, going down the road for a carton of milk. Never seen again. People who loved them grew old and died, never knowing the answer.

She used to be shocked, that a person could just disappear, but now, the more miracles she experienced, the more she could imagine it. Her life no longer fitted her. There was nothing wrong with it, it was just too tight. She was at the mercy of all of them. Will stared at her all day and Gayle didn't come round any more and Frank was still waiting.

'We won't hear from him again,' Will said.

And she laughed and said, 'I wouldn't count on it.'

Her peculiarly vivid image of Tommy – who, at fourteen years old, had perfected his own disappearance – whispered to her that it was time to conquer her fear.

*

One night, Simon got drunk and said to Gayle, 'You know, it's fucking crazy but a while ago I was convinced you'd got something going with Will.'

'What?' she said. 'What do you mean?'

'Sorry. Are you shocked? Yes, I actually thought you might be fucking him.'

'Don't be an arsehole,' she said and turned away. Simon laughed and threw himself on the sofa, scattering newspapers and magazines.

'I thought you were just using Frank,' he continued, more seriously, 'to engineer something – to engineer some sort of a dalliance.' He found his Rizlas and started a roll-up, but his fingers were too drunk and the tobacco strewed itself over the upholstery – little dry brown worms.

'If I wanted to do that, I could do it without Frank Chapman's help,' she said.

'I bet you could.'

'Look, just shut up.'

'Hey,' he said, 'hey, I'm sorry, I'm just pissed. Why don't you come over here and sit down?' He patted the sofa.

'Simon,' she told him then, 'I think it's time you found somewhere else to live.'

He ignored her, or he did not hear.

'I had an amazing dream about you last night,' he said, carefully putting the cigarette in his mouth and feeling around under the cushions for his lighter. He laughed at the memory. She said nothing.

'I did,' he repeated. She turned and walked out of the room.

*

Sometimes, as she went about her work, she shut her eyes and told herself she was a free and blameless person, cleared out of all feeling and responsibility, unafraid. It was easier without Annie. She hated everything that little bit more – did not have to think.

When Florrie Pykett died suddenly in the bath one morning, she scarcely noticed the event. It was no more than another death, barely pricking the bubble of her numbness.

One moment they were soaping her tits and the next she slid under with a seizure, hair lifting out around her, a frost of oxygen clinging to her face and neck. They grabbed at her but she was gone. The surface of the bath became milky with soap.

There was a memorial for Annie that afternoon at her church. It was full of her family. Gayle had not realized she had so much family.

*

When she got home, she made a cup of tea and drank it very slowly whilst Kitty watched *Rupert* on TV. Soon, she knew, the phone was going to ring and it did. 'Is Simon still living there with you?' he asked.

'I don't think so.' She found herself laughing again. 'He's gone off somewhere. He's pissed off with me.'

'Can I come round?'

'Do you think you should?'

'Yes, I do think I should.'

'OK, then, after Kitty's asleep.' She hesitated. 'Will?'

'Yes?'

'I don't know if you should.'

They both laughed.

*

He phoned Donna and told her he'd be going to Betty's party after work, that he'd be late. And he found himself going there, though he hadn't meant to. Notting Hill was well out of his way. Maybe he didn't want to lie to Donna. Maybe he didn't want to disappoint Betty.

Her flat was on the top floor of a mansion block and there was a small roof garden with no plants as yet and a lot of broken slate and bricks. It was an airless night and there was plenty of vodka. And cocaine, he guessed. People were pressed into doorways, kissing. There was no one he knew.

Betty had on very little. Every time she folded her arms, her cleavage squeezed into view.

'Thank God you're here,' she said, shivering despite the heat, and gripped his arm with both hands and kissed him straight away right on the lips. He'd never seen her lips so pale and bare. Her hair was messed and her pupils were very dilated.

'I can't stay long,' he told her.

*

Gayle read Kitty a book about some hippos building a house.

Kitty particularly liked the bit about them fixing the roof guttering on and made Gayle read that whole page several times. She then took the book to bed with her, along with a broken tambourine, a blue plastic hammer and some toy slices of bread from her sandwich set.

Gayle kissed her and put the light out and went down and poured herself the last of a bottle of wine from the fridge. It had been uncorked too long and tasted sour. Starving, she looked in the cupboard and found some unsalted cashews which were for cooking but which were better than nothing, so she ate a handful.

The phone rang and she was surprised to hear Harry. She'd forgotten him completely. 'Nice holiday?' He sounded too relaxed, as if he'd been drinking.

'Fine, thanks.'

'And Kitty?'

'Fine.'

'I'd like to see her, if that's all right.'

'No,' she said, 'I don't think that's a good idea at all.'

'Well,' he said without a trace of disappointment, 'what about us? What about dinner one of these days?'

'You can't be serious,' she said.

'I am.'

'I thought it was Kitty you wanted to see?'

'It was, but you'll do nicely.' He chuckled. She realized then that he was out of his head.

'I can't think of anything I'd like less,' she told him, and dropped the phone back into its cradle.

She sat down. Her arms and back ached. She gulped the wine so it stung the back of her throat and wondered what it would be like for Kitty if Harry was properly her father – if she came in each morning to find him in the big double bed, his Levi's shrugged off on a chair. It was impossible to imagine.

Kitty called out and she took her a drink of water. The phone rang again. She didn't bother to answer it.

*

She opened the door immediately. 'What is it?' she said. 'You look terrible.'

'Too much vodka,' Will kept his head down, 'it'll pass.'

He knew he'd blown it. He'd hoped to fuck her, sweep her off her feet, take up where they'd left off in Suffolk. She took him in the kitchen and made him coffee. He sat watching as she moved around, heaped black powder on a spoon, took a carton of milk from the fridge.

She was wearing boys' jeans which hung low on her hips and an unironed short-sleeved shirt with tiny red birds embroidered around the collar. Her hair was twisted up on top of her head. She looked so real and scowly and perfect he wanted to cry.

They hadn't even touched – he knew he was too drunk.

He was furious with himself for letting Betty get to him first, keep him there, get him pissed. Furious because she had held onto his arm, slid herself against him, stayed by him, without speaking, in the peeling doorway where he had leaned, drinking. His head had been empty, but he knew his hand had at one point been on her hip. He remembered watching the round, shadowy tops of her breasts – letting her know he was watching.

Gayle sat, delicate and blameless, in her bird shirt. The room was hot and the windows were open despite the traffic. Kitty's toys were still strewn over the floor, little red and yellow bricks which clicked under foot. 'I'm sorry,' he said, at last. She said nothing. She seemed unmoved. She seemed to be thinking about something else.

'I really want to touch you,' he told her truthfully, 'but I don't suppose I can.'

But she smiled and moved over to him.

*

In her room an hour or so later, they made love slowly, in a bed for the first time. It wasn't until afterwards, when she lay there naked by his side, that he really understood what was going on.

She saw him looking at her stomach, which bore the fizzy, firework pattern of stretch marks. 'I've had a child,' she said simply, without moving or covering herself, and he couldn't tell if it was sarcasm, or else an indirect criticism of him. He felt she was trying to put him off somehow, and he wasn't having it.

'You're lovely,' he said, 'lovely.'

'You're still drunk,' she accused and it struck him for the first time that she was incapable of hearing praise.

He stroked her, felt how soft she was where the embryo of Kitty had pushed out at her from inside. She turned over on her stomach and held his hand, loosely, like a shy, sensible child.

'Did you love Harry?' he asked her then, hating to ask, but because he had to know. She looked at him quickly.

'You must be joking,' she said.

'But if he'd wanted a child?'

'I'd have said no, of course.'

They were both silent.

'I really regret him,' she added then, transferring his

hand to her other one. 'Apart from Kitty. It was a one-night stand that went on and shouldn't have. I never even thought of caring for him. I don't know why I did it. I'm capable of great coldness, you know.'

'No, you're not,' he said, ecstatic.

'You don't know what I'm capable of,' she told him, and they both stared at the wall for a moment.

'What's the matter?' he asked her then.

She didn't answer. Then she said, 'This is such a mess.'

'Is it that you couldn't come?'

She turned her face away and he stroked her bottom, but really he wanted to see her eyes. He thought how sex always turned out so much better and worse than you dared to imagine.

'No,' she said, 'it's not that.'

'Yes, it is.'

'OK, then, it is.'

He held her tight.

'I'm ashamed of what we're doing,' she said, 'and I haven't been with anyone at all for so long.'

'I'm going to leave Donna,' he said suddenly.

'That's even worse,' she said, and pulled away.

'I don't love her,' he said. 'It's no one's fault that I don't love her any more.'

She said nothing, but kept turned away from him.

'And the other thing is just practice,' he said.

*

Frank walks down into the High Street and past Woolworths and the Tube station and then turns back and heads left up Coldharbour Lane.

He doesn't know where he's walking, or why. Everywhere lights are exploding into the sky – neon lights and flashing lights and hot lights which tempt you off to money and drinking and smoking and gambling and of course sex. 'You don't fool me,' he says aloud, and people glance at him and he stares them out and reminds them of what they must do to secure their Salvation.

A boy in filthy rags sits there in a doorway on a dirty nylon sleeping bag and he stretches out his hand. 'Hallelujah!' Frank shouts. 'Jesus will gather ye unto Him.' He feels a great power well up in him and would like in some ways to strike the boy, to rid him once and for all of demons and tell him of the Way, the Truth and the Life. He stops.

'Get fucked,' says the boy.

Someone has been sick against the wall, and there are three subsequent showers of vomit, each one smaller than the last. Someone's takeaway, no doubt. Frank walks on.

He's been in the flat alone for ten days now without communication from a single soul – munching on crackers and potted meat, barely stopping to wash or sleep. 'What're you staring at?' he eventually asked the red-haired woman from next door when she'd not taken her eyes off him standing in just his trousers and bare feet in the yard. 'Never seen a happy man before?'

Of course, he wasn't happy. He was looking at all the plants which had buggered off after Lola – all those small climbing things which she'd looked after and which had now turned snappy and brown. Should he just pull 'em up?

The woman trained her eyes on him. 'I'll call the police,' she said, 'if you speak to me like that.'

He laughed. 'Call them,' he said, 'go ahead. I could do with a bit of action. I'll introduce them to my Personal Saviour the Lord Jesus Christ. In fact, send your old man round 'n' all.'

*

Later, Will turned Gayle on her back and crept between her legs and licked her. She shivered and tried at first to push his head away, but he gripped her hands and held her till she allowed him to change her mind.

Then he pulled himself back on top of her and stroked her head, smoothing and tucking the wild, black strands of hair behind her ears. She was the most desirable thing he'd ever known and he'd no idea how he should deal with her and this fact alone unhinged him unbearably.

*

Donna perched like a butterfly on the edge of the bath and did what she had done once before. The blue that appeared was a light, abrasive, blotting-paper blue. She regarded it calmly. There were no surprises any more.

*

One day, Miss Freeman comes round. She rings the bell several times, the last time holding it down with such angry force that he is sorely tempted to have her in, to carve small niches in her willing soul and set her aside for the Lord. But he's not up to her today. He lets her go.

He remembers how Kitty used to stand in the doorway, plaiting his plastic curtain. He gets the sharpest knife he has and lops it off, all of it in one fell swoop, and it lies limp in his two hands like Samson's severed hair.

*

'So funny,' Gayle said, 'after all these years.'

'Yes?'

'I never liked you. You were so gruff and serious. I couldn't talk to you.'

'Really? Is that what you felt?'

'Yes, you made me feel boring and you inhibited me. And I found you arrogant.'

'Arrogant? But—'

'Yes?'

'That's what I would have said about you.'

'Oh, come on.'

'So fucking superior.'

'No!'

'The big sister act. Been there, done that. I don't know, bossy and aloof. I suppose I just saw you through Donna's eyes.'

At the mention of her name they were both silent.

Then she placed a circle of fingers around his penis and stroked under the rim, where the sensation made him gasp and then she put her tongue in the same place. He put his arms around her and kissed her and then moved her legs apart and whispered that he was going to fuck her again, and he knew this time by the way her voice dipped and squeaked and moved with him that it was going to be different and she'd do it and she did.

The air around them seemed to go dead.

Afterwards, they went back to discussing what they'd

thought of each other – over and over, round and round, laughing and touching. Their love affair was newborn, in its baby days, and all they wanted to do was dissect and worship and adore this thing which had happened to them.

*

'I used to be a difficult person,' she told Will at two in the morning, just before he went home. 'You've reinvented me.'

'What are you now?' he asked her, smiling, moving the strands of her hair this way and that. She could barely speak, because her mouth was so full of his prick.

'I'm fucking perfect.'

*

Four days later, Donna told him she was pregnant.

'Pretty pregnant, in fact,' she said, 'ten weeks is almost out of the danger zone.'

He was stunned. 'Ten weeks?'

'I've only just tested. I didn't want to know. Can you imagine that? I was frightened to know.'

'I can't believe it,' he said flatly.

'I can,' she said, 'the funny thing is, I can.'

She sat cross-legged on the bed and he could see it all over her body and face – the thing she'd known for weeks and he had not. Her power over him, waiting just under the surface. She smiled and pushed her hair back from her face. Her skin was still rosy with the Suffolk sunshine.

'You look so shocked,' she said quietly. 'You're funny when you're shocked.'

He sorted through all the words he could possibly have used but knew that none of them would do.

*

He crept into a meeting room at work the next day and phoned Gayle. The blinds were drawn and the room was very dark.

'That's that. We have to stop, immediately,' she said. Her voice was falsely level, falsely calm.

'I can't,' he whispered, 'I love you.'

'I feel sick,' she said, 'I feel like I'm going to be sick.'

'Look, we can't have this discussion now,' he told her.

*

Frank appeared at the hospital. 'Hello, stranger.' He moved out of the shadows in the corridor as she was on her way to the canteen and she jumped.

She thought he looked thinner and he seemed to be growing a beard. It was white, with unexpected ginger bits. He smelt unwashed. She did not like the way he looked at her, staring through and into her as if she was his. She wondered, not for the first time, what power he could possibly have had that had helped her sister. Then she noticed he leaned on Donna's stick with the silver knob. 'That's Donna's stick,' she said.

'A gift,' he said, 'remember? A gift for a gift. Very handy.'

'Frank,' she began.

'I've missed you,' he said.

'I've been very busy,' she told him, as coolly as she could, determined not to apologize. 'How are you?'

'You can see how I am,' he said, 'never better.'

*

Will told Gayle he was going to tell Donna, that he was going to leave Donna for her, that it would be the only honest thing, that he had to do it. Donna's pregnancy was an accident. And Gayle, after all, knew all about accidents.

He stayed very calm. When he spoke the words they sounded right and he felt almost sorry for himself. He felt like a man stripped against his will of options, in a tight corner, doing his best to choose the right and moral thing.

Gayle sat and cried at her kitchen table. She didn't stop crying the whole time he was there. When she cried, she looked like someone else.

'We have to plan it out,' he kept saying, 'hurt as few people as possible.'

She looked at him and carried on crying.

'Let's get this in proportion,' he said finally, 'it happened to you. It's only what Harry did to you.'

They ended up in bed. He lay with his weight on her and rocked himself against her till their bones seemed to twine and held her mouth in both hands and kissed it as if he thought with a bit of luck it might feed him and he might be able to walk away from her, sustained.

In the next room, Kitty started to cry. Gayle tried to struggle out from under him, but he prevented her and held her and stroked her and pretty soon the crying stopped.

They fucked slowly and for a long time and, though they

wanted it to feel like love, it wasn't, it was something else: greed and desperation and the sum total of all the troubles they'd both had in their lives.

*

Once he's left Miss Know-It-All at the hospital, he catches a bus which takes him all the way along Stockwell Road and up as far as Budgens and then he alights and walks the rest of the way home.

He walks very jauntily, tapping Donna's stick along the pavement in time with his feet, like a cabaret artiste, the silver knob pleasantly chilling his palm.

*

Afterwards Will was lying with his face against her abdomen where the paths of his semen were already dried and glassy when they heard a key turn in the door. She stiffened and said, 'It's Si.'

'Simon?'

'He still has a key.'

It was too late to do anything, but she got up quickly and locked the bedroom door. She put out her hand to stop him saying anything. There was a soft knock.

'No,' she called out, 'I've gone to bed.'

'I want to talk to you.' He sounded angry, fiddling with the locked door.

'In the morning. Go and sleep.'

'Why can't I come in?'

'None of your bloody business,' she said in a low, even voice. 'Go away.'

Will put out his arms to her, to make her come back to bed, but she just stood there, tense and naked.

*

He sits all alone in his room watching something on the telly – one of those televised discussions. Young people talking about the work of the Devil made flesh – yes, sexual intercourse! Channel Four. He can see Tommy as one of these slightly, dangerously articulate young people. He's better off dead, he really is.

There's a girl with a shaven head, another with a ring through her nose. Mohair jerseys and, on their feet, heavy workmen's boots. They are all pale. Masturbation. Frank leans a little closer. TV makes him jumpy.

When the ad break comes, he goes in the kitchen and lights the gas under the kettle. When the kettle boils, he pours the water over a tea bag and sets the egg timer for four minutes. Otherwise he'll forget and it will be stewed.

When he goes back in, the girl with the ring through her nose is still talking. Where are her inhibitions? How old is she? 'You little madam,' Frank tells her as (before he knows it) his egg timer yells that time's up, 'you little Know-It-All.'

The Holy Ghost is the Spirit of Jesus Christ and God is a Spirit. That's Him all right! Yes, sir! It's so simple! One God and One Name.

*

'Don't do this to me!' Simon shouted. Then the door handle released and they heard him step away. Gayle sat down on the edge of the bed and looked at Will. He put out his hand.

They didn't hear anything for a moment and they thought he might have gone, but then there was an almighty crash and the frail wood around the lock burst and splintered as Simon kicked the plywood door in two with his boot and stood there staring in at them.

Someone screamed. Was it Kitty?

He was very drunk. He was still wearing his jacket and his anger was all over him like an extra garment. His eyes were blank with hatred. He looked at Gayle who was still naked and had not even tried to cover herself.

'I hope you frigging well die,' he told Will.

*

Queen Gayle cold-shouldered him when he visited her at the hospital, really let him know where he stood. Made it clear it was all over between them. That it had never even begun. When he had thought he could count on her as he had never been able to count on Tommy. No skin off his nose.

'Don't know what you want, Frank,' she said snootily as anything, 'I'm extremely busy just now.'

'You can't drop me just like that,' he said, 'not after what Jesus did for your sister.'

'No one's dropping anyone,' she said, 'you've got Jesus. I have a job and a daughter. We'll keep in touch.'

'You've got more than that though, haven't you? Miss All High and Mighty.' It worked, she looked scared.

'I don't have to stand here while you go on at me like

this,' and she walked back onto the ward, where she knew she was safe and he couldn't kick up a fuss.

'You're making a big mistake,' he called after her, 'this is a cry for help. I've found the Light. No power on earth could cause me to go back into Darkness.'

Carnal minds, that's what he meant. Whatsoever you do in word or deed, do all in the name of Jesus Christ.

He watched her move into another room and close the door. He felt his body twitch with anger. He blinked under the fluorescent light, and touched the knob of the stick. She thought she was powerful but she was not. He could turn up wherever he chose, wherever he liked.

He'd wanted to warn her – there ain't no Trinity, only Jesus himself, lovely lad – but she hadn't given him a chance.

*

Gayle insisted to Will that she could sort it out with Simon and she warmed some milk for Kitty who'd woken at the noise and was crying again. She said it would be best if he left. She added that it wasn't that she wanted him to go but it really would be easier if she handled this alone.

He tried to argue with her.

'Easier for who? Anyway, what's "this"? There is no "this",' he whispered to her whilst Simon stomped around in the next room, bumping into things, kicking books across the floor. 'He's behaving like a spoiled kid. It's none of his business. It's atrocious, that he thinks he can burst in here like that.'

'What if he rushes straight to Donna?' she said. 'What about that? I have to calm him down.'

'He rules your life, doesn't he?' he told her. 'I think he fancies you rotten himself – I've thought it before now – has that ever occurred to you?'

Gayle watched the saucepan of milk as if she hadn't heard. Will stood there. He'd pulled on his shirt and jeans and now he felt helpless and outwitted. She was very calm, as if she knew exactly what to do – as if she'd done it all before. Then she turned and smiled at him as if it was something she'd just remembered she had to do.

'It'll be OK,' she said, 'trust me. I'll talk to you tomorrow.'

'When tomorrow?' he countered, more grumpily than he intended.

By the time he left, Simon wasn't saying a word but was sitting on the sofa with his jacket still on, staring at the cold TV screen. Will hesitated in the doorway, because he didn't want to leave her there.

She stood at the cooker in her robe with the pan of milk and her hair all messed around by his hands just twenty minutes ago, and she shook her head and blew a kiss and waved him away.

*

Wait and see, Frank tells himself.

He lifts the curtain. It is a hot, starless night. From here the sky looks almost green, freakish. Tommy has been dead these twenty-one years and he himself has not aged a jot, thanks to TLJC.

Why not go for a walk? Why not cheer himself up?

two

Will walked out of Gayle's flat.

It was about half-past ten and hot, barely dark. The pubs were all still full. He could smell traffic fumes and honeysuckle and the fatty heat of the kebab place.

He wandered off down Clapham Road and looked into the window of an electrical shop. There was a photo of a smiling blonde girl with a cleavage, holding plugs. Everything in the window was covered in a layer of dust. The prices were written in felt tip on jagged day-glo orange card. Some words were misspelt.

He wondered if he should just go to Donna and tell her everything, save Simon the trouble.

He thought about turning his body in the right direction but nothing happened and he just knew he wasn't going home.

*

A girl stands purposelessly outside Kwik-Fit on Acre Lane – only about fifteen or so, a big fat teenager, with joining-up freckles and an anorak and a pack of Silk Cut between her sausage fingers.

He crosses the road, approaches her. Can smell the heat coming off her. 'Come for a walk,' he says.

'How much?' She glances at the stick in his hands.

'It doesn't cost, to talk about Jesus,' he says.

'Tell me what you'll pay.' She stares at his face and then back to the stick. He can smell how sick she is.

'I'll Save you.' He holds out one hand to her. 'Healing for Jesus. That's the biggest prize of all.'

'Fuck off with your crap.' She curls her lips and turns away, but as she does it he strikes her across the shoulders with the stick. She gasps, she almost falls against the brick wall, puts out her hand.

'That's for turning down the opportunity to be Saved,' he proclaims loudly. Before he walks away, he hits her once more in the stomach, this time just a light punch with his hand. The navy-blue night sky hums with angels. When he glances back, she is doubled over, crying like a baby.

'Poor Bubba,' he laughs, 'go to the doctor's. Jesus is better than any GP, I'll tell you that for nothing.'

He thinks of how he's lived a celibate life, more or less, never bothering much with sex once the early attempts with Lola were over. Desire mucks you around and you lose track of the Real Joy and the Real Release which is Jesus Christ.

Twenty-one years since Tommy's death. Twenty-one years since Jesus told him it was better not to wake him up.

And he himself hasn't aged a jot.

*

Will walked up Clapham High Street. He did not know where he was going.

Past the Maharani Restaurant with its purple lights, with the waiters standing by the door smiling into the night. Past the jacket-potato shop and the bookshop with its dim blue light, past McDonald's and past the black hairdresser's with the silvery lettering. Past the Tube station. He thought about getting on a train but he had about twenty pence in his pocket.

The air was hot and thick on his face. He could smell dust and traffic and hot meat.

Men in trainers and short-sleeved shirts spilled out of pubs onto the pavements. They stood in small groups, elbow to elbow, and some leaned against the wall. One stood and pissed into the road. A drink would have been really nice.

There was a fun fair on the Common, he could hear the music wobbling far away, see the dazzle and splotch of lights between the trees. He decided he'd walk across the grass and onto the grey path, and go towards the fair. Then he might turn and think about going home.

Donna would be asleep by now anyway. He'd think about what to say to her in the morning.

*

Gayle settled Kitty and sat down with Simon.

'OK,' she said, 'I've had enough of you in my life and I want you out. I don't care what you do or where you go, but I want you out now.'

He did not move, he just looked at her. There was something heartless and greedy in his look which frightened her. 'I want you out, now,' she said again and stood up.

'Throw me out then,' he said, but as she bent and grabbed his arm he pulled her down and pushed her face into his and put his lips around her mouth.

She screamed and fought him off. She felt his hand go round her buttocks and dip under. She hit him hard across the face and ran across the room.

'Gayle—' he said and she saw he was crying.

'Get out,' she said, 'you don't mean this. You don't know what you're doing. Get out.'

He went, leaving the door wide open. She was shaking from head to toe. She could not move until she heard his feet thump unevenly down to the bottom of the flight of stairs and then she shut the door and bolted it.

*

Suddenly a hand touched Will's shoulder. 'Hello stranger.'

'Frank?' he said. 'What are you doing here?' Though it couldn't be Frank, he felt, because all the evidence was against it.

Frank had the beginnings of a beard, but if anything his face seemed younger, his eyes lighter, brighter.

'Is it you?' he asked him. 'You look different somehow. What have you done to yourself?' He was feeling so alone that even against his better judgement he felt almost glad to see him.

Frank just smiled. 'Jesus is my Saviour and my Guide.'

*

Donna was asleep when the phone rang. The ringing was in her dream and she smiled to herself because it was a pleasant sound, the sound of someone getting in touch. But

Simon's voice was shaky, cold. 'I found them in bed, him and Gayle. Thought you'd want to know. I'm sorry.' His voice was breathy with tears.

She sighed. He went on, from between clenched teeth, 'He's a bastard. I could kill him. You're having a baby.'

'Simon,' she said patiently, 'I know.'

'What?'

'I know all this. I've known for ages. Thank you but you didn't need to wake me up.'

He didn't seem to hear. He was very upset.

'You're my sister. Gayle's my sister.'

She laughed. 'I'll be just like Gayle now.'

'What?' A sob.

'Single mum. Hands full.'

She put the phone down and rolled over and went back to sleep.

She was just like Gayle. It wasn't so far from what she'd had in mind. Miracles had been worked – a million stars exploded, bouncing in her face. She smelled gunpowder, lanolin, carbolic. Her limbs were warm, her spine supple, and her own particular angels waited in her dreams to comfort her.

*

Kitty said her head was hurting and she could not sleep. She'd been woken twice and now she sat up in bed holding Rabbit and scowling at the light.

'I want Calpol,' she said. Gayle gave her some and then got her to drink some water.

'Mummy's very tired,' she said, 'will you let Mummy go to sleep?' Kitty just looked at her.

Finally, she said, 'Do you want to sleep in my bed?'

Without a word, Kitty slipped down and padded across the landing. Gayle smoothed the pillows where Will had lain with her earlier. She tucked Kitty in.

It was only half-past eleven. The evening seemed to have lasted a week.

*

'I'll walk with you,' Frank said.

They moved towards the middle of the Common, leaving the fair on their left, moving into a dark, treeless space he hadn't been in before. He noticed Frank was using Donna's stick. He resented it slightly, even though he knew she'd given it to him. He had chosen it specially for her. It seemed wrong that it should end up with Frank.

'It was good,' Frank remarked at last, 'at the seaside. I enjoyed that.'

'Good,' Will said. Already, he was trying to think of a reason to leave Frank now and head off in the opposite direction.

'Yes, ' said Frank, 'and Karin's a fine woman.'

Will felt cold. The wind was warm, but his neck was cold. Suddenly, Frank said, 'How's the bride-to-be?'

Will said nothing, started walking again. Frank followed him, in silence. Will could hear the older man's breath behind him, hah, hah, hah, squeezing out of his lungs and into the night.

They were a long way away from everything now. It was very dark, away from the street lights. The cycle path was the only luminous thing – a ribbon of white – though the sky was washed with lilac and there were at last one or two stars.

For no reason he could understand, Will suddenly remembered a small red Scottie dog his mother had stitched onto his school bag before he could read his name, and how rubbing his thumb over the satin sheen of the dog's shape had comforted him. He wished he could conjure up Gayle in the same way, her face when he had kissed her – and then he felt sad because he realized that very few things had given him any sort of proper comfort in his life.

He looked around and saw Frank was smiling at him, fingering the knob of the stick. It was a balmy night.

There was the fair again. You could just see the yellow top of the helter-skelter through the trees.

*

She did not feel distressed or ashamed or worried. Her heart was strangely clean, just like a weight had been lifted away.

She'd felt very sorry, ultimately, for Simon, but she'd thrown him out because she knew it was the right thing for him and for her. She knew she would not see him for a very long time. She did not give him another thought – nor did she think about Donna or the baby or Frank Chapman or her mother or Annie and her shocking, purposeless death.

In her bed, she set the alarm and pulled the sheets up around her and kissed Kitty's silky brow and thought about how love had altered the way she looked at things and how somehow the next day she was going to manage to touch and talk to Will.

*

'Do you believe in Christ's Holy Angels?' he asks Will.

'No,' the young man unwisely says, 'you know I don't.'

'There ain't no such thing as the Holy Trinity,' he tells him, 'no such thing as the Three. Jesus lived and died under the period of Law – He preached the coming Kingdom, which was to come about by His death and resurrection—'

'Frank,' the ignoramus says, 'you're wasting your breath.'

Big mistake, that.

*

They stopped again. All around them the undergrowth was ragged and dark.

'I saw Jesus once,' Frank said, 'you know that?' He held the stick within the fingers of one hand and twirled it with the other.

'No,' Will sighed, 'I didn't know.'

He did not feel happy. He could barely breathe, they were standing so close and still together. He wanted to move away, but he kept on wondering about things, he couldn't stop himself. It was as if all the thoughts in his head were preventing him from acting, from walking away from Frank. He was paralysed by all that had happened. He wondered what Gayle had said to Simon, what Simon was going to say to Donna. Whether Donna would make it possible for him to leave. Whether the baby would be a boy or a girl.

'Oh, yes,' Frank was going on again, and his voice sounded fragile in the darkness, almost female in tone now, 'I saw him in my yard, quite an ugly sight really.'

Will said nothing.

'Yes. The day my Tommy died. And now I just do as

I'm told.' He continued to twirl the stick, cheerleader-style, with a grin.

Will looked at him and felt frightened suddenly. There was a sneer in Frank's voice.

'I'm going home now,' he said quietly.

'No, you're not,' said Frank.

*

He carried on smiling, and as he smiled, he raised Donna's stick up – whish – in the air and that's when Will knew he was going to die.

And he realized it was his own fault and he should have known – that they'd all known all along if only they'd looked at the facts – that Frank Chapman was capable of just about anything.

He thought what a waste of time it all was, all that visiting and befriending, if Frank was just going to turn out to be a maniac, after all. But then if it hadn't been for Frank, Donna would never have been cured and well enough to conceive a child – and maybe his love affair with Gayle would never have happened.

In the few seconds it took Frank to catch hold of his shoulder and swing the hard silver knob of the stick up, he thought only of the cold crack of the metal and how shit-scared he was and how much it was going to hurt him.

Frank grunted with the effort of bringing it down.

'Do you not know who I am?' he shouted as he struck Will hard on the side of the head.

There was not much pain at first, but he felt himself staggering and he could not speak. He knew it would take more than a single blow to kill him and so it was almost certainly going to happen again.

'No!'

'No.' Frank paused to watch as Will stayed upright, put out his hands, moved to grab at the stick. Frank whipped it away with a snarl. 'I bet you don't. I am the Light. I tried to tell you earlier.'

Will did not know how you fought a big man like Frank. He felt his fingers close over into fists.

'Hallelujah.' Frank spun the stick, gripping it at its very tip for maximum force, and this time Will fell under the blow.

He felt his knees hit the cool, bendy ground and saw the grass turn black with his own blood.

*

Jesus said, 'If you speak the Words I put into your mouth, I will confirm them with signs and wonders.'

But how many signs and wonders do you have to be given before you sit up and take note? How many? Frank's patience is not limitless. Like any Father, he eventually runs out – goes bananas and kicks up an Almighty Fuss.

*

He was being murdered – but must survive – so forced himself to begin to crawl.

There was a metallic lolly wrapper on the grass with a rocket on and he saw the rocket was already obscured by a great deal of his blood.

'I tried to tell you,' someone said, 'I tried to tell yooo—'

He was crawling over the dark grass with wet wrists –

slowly, painfully, thighs and buttocks dragging – but then Frank clobbered him twice more in quick succession and he couldn't shout at him to stop because his mouth was gone, caved in, teeth smashed, and now he was putting all his effort into trying to breathe without swallowing them.

Frank had belted him with the end of the stick about nine times altogether. The last blow was in the soft space between his neck and jaw as he lay face up staring through the trees, nerves blasted and ripped, but still not exactly dead.

He kept his eye on one small, particular star.

*

Frank left him for dead but he was not dead. He was not anywhere.

There were bits of his life everywhere, all over, floating in the air around him and he put out his hands and reached for them, but they dodged and dashed a little too fast, so he gave in, gave up and closed his eyes (or were they already closed?) and saw many brilliant, forgotten things from a long time ago, things dropped from his consciousness, now haphazardly retrieved.

He thought of Gayle and Donna and how he envied Simon for growing up with two such different, interesting women. He wished he'd been able to move in with Gayle and be a father to Kitty and that Donna had been able to forgive him.

He realized none of this would happen now.

He tried to move his head and take in some of the dark air around him, but he couldn't see anything, not even the star.

He wondered whether his face was still recognizable, but when he tried to think seriously about what it had been like before, found he didn't know.

*

He saw Gayle quite clearly.

*

He heard the sea pounding in his head and ears and on Kessingland beach, heard Kitty asking questions, smelled Gayle's face and his fingers when they were still wet from her sweet, muted excitement.

He felt himself going somewhere and tried with all his strength and passion and intelligence to come back.

*

He waited for Gayle to come and find him, as he knew she would. It might take longer this time, because it was the middle of the night. It seemed fairly stupid to die because of Frank Chapman. He was no longer in pain. It was lucky she was a nurse. And that he was prepared to wait.

He knew just about enough by now to know she'd come.